DEATH of a
VILLAGE

The Hamish Macbeth series

DEATH of a VILLAGE

A Hamish Macbeth Murder Mystery

M. C. BEATON

ROBINSON
London

Constable & Robinson Ltd
3 The Lanchesters
162 Fulham Palace Road
London W6 9ER
www.constablerobinson.com

First published in the USA by Grand Central Publishing,
a division of Hachette Book Group USA, Inc.

This edition published by Robinson,
an imprint of Constable & Robinson, 2009

A copy of the British Library Cataloguing in
Publication data is available from the British Library

UK ISBN: 978-1-84901-276-8

Printed in Great Britain by Clays Ltd, St Ives plc

3 5 7 9 10 8 6 4

To my friend David Lloyd of
Lower Oddington, Gloucestershire,
with affection

Hamish Macbeth fans share their reviews . . .

Share your own reviews and comments at
www.constablerobinson.com

Chapter One

In all my travels I never met with any one Scotchman but what was a man of sense. I believe everybody of that country that has any, leaves it as fast as they can.
— Francis Lockier

The way propaganda works, as every schoolboy knows, is that if you say the same thing over and over again, lie or not, people begin to believe it.

Hamish Macbeth, police constable of the village of Lochdubh and its surroundings, had been until recently a happy, contented, unambitious man. This was always regarded, by even the housebound and unsuccessful, as a sort of mental aberration. And he had been under fire for a number of years and from a number of people to pull his socks up, get a life, move on, get a promotion, and forsake his lazy ways. Until lately, all comments had slid off him. That was, until Elspeth Grant, local reporter, joined the chorus. It was the way she

1

laughed at him with a sort of affectionate contempt as he mooched around the village that got under his skin. Her mild amazement that he did not want to 'better himself', added on to all the other years of similar comments, finally worked on him like the end result of a propaganda war and he began to feel restless and discontented.

Had he had any work to do apart from filing sheep-dip papers and ticking off the occasional poacher, Elspeth's comments might not have troubled him. And Elspeth was attractive, although he would not admit it to himself. He felt he had endured enough trouble from women to last him a lifetime.

He began to watch travel shows on television and to imagine himself walking on coral beaches or on high mountains in the Himalayas. He fretted over the fact that he had even taken all his holidays in Scotland.

One sunny morning, he decided it was time he got back on his beat, which covered a large area of Sutherland. He decided to visit the village of Stoyre up on the west coast. It was more of a hamlet than a village. No crime ever happened there. But, he reminded himself, a good copper ought to check up on the place from time to time.

After a winter of driving rain and a miserable spring, a rare period of idyllic weather had arrived in the Highlands. Tall twisted mountains swam in a heat haze. The air through the open window of the police Land

Rover was redolent with smells of wild thyme, salt, bell heather, and peat smoke. He took a deep breath and felt all his black discontentment ebb away. Damn Elspeth! This was the life. He drove steadily down a winding single-track road to Stoyre.

Tourists hardly ever visited Stoyre. This seemed amazing on such a perfect day, when the village's cluster of whitewashed houses lay beside the deep blue waters of the Atlantic. There was a little stone harbour where three fishing boats bobbed lazily at anchor. Hamish parked in front of the pub, called the Fisherman's Arms. He stepped down from the Land Rover. His odd-looking dog, Lugs, scrambled down as well.

Hamish looked to right and left. The village seemed deserted. It was very still, unnaturally so. No children cried, no snatches of radio music drifted out from the cottages, no one came or went from the small general stores next to the pub.

Lugs bristled and let out a low growl. 'Easy, boy,' said Hamish. He looked up the hill beyond the village to where the graveyard lay behind a small stone church. Perhaps there was a funeral. But he could see no sign of anyone moving about.

'Come on, boy,' he said to his dog. He pushed open the door of the pub and went inside. The pub consisted of a small whitewashed room with low beams on the ceiling. A few wooden tables scarred with cigarette burns were dotted about. There was no one behind the bar.

'Anyone home?' called Hamish loudly.

To his relief there came the sound of someone moving in the back premises. A thickset man entered through a door at the back of the bar. Hamish recognized Andy Crummack, the landlord and owner.

'How's it going, Andy?' asked Hamish. 'Everybody dead?'

'It iss yourself, Hamish. What will you be having?'

'Just a tonic water.' Hamish looked round the deserted bar. 'Where is everyone?'

'It's aye quiet this time o' day.' Andy poured a bottle of tonic water into a glass.

'Slainte!' said Hamish. 'Are you having one?'

'Too early. If ye don't mind, I've got stock to check.' Andy made for the door behind the bar.

'Hey, wait a minute, Andy. I havenae been in Stoyre for a while but I've never seen the place so dead.'

'We're quiet folks, Hamish.'

'And nothing's going on?'

'Nothing. Now, if ye don't mind . . .'

The landlord disappeared through the door.

Hamish drank the tonic water and then pushed back his peaked cap and scratched his fiery hair. Maybe he was imagining things. He hadn't visited Stoyre for months. The last time had been in March when he'd made a routine call. He remembered people chatting on the waterfront and this pub full of locals.

He put his glass on the bar and went out into the sunlight. The houses shone white in the glare and the gently heaving blue water had an oily surface.

He went into the general store. 'Morning, Mrs MacBean,' he said to the elderly woman behind the counter. 'Quiet today. Where is everyone?'

'They'll maybe be up at the kirk.'

'What! On a Monday? Is it someone's funeral?'

'No. Can I get you anything, Mr Macbeth?'

Hamish leaned on the counter. 'Come on. You can tell me,' he coaxed. 'What's everyone doing at the church on a Monday?'

'We are God-fearing folk in Stoyre,' she said primly, 'and I'll ask you to remember that.'

Baffled, Hamish walked out of the shop and was starting to set off up the hill when the church doors opened and people started streaming out. Most were dressed in black as if for a funeral.

He stood in the centre of the path as they walked down towards him. He hailed people he knew. 'Morning, Jock ... grand day, Mrs Nisbett,' and so on. But the crowd parted as they reached him and silently continued on their way until he was left standing alone.

He walked on towards the church and round to the manse at the side with Lugs at his heels. The minister had just reached his front door.

He was a new appointment, Hamish noticed, a thin nervous man with a prominent Adam's apple, and his black robes were worn and dusty. He had sparse ginger hair, weak eyes and a small pursed mouth.

'Morning,' said Hamish. 'I am Hamish Macbeth, constable at Lochdubh. You are new to here?'

The minister reluctantly faced him. 'I am Fergus Mackenzie,' he said in a lilting Highland voice.

'You seem to be doing well,' remarked Hamish. 'Church full on a Monday morning.'

'There is a strong religious revival here,' said Fergus. 'Now, if you don't mind . . .'

'I do mind,' said Hamish crossly. 'This village has changed.'

'It has changed for the better. A more God-fearing community does not exist anywhere else in the Highlands.' And with that the minister went into the manse and slammed the door in Hamish's face.

Becoming increasingly irritated, Hamish retreated back to the waterfront. It was deserted again. He thought of knocking on some doors to find out if there was any other answer to this strange behaviour apart from a religious revival and then decided against it. He looked back up the hill to where a cottage stood near the top. It was the holiday home of a retired army man, Major Jennings, an Englishman. Perhaps he might be more forthcoming. He plodded back up the hill, past the

6

church, and knocked on the major's door. Silence greeted him. He knew the major lived most of the year in the south of England. Probably not arrived yet. Hamish remembered he usually came north for a part of the summer.

When he came back down from the hill, he saw that people were once more moving about. There were villagers in the shop and villagers on the waterfront. This time they gave him a polite greeting. He stopped one of them, Mrs Lyle. 'Is anything funny going on here?' he asked.

She was a small, round woman with tight grey curls and glasses perched on the end of her nose. 'What do you mean?' she asked.

'There's an odd atmosphere and then you've all been at the kirk and it isn't even Sunday.'

'It is difficult to explain to such as you, Hamish Macbeth,' she said. 'But in this village we take our worship of the Lord seriously and don't keep it for just the one day.'

I'm a cynic, thought Hamish as he drove off. Why should I find it all so odd? He knew that in some of the remote villages a good preacher was still a bigger draw than anything on television. Mr Mackenzie must be a powerful speaker.

When he returned to Lochdubh, Hamish found all the same that the trip to Stoyre had cheered him up. The restlessness that had

7

plagued him had gone. He whistled as he prepared food for himself and his dog, and then carried his meal on a tray out to the front garden, where he had placed a table with an umbrella over it. Why dream of cafés in France when he had everything here in Lochdubh?

He had just finished a meal of fried haggis, sausage and eggs when a voice hailed him. 'Lazing around again, Hamish?'

The gate to the front garden opened and Elspeth Grant came in. She was wearing a brief tube top which showed her midriff, a small pair of denim shorts, and her hair had been tinted aubergine. She pulled up a chair and sat down next to him.

'The trouble with aubergine,' said Hamish, 'is that it chust doesnae do.'

'Doesn't do what?' demanded Elspeth.

'Anything for anyone. It's like the purple lipstick or the black nail varnish. Anything that's far from an original colour isn't sexy.'

'And what would you know about anything sexy?'

'I am a man and I assume you mean to attract the opposite sex.'

'Women dress and do their hair for themselves these days.'

'Havers.'

'It's true, Hamish. You've been living in this time warp for so long that you just don't know what's what. Anyway, I'm bored. There's really nothing to report until the Highland Games over at Braikie and that's a week away.'

'I might have a wee something for you. I've just been over at Stoyre. There's a religious revival there. They were all at the kirk this morning. Seems they've got a new minister, a Mr Mackenzie. I was thinking he must be a pretty powerful preacher.'

'Not much, but something,' said Elspeth. 'I'll try next Sunday.'

'The way they're going on, you may not need to wait that long. They've probably got a service every day.'

'Want to come with me?'

Hamish stretched out his long legs. 'I've just been. Have the Currie sisters seen you in that outfit?'

The Currie sisters were middle-aged twins, spinsters, and the upholders of morals in Lochdubh.

'Yes. Jessie Currie told me that I should go home and put on a skirt and Nessie Currie defended me.'

'Really! What did she say?'

'She said my boots were so ugly that they made everything else I had on look respectable.'

Hamish looked down at the heavy pair of hiking boots Elspeth was wearing. 'I see what she means.'

Elspeth flushed up to the roots of her frizzy aubergine hair with anger. 'I don't know why I bother even talking to you, Hamish Macbeth. I'm off.'

When she had gone, Hamish lay back in his chair, his hands clasped behind his head. He shouldn't have been so rude to her but he blamed her remarks about him being unambitious for having recently upset the lazy comfort of his summer days.

The telephone in the police station rang, the noise cutting shrilly through the peace of the day.

He sighed, got to his feet, and went to answer it. The voice of his pet hate, Detective Chief Inspector Blair, boomed down the line. 'Get yoursel' over to Braikie, laddie. Teller's grocery in the High Street has been burgled. Anderson will be there soon.'

'On my way,' said Hamish.

He took his peaked cap down from a peg on the kitchen door and put it on his head. 'No, Lugs,' he said to his dog, who was looking up at him out of his strange blue eyes. 'You stay.'

He went out and got into the police Land Rover and drove off, turning over in his mind what he knew of Teller's grocery. It was a licensed shop and sold more upmarket groceries than its two rivals. He was relieved that he would be working with Detective Sergeant Jimmy Anderson rather than Blair.

He parked outside the shop and went in. Mr Teller was a small, severe-faced man with gold-rimmed glasses. 'You took your time,' he said crossly. 'They've taken all my wine and spirits, the whole lot. I found the lot gone when I opened up this morning, and phoned the police.'

'I was out on another call,' said Hamish. 'How did they get in?'

'Round the back.' Mr Teller raised a flap on the counter and Hamish walked through.

A pane of glass on the back door had been smashed. 'The forensic people'll be along soon,' said Hamish. 'I can't touch anything at the moment.'

'Well, let's hope you hurry up. I've got to put a claim into the insurance company.'

'How much for?'

'I'll need to total it up. Thousands of pounds.'

Hamish looked blankly down at the shop-keeper. He had been in the shop before. He could not remember seeing any great supply of wine or spirits. There had been three shelves, near the till, that was all.

He focused on Mr Teller. 'I haven't been in your shop for a bit. Had you expanded the liquor side?'

'No, why?'

'I remember only about three shelves of bottles.'

'They took all the stuff out of the cellar as well.'

'You'd better show me.'

Mr Teller led the way to a door at the side of the back shop. The lock was splintered. Hamish took out a handkerchief and put it over the light switch at the top of the stairs and pressed. He stood on the top step and looked down. The cellar was certainly empty. And dusty.

11

He returned to the front to find that Jimmy Anderson had arrived.

'Hello, Hamish,' said the detective. 'Crime, isn't it? A real crime. All that lovely booze. Taken a statement yet?'

'Not yet. Could I be having a wee word with you outside?'

'Sure. I could do with a dram. There's a pub across the road.'

'Not yet. Outside.'

Under the suspicious eyes of Mr Teller, they walked out into the street.

'What?' demanded Jimmy.

'He is saying that thousands of pounds of booze have been nicked. But when I pointed out to him that he only kept about three shelves of the stuff, he said they had cleared out the cellar as well.'

'So?'

'The cellar floor is dusty. Even dust. No marks of boxes and, what's more to the point, no drag marks. It is my belief he had nothing in that cellar. He could have been after the insurance.'

'But the insurance will want to see the books, check the orders.'

'True. Well, we'd best take a statement and then talk to his supplier.'

They returned to the shop. Hamish took out a notebook. 'Now, Mr Teller, you found the shop had been burgled when you opened up. That would be at nine o'clock?'

'Eight-thirty.'

12

'You didn't touch anything?'

'I went down to the cellar and found everything gone from there.'

'We'll check around and see if anyone heard or saw anything. What is the name of your supplier?'

'Frog's of Strathbane. Why?'

'The insurance company will want to see your books to check the amount of the lost stores against your record of deliveries.'

'They're welcome to look at them anytime.'

'Have you seen anyone suspicious about the town?'

'Now, there's a thing. There were two rough-looking men came into the shop two days ago. I hadn't seen them before. They asked for cigarettes and I served them but they were looking all around the place.'

'Descriptions?'

'One was a big ape of a man. He had black hair, foreign-looking. Big nose and thick lips. He was wearing a checked shirt and jeans.'

'Did he sound foreign?'

'I can't remember.'

Two men in white overalls came into the shop carrying cases of equipment. 'We'll stop for a moment while you take the forensic boys through the back to check the break-in,' said Hamish.

'What do you think?' Hamish asked Jimmy when the shopkeeper had gone through to the back shop with the forensic team.

'Seems a respectable body. Still, we'll check with Frog's. If he'd had the stuff delivered, then he must be telling the truth.'

'I don't like the look o' that cellar floor.'

'Well, if there's anything fishy, the forensic boys will find it.'

They waited until Mr Teller came back. 'Now,' said Hamish, 'what did the other fellow look like?'

'He was small, ferrety. I remember,' said Mr Teller, excited. 'He was wearing a short-sleeved shirt and he had a snake tattooed on his left arm.'

'Hair colour?'

'Maybe dark but his head was shaved. He had a thin face, black eyes, and a long nose.'

'Clothes?'

'Like a told you, he had a short-sleeved shirt on, blue it was, and grey trousers.'

Hamish surveyed the shopkeeper with a shrewd look in his hazel eyes. 'I'm puzzled by the state of your cellar floor.'

'How's that?'

'There were no marks in the dust. No signs of dragging.'

'Well, maybe they just lifted the stuff up.'

Jimmy Anderson was exuding the impatient vibes of a man dying for a drink.

'Come on, Hamish,' he said impatiently. 'Let forensics get on with it while we go over what we've got.'

Hamish reluctantly followed him over to the

pub. 'Maybe I'll nip back and tell those chaps from forensic about that cellar floor.'

'Och, leave them. They know their job.' Jimmy ordered two double whiskies.

'Just the one, then,' said Hamish. 'I don't trust that man Teller one bit.'

Finally he dragged a reluctant Jimmy away from the bar. Mr Teller was serving a woman with groceries.

'I think you should close up for the day,' said Hamish.

Mr Teller jerked a thumb towards the back shop. 'They said it was all right.'

'Let us through,' said Hamish.

Mr Teller lifted the flap on the counter.

Hamish and Jimmy walked through to the back shop.

'How's it going?' Jimmy asked one of the men.

'Nothing much,' he said. 'Looks like a straightforward break-in. Can't get much outside. There's gravel there. Nothing but a pair of size eleven footprints at the top of the cellar stairs.'

'Those are mine,' said Hamish. 'But what about the cellar itself, and the stairs? When I looked down, there seemed to be nothing but undisturbed dust.'

'Then you need your eyes tested, laddie. The thieves swept the place clean and the stairs.'

'What?' Hamish had a sinking feeling in his stomach.

'Have a look. We're finished down there.'

Hamish went to the cellar door, switched on the light, and walked down the steps. He could see sweeping brush marks in the dust.

'Those weren't there before,' he said angrily. 'Teller must have done it when you pair were out the back.'

Hamish retreated wrathfully to the shop, followed by Jimmy. 'Why did you sweep the cellar?' he demanded angrily.

Mr Teller looked the picture of outraged innocence. 'I never did. I went back outside to ask them if they wanted a cup of tea. I am a respectable tradesman and a member of the Rotary club and the Freemasons. I shall be speaking to your superior officer.'

'Speak all you want,' shouted Hamish. 'I'll have you!'

'Come on, Hamish.' Jimmy drew him outside the shop. 'Back to the bar, Hamish. A dram'll soothe you down.'

'I've had enough and you'd better not have any more. You're driving.'

'One more won't hurt,' coaxed Jimmy, urging Hamish into the dark interior of the bar. When he had got their drinks, he led Hamish to a corner table. 'Now, Hamish, couldn't you be mistaken? When anyone mentions Freemasons, my heart sinks. The big cheese is a member.' The big cheese was the chief superintendent, Peter Daviot.

'I'm sure as sure,' said Hamish.

'So what do you suggest we do if the wee

man's books are in order and tie in with Frog's records of deliveries?'

'I don't know,' fretted Hamish.

'It's your word against his.'

'You'd think the word of a policeman would count for something these days.'

'Not against a Freemason and a member of the Rotary,' said Jimmy cynically.

Hamish made up his mind. 'I'm off to Frog's. You can have my drink.'

Jimmy eyed the whisky longingly. 'I should report what you're doing to Blair.'

'Leave it a bit.'

'Okay. But keep in touch. I'll see if I can sweat Teller a bit. The wonders o' forensic science, eh?'

'There's something up with that lot from Strathbane. It seems to me they're aye skimping the job because they've got a football match to go to or something.'

Hamish drove to Strathbane after looking up Frog's in a copy of the Highland and Islands phone book he kept in the Land Rover. Their offices were situated down at the docks, an area of Strathbane that Hamish loathed. The rare summer sunshine might bring out the beauty of the Highland countryside but all it did was make the docks smell worse: a combination of stale fish, rotting vegetables, and what Victorian ladies used to describe as something 'much worse'.

The offices had a weather-faded sign above the door: FROG'S WHISKY AND WINE DISTRIBUTORS. He pushed open the door and went in. 'Why, Mary,' he exclaimed, recognizing the small girl behind the desk, 'what are you doing here?'

Mary Bisset was a resident of Lochdubh, small and pert. Her normally cheeky face, however, wore a harassed look. 'I'm a temp, Hamish,' she said. 'I cannae get the hang o' this computer.'

'Where's the boss?'

'Out in the town at some meeting.'

'Who is he?'

'Mr Dunblane.'

'Not Mr Frog?'

'I think there was a Mr Frog one time or another. Oh, Hamish, what am I to do?'

'Let me see. Move over.'

Hamish sat down at the computer and switched it on. Nothing happened. He twisted his lanky form around and looked down. 'Mary, Mary, you havenae got the damn thing plugged in.'

She giggled. Hamish plugged in the computer. 'What do you want?'

'The word processing thingy. I've got letters to write.'

'Before I do that, do you know where he keeps the account books?'

'In the safe.'

Hamish's face fell.

'But you're the polis. I suppose it would be all right to open it up for you.'

'Do you know the combination?'

'It's one of thae old-fashioned things. The key's on the wall with the other keys in the inner office.'

Hamish went into the inner office. 'Where is everyone?' he asked over his shoulder.

'Tam and Jerry – they work here – they've gone into town with Mr Dunblane.'

Hamish grinned. There on a board with other keys and neatly labelled 'Safe' was the key he wanted. 'Come in, Mary,' he said. 'You'd better be a witness to this.'

Hamish opened the safe. There was a large quantity of banknotes on the lower shelf. On the upper shelf were two large ledgers marked 'Accounts'. He took them out and relocked the safe. He sat down at a desk and began to go through them. 'Keep a lookout, Mary,' he said, 'and scream if you see anyone.'

'What's this all about?'

He grinned at her. 'If this works out, I'll take you out for dinner one evening and tell you.'

Chief Superintendent Peter Daviot had finished his speech to the Strathbane Businessmen's Association. He enjoyed being a guest speaker at affairs such as these. But his enjoyment was not to last for long. He had just regained his seat to gratifying applause when his mobile phone rang. He excused himself

19

from the table and went outside to answer it. It was Detective Chief Inspector Blair. 'Macbeth's landed us in the shit,' growled Blair.

'Moderate your language,' snapped Daviot. 'What's up?'

'Teller's shop up in Braikie was broken into and all his booze stolen. Macbeth's accusing Teller of covering up evidence and Teller is threatening to sue.'

'Dear me, you'd better get up there and diffuse the situation.'

'Anderson's up there.'

'Go yourself. This requires the attention of a senior officer. And tell Macbeth to report to me immediately.'

When Daviot returned to police headquarters, he was told to his surprise that Hamish Macbeth was waiting to see him. 'That was quick,' he said to his secretary, Helen. 'Where is he?'

'In your office,' said Helen sourly. She loathed Hamish.

Daviot pushed open the door and went in. Hamish got to his feet clutching a sheaf of photocopied papers.

'What's this all about, Macbeth? I hear there has been a complaint about you.'

'It's about Teller's grocery,' said Hamish. 'He claims to have had all his booze stolen, booze that was supplied by Frog's. These are photocopies of the account books at Frog's. They are an eye-opener. The last delivery to Teller is recorded in one set of books. But this other set shows five more shopkeepers from all over who claimed insurance and were paid fifty per cent of the insurance money.'

'How did you come by this?'

'Dunblane, the boss, and two others were out. I know the temp. She let me into the safe.'

'Macbeth! You cannot do that without a search warrant!'

'So I need one now. The temp won't talk. We'd better move fast.'

'I sent Blair up to Braikie because Teller was threatening to sue. I'll issue that search warrant and we'll take Detective MacNab and two police officers and get round there.'

It was late evening by the time Hamish Macbeth drove back to Lochdubh. He was a happy, contented man. Blair had returned from Braikie in time to hear about the success of the operation. The five other shopkeepers were being rounded up. They had claimed on supposedly stolen stock, taken it themselves and hidden it. So they gained half the insurance money and still had their stock after they had paid Dunblane.

That strange half-light of a northern Scottish summer where it never really gets dark bathed the countryside: the gloaming, where, as some of the older people still believed, the fairies lay in wait for the unwary traveller.

As Hamish opened the police station door, Lugs barked a reproachful welcome. Hamish took the dog out for a walk and then returned to prepare them both some supper. There came a furious knocking at the kitchen door just as he had put Lugs's food bowl on the floor and was sitting down at the table to enjoy his own supper.

He opened the door and found himself confronted with the angry figure of Mary Bisset's mother.

'You leave my daughter alone, d'ye hear?' she shouted. 'She's only twenty. Find someone your own age.'

Hamish blinked at her. 'Your daughter was of great help in our inquiries into an insurance fraud,' he said. 'I couldn't tell her what it was about but promised to take her out for dinner by way of thanks and tell her then.'

'Oh, yeah,' she sneered. 'Well, romance someone of your own age. You ought to be ashamed of yourself. Casanova!'

And with that she stormed off.

Hamish slammed the door. Women, he thought. I'm only in my thirties and I've just been made to feel like a dirty old man.

Chapter Two

The wife was pretty, trifling, childish, weak;
She could not think, but would not cease to
speak.

– George Crabbe

Hamish sat down at his computer in the morning to type out a full report of the insurance frauds. His long fingers flew rapidly over the keys. It was still sunny outside and he was anxious to get out and go about his normal business of sloping around and gossiping with the villagers.

The phone rang. He looked at it reluctantly for a few moments and then picked it up. 'Hamish?' said a scared little voice. 'It's me, Bella Comyn.'

'Morning, Bella. What can I do for you?'

'I'm frightened, Hamish. I want to leave him but I'm frightened of what he'll do.'

'Where is he at the moment?'

'He's down at the slaughterhouse in Strathbane.'

23

'Give me half an hour and I'll be over.'

Hamish typed busily, finished the report, sent it over to police headquarters, and then decided to find out what was up with Bella.

He turned over in his mind what he knew about her and her husband, Sean, while he drove out in the direction of their croft. Sean had reached the age of forty, two years before. He was a quiet, taciturn man. Then he came back from a trip to Inverness with a new bride – Bella. Bella was fifteen years younger than he, and the locals had murmured that never was there a more unsuitable crofter's wife. She wore flimsy, flirty clothes and could be seen teetering around Lochdubh in unsuitable high heels. She giggled and prattled and had seemed relatively happy.

Hamish parked his car outside their white-washed croft house and knocked on the door. Bella opened it. 'I'm right glad you've come,' she said. 'I've been wondering what to do.'

Hamish removed his cap and followed her into the kitchen.

'Would you like a cup of tea?'

'Maybe later. Tell me what's up.'

She sat down at the kitchen table. Her once-dyed-blonde hair was showing nearly two inches of black at the roots and was scraped back from her face. Her pale blue eyes were red with recent weeping.

'I can't take it any more,' she said. 'It's like being in prison. I can't go out anywhere. No

24

movies, no meals out. Just stuck here, day in, day out.'

'Does he beat you?'

'No, he doesn't have to. He just threatens to and I do what he wants. Look at my hair,' she wailed, holding out a strand for Hamish's inspection. 'He says if I dye it again, he'll kill me.'

'What about marriage counselling?'

'Can you see Sean going to a marriage counsellor? We keep ourselves to ourselves, that's what he says, day in and day out.'

'Where would you go?'

She nervously twisted her gold wedding ring around her finger. 'I've got a friend in Inverness. I should have married him. I phoned him. He said I could come to him anytime I wanted.'

'So why do you need me?'

'Folks round here say you're prepared to bend the rules a bit to help people out. I want time to pack up my things and get out.' She looked anxiously at the clock. 'We've only got about half an hour. I can't drive. I thought you could lock him up for something and then give me a lift down to the bus in Lochdubh.'

'I cannae do that,' exclaimed Hamish, whose accent always became broader when he was upset. 'You'll need to talk to one of the women.'

'I don't know any of them.'

'And I cannae interfere in a marriage. Och, I tell you what. Leave it with me. I sometimes see you around the village. How do you get down there?'

'Sean drives me down. Then he goes off to the pub while I get the shopping.'

'So next time, just get on the bus.'

'And leave all my things? I've got my mother's jewellery.'

'You could put that in your handbag or in the bottom of a shopping bag.'

'He searches my bags the whole time in case someone's been slipping me letters. He checks the phone bill. If I'm still here when it next comes in, he'll ask me what I was doing phoning the police station. I'll need to tell him I saw someone suspicious hanging around.'

'So how did you get in touch with this fellow in Inverness?'

'Last time I was down in Lochdubh, I phoned from the telephone box on the front as soon as Sean was in the pub. A couple of pounds it took and that was the very last of my own money. He doesn't allow me any except for the shopping, and when he gets home, he ticks every item off on the list.'

'You need some friends here, women friends. Let me try to fix something.'

'It won't do any good. He'll send them off.'

Hamish suddenly grinned. 'He doesn't know Mrs Wellington, then.'

* * *

Hamish drove back to the police station and put Lugs inside. He was walking up to the manse to see Mrs Wellington, the minister's wife, when Elspeth caught up with him.

'It's about Stoyre,' she said.

'Later, Elspeth,' said Hamish curtly. 'I'm busy.'

She gave him an odd, disappointed look and turned away.

I shouldn't have been so rude to her, thought Hamish. But one thing at a time. Stoyre can wait.

He went on to the manse.

Mrs Wellington was a formidable woman dressed as usual, despite the heat, in a tweed jacket, silk blouse and baggy tweed skirt, thick stockings and brogues.

'Oh, it's you,' she said ungraciously.

'I want to talk to you about a delicate matter,' said Hamish.

'In trouble with the ladies again?' she boomed. 'Mary Bisset's mother is going around saying you're chasing her daughter.'

'That's rubbish. Can I come in?'

Hamish followed her into the manse kitchen, a gloomy room which smelled strongly of disinfectant. Manse houses were always dark, he reflected, as if light were considered unholy.

He explained Bella's problem. Mrs Wellington listened carefully and said, 'She's a flighty little thing and he should never have married her, but she does need to get out a bit and the Mothers' Union always needs new members.'

'She doesn't have children.'

'Neither do the Currie sisters,' said Mrs Wellington dryly. 'But that doesn't stop them from trying to run everything. Leave it with me, Hamish.'

Hamish walked back down to the *Highland Times* office to look for Elspeth. He found her sitting at her desk, moodily stabbing a pencil into her hair.

'So what about Stoyre?' he asked.

'I took a run over there,' she said. 'Nothing. No one in the church.'

'So that's all you wanted to tell me?'

'I think you should go back. There's an odd feeling about.'

'What sort of feeling?'

'Fear.'

'It's probably the fear of some Calvinistic God. They seem to have gone all religious.'

'Could be. But I smell something else.'

Hamish suddenly felt ravenously hungry. He had not eaten any breakfast. To make up to Elspeth for his recent rudeness, he was about to ask her to join him at the Italian restaurant, but she looked up at him and grinned and said. 'What's all this about you romancing Mary Bisset?'

'There iss nothing in that,' said Hamish stiffly, and walked out. Irritating lassie.

Hamish went back to the police station and took a trout out of his freezer to defrost. Lugs let out a low grumbling sound. He did not like fish and felt his master was being selfish, but he brightened when Hamish began to fry up some lamb's kidneys for him.

Food ready, he loaded it all on to a tray and carried it out to the front garden. He placed Lugs's bowl on the grass and settled down to enjoy a meal of trout dipped in oatmeal, salad and chips.

The foxy face of Jimmy Anderson peered over the hedge. 'That looks good,' he said. He opened the gate and came in.

'I hope you've eaten,' said Hamish. 'I don't feel like cooking any more.'

'No, I'm fine.' Jimmy sank down in a chair next to him. He looked around: at the rambling roses tumbling over the front door and then over the hedge to where the loch sparkled in the sun. 'You've got the life o' Riley here, Hamish,' he said. 'Enjoy it while you can.'

'What do you mean?' demanded Hamish sharply.

'Well, because of you solving that big insurance case, Daviot's beginning to make noises about you being wasted up here, and Blair's encouraging him.'

'Why? He loathes my guts.'

'He feels if you were transferred to Strathbane, well, you'd just be another copper and he'd be more on hand to take the credit for anything you found out.'

'And what brings you up here?'

'Day off. I came to warn you about what was brewing, and I think you should be offering me something to drink.'

Hamish sighed but went into the house and came back with a bottle half full of whisky and a glass, which he set on the table. 'Help yourself.'

'Thanks.'

'So what do I do to stop getting a promotion?' asked Hamish.

'I dunno. Disgrace yourself – mildly.'

'How do I do that?'

Jimmy took a mouthful of whisky. 'You've always managed before,' he said.

'I do not want to go to Strathbane,' mourned Hamish. He waved his hand round about. 'Look what I've got to lose.'

'It's grand today, I'll give you that. But what about the long winters?'

'Believe me, long winters in Strathbane would seem worse than they do here.'

'Have it your way. Once a peasant, always a peasant. Stuck up here talking to the sheep would kill me.'

'If the bottle doesn't get to you first.'

'I can take it. Wait a wee bit: I've got an idea.'

Jimmy drank more whisky. 'There's a pet o' Blair's just joined the force. Red-hot keen. Arrest anyone on sight. Today, he's standing out on the main road afore you get to Strath-bane with a speed camera. You could pelt past him at a hundred miles an hour.'

'In a police vehicle? He wouldnae do a thing. He'd think I was chasing someone.'

'Get a private car, get drunk enough, and see what happens.'

'I'd lose my licence!'

'A policeman! He'd be told to hush it up.'

Hamish snorted in disbelief. 'By Blair? Come on, Jimmy. Have some sense.'

'No, by me. He crawls to me because he wants to make CID. I'll be on hand to tell him to drop it and leak it to Daviot. Daviot hates drunken drivers but I'll tell him it'll be bad for the police image if it ever gets in the papers.'

Hamish looked at Jimmy thoughtfully and then said, 'I'll get another glass.'

PC Johnny Peters stifled a yawn. He was bored and tired. Nearly the end of his shift. Like Blair, he was originally from Glasgow and dis-trusted all Highlanders. He guessed that in their primitive, almost telepathic way, the news of his speed trap had spread far and wide. Cars had passed him doing a mere thirty miles an hour although it was a sixty-mile-an-hour area.

His radio crackled. 'Peters here,' he said.

'Anderson here,' came the voice. 'Just had a report of a stolen car. A white Ford Escort belonging to Mrs Angela Brodie of Lochdubh.' Peters had just taken down a note of the registration number when his sharp eyes spotted a small white car on the horizon. He signed off, ran to his car, and swung it across the road.

At first it seemed as if the approaching car, which was coming at great speed, would hit him but the driver braked about one foot from him and sat behind the wheel, smiling inanely.

Peters climbed out and approached the car and rapped on the driver's window. Hamish Macbeth wound down the window and let a strong smell of whisky out into the air.

'Out!' shouted Peters.

Hamish was breathalyzed, handcuffed, charged with being drunk and driving a stolen vehicle. He felt relieved to be out of Angela's car. He had driven painfully carefully until just before the speed trap, when he had accelerated.

As Hamish was led out of the police car, Jimmy Anderson was waiting. 'Peters,' he said. 'What are you doing arresting Hamish Macbeth? He's the hero of the hour. He's the one that solved that big insurance case.'

'I am just doing my duty,' said Peters primly. 'He is drunk and was driving a stolen car.'

'Was it that Ford Escort?'

'Yes.'

'Oh. Dr Brodie has just phoned. It was his wife who reported the car stolen, not knowing her husband had given Hamish permission to drive it.'

'Nonetheless . . .'

'Here. Take the handcuffs off. You'll learn that we try to keep things like this away from the press. I'll talk to Daviot. Let him handle it.'

Peters looked doubtful but was obviously impressed by the fact that Anderson appeared to be on easy terms with the boss. He unlocked the handcuffs on Hamish's wrists.

'Come on, Hamish,' said Jimmy.

Hamish followed him with the stiff, stork-like walk of the drunk.

'Lots of water, Jimmy,' he whispered. 'And coffee.'

'I'll leave you in the canteen while I talk to Daviot.'

Peter Daviot listened grimly to Jimmy's tale.

'I hope he has been charged,' he said.

'Well, that's why I came to see you, sir. Macbeth's a popular man with a lot o' friends in the press. If he's charged, it'll go to the sheriff's court and get in the papers. Bad for our image, sir. Besides, we don't want some reporter remembering how that drunk-driving episode of Chief Inspector Blair's was hushed up.' Blair had wrapped his car round a tree

33

the year before after drinking heavily at a police party.

'Where's Macbeth now?

'In the canteen.'

'To think I was going to promote that man. That such ability should be allied to such dangerous behaviour.'

'May I offer a suggestion, sir?'

'Go on.'

'Macbeth manages to do very well where he is. He's never been one for the bottle. This was a one-off. Remember that fiancée o' his, Priscilla Halburton-Smythe?'

'Yes.'

'Well, he's learned she's getting married and maybe that's what upset him.'

'Send him to me. And get a police officer over to Lochdubh to pick up Mrs Brodie so that she may reclaim her car.'

Five minutes later, awash with mineral water and black coffee, a slightly more sober Hamish Macbeth faced his boss.

'Sit down,' barked Daviot. 'I am sure standing must be difficult for you. This is a bad business. You should have your licence removed and be suspended from duty.'

Hamish let out a giggle.

'And just what is so funny, Officer?'

'I couldnae help thinking o' all the cases I would solve if I were suspended. Thae detectives and policemen on the television are always being suspended from duty and that's when they solve cases.'

'Pull yourself together, man. This must be hushed up for the sake of our reputation. Do you know I was going to promote you? That's all off now. You are only fit to be a village policeman. I am sorely disappointed in you.'

'I am very sorry, sir.'

'Don't let it happen again. Get out of here. And sober up!'

'I hope it worked,' said Angela Brodie as she drove Hamish back to Lochdubh.

'Oh, it worked, all right. Thanks, Angela. Keep your eyes on the road and stop staring at me.'

'How drunk are you?'

'Nearly sober. I drank just enough to get over the limit.'

'This car reeks of booze.'

Hamish looked guilty. 'I spilled some on the seats.'

'Then when you get back, you can get some upholstery cleaner from Patel's and clean the lot.'

'Yes, Angela.'

'Mrs Wellington called on me before the police came to collect me. Seems you've launched her on a crusade to help Bella Comyn. She says she's a battered wife.'

'Not yet. But I gather her husband bullies her and won't allow her any freedom.'

'He does seem besotted with her. Do you really think he might harm her one day?'

'She seems to think so.'

'I'm going out there tomorrow with Mrs Wellington to see her.'

'Let me know how you get on.'

Back in Lochdubh, Hamish bought upholstery cleaner and diligently cleaned out the front seats of Angela's car. His mouth was dry and had a foul taste and his head was throbbing. At last he had finished. All he wanted now was two aspirin and a long sleep.

He was heading for the police station when Elspeth came running up to him. 'Hamish, there's a bit more about Stoyre.'

His headache was now dreadful. 'Is anyone dead or hurt or burgled?'

'No, it's not that. It's . . .'

'Leave it, Elspeth. Talk to me tomorrow.'

He strode off, leaving the reporter staring after him.

In the morning he awoke refreshed and with a hearty appetite. He went along to Patel's to buy bacon. As he entered the shop door, he could hear the voices of the Currie sisters, Nessie and Jessie, shrill with excitement.

'I tell you, he was cleaning out her car and stinking of the booze,' Nessie was saying. 'Why would he be doing that?'

'Why don't you ask him?' said Patel.

'Because he'll just lie, just lie,' said Jessie.

'If you want to know,' said Hamish angrily, 'I was taking some whisky to a sick friend in Strathbane and Mrs Brodie was driving me. She hit a rock and the top was loose and some of it spilled on the upholstery.'

The shop fell silent. The Currie sisters, who hated being caught out gossiping – a thing they were fond of saying that they never did – paid for their groceries and hurried out. Hamish bought a packet of bacon and headed home. He had no need to buy eggs; his hens supplied him with plenty.

He turned over the events of the day before and then remembered Elspeth. He simply must stop being rude to her. After breakfast he went to the local newspaper office, to be told she was out reporting on a flower show over at Dornoch. He wondered whether to drive over to Stoyre but then dismissed it. He had other villages on his beat to visit and it wasn't as if anything criminal had taken place in Stoyre.

He returned with Lugs in the late evening, satisfied that things on his beat were as quiet as they had been earlier that summer. He cooked a meal for himself and his dog and then was picking up the phone to call Elspeth when it rang. Mrs Wellington's voice boomed down the line. 'You've got to do something.'

'What's happened?'

'Sean's left Bella. I was up there early in the day with Angela Brodie to suggest that Bella should start attending the Mothers' Union meetings. Sean was there. He seemed pleased at the idea. Everything seemed normal. But Bella's just phoned in a state. She says he just walked out. Said he wasn't coming back.'

'I'll go right now and see her.'

'I'll meet you there.'

Bella's eyes were again red with recent weeping and she had a black eye. Mrs Wellington held her hand while she blurted out her story. Sean, she said, had pretended to be delighted at the invitation for her to join the Mothers' Union. After Angela and Mrs Wellington had left, he began to rant and say she had set it up so that she would have an excuse to slip out and meet other men, then he had blacked her eye and said he was sick of her and he was leaving her forever.

'You're better off without him,' said the minister's wife.

'How will you manage?' asked Hamish. 'For money, I mean.'

'We have a joint account. I can draw on that.'

'I thought Sean didn't let you have any money of your own.'

'He wouldn't let me draw any without his permission. But believe me, this is one time I'm not going to ask.'

'So what time did he leave?'

'About eleven o' clock.'

'But you didn't phone Mrs Wellington until this evening!'

Bella hung her head. 'I thought he would come back. I thought he'd never leave me. I'd given up the idea of running away.'

There came a long howl from outside. Bella jumped nervously. 'What's that?'

'It's my dog,' said Hamish. 'I'll see what's up.'

Mrs Wellington tut-tutted her disapproval. 'You shouldn't take that dog with you everywhere.'

Hamish went out to the Land Rover. He opened the passenger door and Lugs stumbled down to the ground. He raised his leg against the wheel.

'So that's all it was.' Hamish went back inside.

'Maybe Sean's just taken himself off to cool down,' he said. 'Mind if I have a look around the house?'

Was there a flicker of apprehension in Bella's eyes? 'Go ahead,' she said.

Hamish went through to the living room. A nearly new three-piece suite in a mushroom shade dominated the small room. There was a display cabinet with various pieces of china against one wall. No open fire; just a bar heater. Obviously the room was kept for 'best': a visit from the minister, the rare party.

He went next door to the bedroom. The double bed was covered in a blood-red shiny quilt. What was obviously Bella's side of the bed had a bedside table with film magazines and paperback romances stacked on it. He went to the table at Sean's side. On top was an alarm clock and nothing else. He jerked open the top drawer. A Gideon Bible and several packets of condoms. Hadn't Sean wanted children? He went out and through to the back of the small house and pushed open a door. This was Sean's office. There was an old-fashioned roll-top desk with neatly stacked papers beside a computer. He sifted through them. Farm accounts, sheep-dip papers, electricity and phone bills, nothing that could give him a clue to Sean's disappearance. He opened the drawers and carefully went through the contents until in the bottom drawer he found two passports, one belonging to Sean and the other to Bella. He opened Bella's. It was still in her maiden name – Bella Wilson.

He went through everything again but without finding a single clue to explain why Sean had left.

The man hadn't been gone long, he thought. It was surely a waste of police time, panicking so early over his disappearance.

* * *

40

He was driving back along the waterfront when he saw Elspeth Grant. He screeched to a halt. 'Want to come to the station for a cup of tea?'

'Why?'

'I've been a bit rude to you. But I've had other things on my mind.'

Elspeth swung round in the direction of the police station. 'Meet you there,' she said over her shoulder.

Hamish drove on. She was walking quickly, and by the time he had parked the Land Rover, she was waiting at the kitchen door.

He unlocked the door and ushered her into the kitchen.

'Any crime for me?' asked Elspeth as Hamish plugged in the kettle, a recent purchase. The summer had been so warm that there had been little need to light the stove every day.

Hamish told her about the insurance fraud. When he had finished, she asked, 'Do you know when that will come up in court?'

'I'll find out for you. I've just been up to see Bella Comyn.'

'Lochdubh's dizzy blonde. What's up with her?'

'Her husband's cleared off. Mind you, he only left this morning. He'll probably be back. She claims he bullied and threatened her.'

'I saw them at the Highland Games last year. He seemed besotted with her.'

'I'm sure he's all that. Maybe that's why he keeps such a strong grip on her. Here's your tea. Help yourself to milk and sugar.'

'Why is Lugs pawing at my skirt?'

'He likes tea a lot,' said Hamish. 'It's unnatural in a dog. I give him some on his birthday and at Christmas.'

Elspeth hooted with laughter. 'You treat that dog like a bairn, but then the childless always do.'

Hamish flushed with anger. 'I'm getting a bit weary of your personal remarks, Elspeth.'

'Sorry. I think you ought to take another look at Stoyre.'

'Why? Because you sense they're frightened? I need facts.'

'Well, there's a Mr and Mrs Bain from Stoyre. They've moved into a cottage up the back.'

'So?'

'They seem scared and won't talk about Stoyre.' Elspeth brushed a stray lock of hair from her face. 'Tell you what: let's go together to a church service on Sunday. Suss out the place.'

'I may be busy,' said Hamish loftily.

'You're just cross because I teased you about your dog. Come on, Hamish. Might be a laugh.'

'All right,' he said reluctantly. 'The service is usually at eleven in the morning. I'll pick you up at ten.'

'Right you are, copper. I'd best be going.'

She turned in the doorway and looked at him thoughtfully. Then she said, 'If it were me, I wouldn't believe a word Bella says.'

'And what makes you say that?'

She grinned. 'Just a feeling.'

Hamish went through to the police office after she had left and switched on his computer.

After typing in a password, he typed in the name Bella Wilson. He stared at the screen. Bella Wilson of Donnel Street, Inverness, had been charged, aged thirteen, at the juvenile court, with bullying one Aileen Hendry by repeatedly punching and kicking her. At age eighteen, she had been charged with hitting one Henry Cathcart on the head with a poker. Hamish leaned back in his chair and scowled horribly. Sean was gone and Bella was in charge of the joint account. Where was Sean?

Chapter Three

Come away, come away, death,
And in sad cypress let me be laid;
Fly away, fly away, breath;
I am slain by a fair cruel maid.
— William Shakespeare

The next day, Hamish went up to talk to Bella. He heard her singing in the kitchen as he approached the front door. He knocked, and while he waited for her to answer, he turned and looked around. There was no garden, just sheep-cropped turf and old rusting machinery. But over by the wall was a freshly dug patch of earth.

Bella opened the door. Her hair was newly blonded and she looked fresh and pretty. 'Have you found him?' she asked.

'Not yet. Can I come in?'

'All right.' She stood back reluctantly.

Hamish walked into the kitchen and took off his cap. 'Sit down, Bella,' he said.

'What's this all about?'

45

'It iss about your police record,' said Hamish, his accent becoming more sibilant with worry.

'That was a long time ago,' she said defiantly. 'And on both occasions I was provoked.'

Hamish took a deep breath. 'Have you been battering your husband?'

'What!' she shrieked. 'A wee thing like me wi' a big man like that!'

'It does happen.'

'No, I told you the truth. He's the bully.'

'There's a freshly dug patch in the ground outside. Who dug it?'

'Me. I was going to put in some flowers.'

'So you won't mind if I take a spade and have a look.'

Bella's face hardened. 'You'll need a search warrant.'

'Oh, I'll get one. But in order to get one, I'll need to report your criminal record, and it won't just be me but the top brass from Strathbane who'll question you, and a forensic team will be going over your house.'

'Oh, dig it up, then,' she snarled. 'The spade's by the kitchen door.'

Hamish went to the door and seized the spade. He went out into the bright sunlight. He began to dig in the freshly turned earth. Only about two feet below the surface, he uncovered a dead collie. He picked out the body and laid it on the turf. It had died recently – been killed, for its head had been smashed in. He sat back on his heels, feeling sick.

He turned his head. Bella was standing by the kitchen door. 'You did this,' he said flatly.

'Sean did it,' she said. 'I didn't want you to know.'

Hamish rose and went to the Land Rover, called Strathbane, and spoke rapidly. Then he returned and stood guard over the dead dog. 'You interfering bastard,' hissed Bella, her face now ugly with rage. 'I tell you, he walked out and said he wasn't coming back.'

'You will be asked by police from Strathbane, who will be here soon, to go with them to police headquarters for questioning.'

'I thought you were the policeman here,' she jeered.

'Not when it iss a question o' murder,' said Hamish quietly.

After Bella had been taken away, he returned to the police station to type out his report. Then once he had finished, he leant back in his chair. What if Sean had really run off because he was frightened of her? He would need money. Hamish put on his cap and went out and walked along to the bank and asked to see the manager, Mr MacCallum.

'It's about Sean Comyn,' said Hamish. 'He's gone missing, feared dead. But has he drawn out any money recently?'

47

'I should not be discussing a customer's account. That's confidential.'

'A possible murder does not keep anything confidential.'

'I suppose if I don't help you, you'll get a warrant.' The bank manager switched on the computer on his desk. Hamish waited patiently while he typed in various codes. 'Ah, here we are,' said Mr MacCallum. 'Sean Comyn made out a cheque to Queen and Barrie, estate agents in Strathbane.'

'When?'

'Yesterday.'

'Anything else?'

'Two hundred pounds out of a cash machine in Strathbane the same day.'

'Well, it looks as if the man is still alive, thank God.'

Hamish went back to the police station and dialled the estate agents. He explained the police were trying to contact a Sean Comyn.

'We rented him a cottage. He wanted somewhere cheap. We got him a place in Stoyre.'

'Address?'

'Number six, the waterfront.'

'Thanks.' Stoyre again, thought Hamish as he drove off, leaving behind a sulky Lugs.

When he descended into the huddle of houses which made up the tiny village of Stoyre, he was relieved to see people moving about and men working at the nets. Elspeth and her fears! He parked outside the pub and walked along the waterfront to number 6. It had been a fisherman's cottage and had a run-down appearance, unlike its neighbours. He knocked on the door.

To his relief, Sean Comyn himself answered it. He was unshaven and red-eyed.

'What's the matter?' he asked. 'Bella?'

'A word with you. Let me in.'

Sean led him into a front room. It was dark and sparsely furnished with a few shabby chairs and a sofa.

'Before we start,' said Hamish, taking out his mobile phone, 'I'll phone police headquarters and say you've been found.'

Sean tried to say something but Hamish held up a hand for silence. 'In a minute,' he said. He reported to Jimmy Anderson that Sean had been found. 'If she's been beating him,' said Jimmy, 'will he press charges?'

'I'll see what I can do.'

Hamish rang off and turned to Sean. 'Before I begin, I want you to take this phone and call your bank manager and freeze your account or, if I'm not mistaken, she'll clean you out.'

Sean took the phone from him. He did not ask questions or protest, simply phoned the bank and did what Hamish had suggested. Then he handed the phone back and sat with his hands between his legs, slumped forward.

'Now,' said Hamish gently, 'she'd been beating you, hadn't she?'

There was a long silence and then Sean said wearily, 'How was I to know? She seemed so pretty, so fragile, like a wee bird. It started soon after we were married. She'd get this blank look in the eyes and then start hitting me with anything that was handy. The other day, I said I wasn't taking any more, I was leaving her. She laughed in my face. And then still looking at me, she punched herself in the eye – hard. "I'll say you did that," she said.'

'You'll need to file charges.'

'I cannae do that, Hamish. I'd be the laughing stock o' the Highlands.'

'She killed one of your collies.' Hamish told him about the grave.

He turned a muddy colour but said, 'I can't let folks know she was beating me.'

'They'll know soon enough. Police and forensic have been crawling over your croft house looking for your dead body.'

'But if it goes to court, it'll be in all the papers. I cannae do it.'

Hamish sighed and looked around. 'Who owns this place?'

'Some couple. They rent it out to summer visitors. They havenae been able to rent it for a while.'

'Do you have a phone?'

'Over there. It's a coin box phone. Everything's got a coin box – the gas and the electric.'

'You can't go on living here. Think of your beasts. It's hot weather and Bella's more likely to take a hammer to them than give them water.'

He shuddered. 'Give me a bit o' peace, Hamish, till I get my courage back. But I'm not pressing charges.'

Hamish took a note of his phone number. 'I'll be back,' he said.

Once outside, Hamish walked back to the Land Rover and phoned Jimmy again. 'So far, he won't press charges.'

'Well, the RSPCA will,' said Jimmy, meaning the Royal Society for the Prevention of Cruelty to Animals. 'We found a bloodied hammer. Haven't got a report back yet on where the blood came from, but it's got her fingerprints on it, and if Sean's alive, then it stands to reason it's the dog's blood. And Sean will pay her fine and be stuck in Stoyre until his croft rots.'

'Where is she now?' asked Hamish.

'Johnny Peters is driving her home.'

'Good luck to him. I'll go and see her.'

Once more to Lochdubh to file another report and out to Sean's croft. As he approached the door, he knew instinctively that there was no one at home. He tried the door. Locked. Maybe

51

she wasn't back yet. And yet he had taken his time over the report.

He got back in the Land Rover and drove down into Lochdubh and stopped outside Patel's grocery store. A daily bus would have left for Inverness half an hour ago. He went into the shop and asked Mr Patel, 'Did anyone see if Bella Comyn left on the bus?'

Nessie Currie appeared behind him, her eyes gleaming behind thick glasses. 'The poor wee thing left on the bus with two big suitcases. A policeman drove her to Lochdubh. What's been happening?'

Hamish didn't answer. He went back to the police station and phoned Jimmy.

'Bella Comyn left for Inverness on the bus. Johnny Peters drove her there. What was he on about?'

'I'll see if he's back yet and ring you.'

Hamish took Lugs out for a walk and then fed the dog. He was just wondering whether to ring Jimmy again when the phone rang. It was Jimmy.

'Peters didn't know anything about why she was at police headquarters,' he said. 'He'd just come on duty and was simply told to take her back to Lochdubh. She spun him a story that she had gone to report her husband missing and that she was so upset, she wanted to stay with relatives in Inverness. She packed in a short time and he drove her to Lochdubh.

She'd called the bank and whatever she heard upset her.'

'I told Sean to tell the bank to freeze the account. It was a joint account.'

'Anyway, she got on the bus and off she went.'

'You'd best phone Inverness police. We'll get her for the dog if nothing else.'

'Will do.'

'Thank God she couldnae drive or she'd have taken Sean's car as well. I'll get over to Stoyre and give him a lift home.'

'Why Stoyre?' asked Hamish as he drove the crofter towards Lochdubh.

'It was the cheapest rent I could find,' said Sean. 'I only took it for a month – holiday let.'

'Have you any idea where Bella might have gone?'

'She's an only child and her mother and father are dead.'

'What about relatives at your wedding?'

'There weren't any. We were married in the register office and two of my cousins acted as witnesses.'

'Any friends?' Hamish wondered whether to ask about the man in Inverness that Bella had said she ought to have married but decided against it.

'Not that I know of.'

'Didn't that strike you as odd?'

'No, I thought she just wanted to be with me. I couldnae get over the fact that someone so young and pretty could fancy me.'

'I hope you're over her, Sean. And if she comes back, you're to phone me immediately.'

'I'll do that. She shouldnae have killed my dog. Which one?'

'Don't know.'

'Probably Bob,' he said gloomily. 'Always was a friendly dog. Now, Queenie, the other, was mortal scared of her.'

As they approached Sean's croft, Sean said, 'It's odd. Things'll be the same as they were afore I married her. But not the same, if you know what I mean. I'll aye be frightened I'll turn round and see her standing there.'

'She's wanted on a charge for killing the dog – cruelty. She's made a run for it. I doubt if she'll be back. Get yourself a lawyer and get a divorce.'

Hamish parked the Land Rover and Sean climbed stiffly down and then heaved his suitcase out of the back. 'Thanks, Hamish.'

'I'd best come in with you,' said Hamish. 'See if she's taken anything she shouldn't have.'

Sean unlocked the door. Hamish waited in the kitchen while Sean looked around the place. 'Nothing taken but her clothes and things,' he said. He went to the door and gave a shrill whistle. A collie came bounding up to him. 'This is Queenie,' he said, fondling the animal's coat. 'I'll be all right now, Hamish.'

'Don't keep the truth of the matter to yourself, Sean. She's put it about that you were the one who was bullying her. There's no shame in it. Folks wouldn't expect you to hit back at a lassie.'

'I'll think about it.'

Hamish went back to the police station and phoned Jimmy Anderson. 'Any news?'

'Not a sight of her,' said Jimmy. 'Police were waiting at Inverness station but she never got off the bus. The driver said she got off at Dingwall. No record of her having taken another bus or even the train from Dingwall. She's gone to ground somewhere.'

'Are the police at Dingwall checking the taxi services?'

'Nobody's checking anything any more, Hamish.'

'Why?'

'Blair says it's a waste o' manpower looking for a lassie who killed a dog. He instructed us all to have nothing more to do with it.'

'Doesn't the silly cheil know she might kill a man or woman the next time?'

'He doesn't care.'

'While you're on the phone, have you heard any reports of anything going on in Stoyre?'

'Where's Stoyre?'

'It's a wee village up on the coast.'

'That's your beat. No, I haven't heard anything.'

Hamish thanked him and rang off. Then he phoned Mrs Wellington and told her the truth about Sean's marriage. At first she wouldn't believe him until he told her about the death of the dog. 'A woman who would do that is capable of anything,' said Mrs Wellington.

Hamish then phoned Angela Brodie with the same information and then asked, 'There's a new family in Lochdubh called Bain. Where's their house?'

'Up the back. The one that belonged to the dustman's wife, Martha Macleod. Remember, she and your ex-policeman moved up to live in the Tommel Castle Hotel after they got married.'

Clarry, Hamish's policeman when Hamish had last, briefly, been elevated to the rank of sergeant, had left the force to become a chef at the hotel.

'I'll call on them tomorrow,' said Hamish.

'Why?'

'Just to be friendly, that's all.'

But Hamish remembered that Elspeth in her psychic way had not trusted Bella. And Elspeth had said the Bains were frightened.

Hamish walked past Patel's and up the lane at the back to the Bains's cottage. He knocked on the door and it was answered by a small, thin woman. She had sallow skin and small black eyes, which regarded him warily.

'Mrs Bain?'

'Yes, what's happened? It's not Mairie, is it? I sent her down to the shop.'

'No, it's only a friendly call. I heard you had moved from Stoyre.'

'Yes, that's right. We're fine.' She made to close the door.

'I chust wanted a word with you,' said Hamish, not used to unfriendliness. 'Is your man at home?'

'He's asleep. He's been out all night at the fishing.'

A small voice behind Hamish piped, 'I got the milk, Ma.'

Hamish swung round. A little girl, about ten years old, stood there.

'Get in the house this minute!' ordered her mother.

The girl slid past them and vanished into the cottage.

'And is everything all right with you?' pursued Hamish.

'Yes, yes. Fine. Now, if you don't mind . . .'

'Was anything going on at Stoyre?'

She had been about to close the door but hesitated. 'No, why?'

'There was a strange atmosphere when I was there.'

'Well, ye cannae be arresting an atmosphere,' and with that she closed the door firmly.

Hamish pushed back his cap and scratched his fiery hair. He turned and walked back down to the waterfront and along to the harbour. Archie Maclean, a fisherman, was sitting on the wall outside his cottage, puffing on a hand-rolled cigarette.

'Grand morning, Archie,' said Hamish, sitting down next to him.

'Aye, it is that.'

'Don't you ever sleep?'

'I will be having a kip this afternoon. Herself is cleaning again.'

The sound of frantic activity sounded from the cottage behind them.

'I went up to see the Bains,' said Hamish.

'Aye, Harry Bain was out with us last night.'

'What's he like?'

'Quiet wee man. Nothing much to say for himself. But a good worker.'

'He's just moved here from Stoyre. Have you heard anything about Stoyre, Archie?'

'Nothing much except they seem to have a rare powerful preacher. The kirk is aye full.'

'If you get talking to Harry, see if you can find out anything.'

'I'll do that. But why? You think something criminal's going on?'

'I don't know. Just a feeling.'

Hamish went back to the police station after collecting the newspapers from Patel's. Time to relax and forget about Bella and about Stoyre. He took a deck chair out to the garden and, with Lugs at his feet, settled down to read.

The phone rang in the police station. Hamish rustled a newspaper impatiently. Let the answering machine pick it up. The window to the police office was open. The answering machine clicked on. Blair's voice broke the peace of the day. 'Get yourself over to Stoyre. Major Jennings's cottage has been blown up.'

'Where is the major?' asked Hamish as he and Jimmy stood with detectives and police officers surveying the burnt-out shell that had once been the major's bungalow.

'Flying up from the south. We'll have the anti-terrorist squad here.'

'Can't be the IRA this far north.'

'The major's retired but he was once in army intelligence. May have had something to do with Northern Ireland.'

'Are they sure it was some sort of explosive? Couldn't have been a faulty Calor gas tank?'

'Too early to say. Could just be some anti-English bastards. You mind that film *Braveheart*?'

'Of course,' said Hamish. 'And what a load of inaccurate historical rubbish it was, too.'

'Aye, but you know it caused a lot of anti-English feeling in some weak heads. Then there was that showbiz chap, Cameron

McIntosh over in Mallaig. His cottage got destroyed.'

'Well, we'll see,' said Hamish uneasily. All the while he thought, This can't be happening in Stoyre. He looked down at the calm sea and the sun-warmed stone harbour. Something evil was going on here.

Blair came marching up to him. 'Move your lazy bum, Macbeth, and see what you can get out of the local yokels.'

Hamish set off down the slope from the ruins of the major's cottage.

He decided to try the manse first. The door was eventually answered by what he at first thought was a young girl. She was wearing a short summer dress and her hair was in pigtails. Her thin legs ended in white ankle socks and black flat shoes. Her features were small but then he noticed the thin, spidery lines on her face. 'Mrs Mackenzie?'

'Yes, Officer. Won't you come in? My husband is going about his parochial duties.' Her voice was soft and lilting.

Hamish took off his cap and followed her along a stone-flagged passage to the manse kitchen. The long sash windows were open and a breeze fluttered the crystal-white net curtains. A scarlet Raeburn cooker stood against one wall and a dresser with brightly patterned plates against another. There was a scrubbed wooden kitchen table in the centre surrounded with ladder-back chairs.

'Sit down, Officer,' said the minister's wife. 'Coffee?'

'That would be grand.'

She put instant coffee in two mugs and poured boiling water from a kettle on top of the stove. 'Help yourself to milk and sugar,' she said, sitting down opposite him. 'I suppose you've come about that terrible business.'

'The major's cottage, yes. What can you tell me about it?'

'Nothing.' Her eyes were greyish blue and slightly slanted, the sort of Highland eyes which reflected everything back, in a way, without betraying their owner's feelings. 'We were woken up about dawn with this tremendous blast, and the windows of the manse rattled.'

'So you got up and went out to have a look?'

'Well, no. We were both still tired, so we went back to sleep.'

'Heavens, woman! Surely natural curiosity would ha' impelled you to go out of doors to see what had happened.'

'Odd things happen every day,' she said serenely. 'It is God's will and it is not up to us to question the will of God.'

'I would think it was up to everyone to question the will of man,' said Hamish dryly. He looked at her curiously. 'I mean, God didn't blow up the major's cottage. Some villain or villains did it.'

61

'It could have been lightning or a thunderbolt.'

'Meaning God zapped the major's cottage? Havers. And what do you think a douce body like the major would have done to incur the wrath of God?'

Her thin lips became even thinner as she folded them into a reproving line. 'He did not attend the kirk when he was here.'

'The kirk is Free Presbyterian. Stands to reason, the major is probably a member o' the Church of England.'

'That is as may be.'

'And what's that supposed to mean?'

She sipped her coffee in silence while Hamish gave her a frustrated look. At last he said, 'So you've nothing to tell me?'

'There's nothing I can tell you.'

He stood and picked up his cap. 'If you think of anything, let me know.'

'You can find your own way out?'

'Aye.'

Baffled, Hamish went off. He stood outside the door of the manse and looked down on the village of Stoyre, a huddle of houses before a tranquil sea. The air smelled fresh and clean. Somewhere up on the hill a sheep bleated.

He walked down into the village and into the pub. A few locals were sitting at tables. When he came in, they rose to their feet and went out. Andy Crummack, the landlord, was polishing glasses.

'I seem to be bad for business,' commented Hamish.

'We keep ourselves to ourselves in this village,' said Andy, 'and we don't like nosy coppers asking questions.'

'Then get used to it,' snapped Hamish. 'Because I'm the first of many.' He took out his notebook. 'Now, where were you when the major's cottage was blown up?'

'I was in my bed.'

'And did you go out to see what happened?'

'No, I thought it was thunder.'

'Man, the blast must have been horrendous. What time did you hear it?'

'I looked at the clock. It was just after five.'

'Andy, something's going on in this village and I mean to get to the bottom of it.'

'Aye, well, that's your job.'

The pub door opened and Elspeth came in. Hamish was relieved to see someone, anyone, from outside this strange village. 'Come and have a drink,' he hailed. He jerked a thumb at Andy. 'No use asking him anything.'

Hamish ordered a tonic water for himself and a whisky for Elspeth and carried them to a corner table. 'Got any news for me?' he asked.

'Not a thing. They all heard that blast at dawn and inexplicably no one admits to going out to see what happened or even to looking through a window.'

'Do you still think they're scared of something?'

'No, that's the odd thing. They've got carefully blank faces, but underneath they're elated about something – elated and secretive, like children hiding something.'

'Don't you think,' asked Hamish, surveying her outfit, 'that you might get a bit more out of the locals if your clothes weren't so strange?'

Elspeth was wearing a grey chiffon blouse with a pair of cut-off denim shorts and clumpy hiking boots.

'No, you old fuddy-duddy. No one is going to get anything out of this lot.'

Hamish looked across her out the window and saw a familiar figure heading for the pub door. 'Blair,' he hissed. 'Don't say you saw me.'

He vaulted the bar and made his way through to the back premises just as the detective chief inspector came through the door. There was a back storeroom with a door opening on to a weedy garden. In the middle of the storeroom, clutching a Bible and on his knees in prayer, was the landlord. Hamish edged round him and darted out into the sunlight. Andy seemed unaware of his existence.

Hamish then went diligently from cottage to cottage, asking questions and getting the same replies as Elspeth had received. He had just left one of the cottages when he heard himself being hailed by Jimmy Anderson. 'Get anything?' asked Jimmy.

Hamish sighed. 'I get the impression they all believe it was the wrath of God. They've never actually attacked anyone English up here before. I mean, they don't even like people from anywhere south of Perth.'

'See Blair?'

'He was heading for the pub. He's probably still there.'

'Well, that'll keep him away for a bit. The major should be here this afternoon. I wonder what he'll have to say. The bomb squad is combing the ruins. They think it was one of those fertilizer bombs like the IRA uses.'

'Now, why don't I believe it was the IRA?' muttered Hamish. 'There's something odd going on here, Jimmy.'

'I agree with you. I think one of them did it out of spite. Maybe the Lord told them to do it. Is there a lot of inbreeding in these parts?'

'Not now. No.'

'It would drive me daft living in a place like Stoyre. Think what it's like in the winter when the sun rises at ten in the morning and sinks at two in the afternoon.'

'It does that in Strathbane.'

'Aye, but there's life there, man. Lights, traffic, theatre, cinema, clubs.'

'And crime and drugs.'

'Maybe, but we haven't had anything as dramatic as this.'

'Oh, here's the boss,' said Hamish.

Blair, red in the face and breathing whisky fumes, came up to them. 'You,' he said to Jimmy, 'come back up to the major's with me. You, Macbeth, get back to your local duties. We've enough men here.'

Hamish trotted off. He knew that Jimmy would probably fill him in later and he also knew that he wasn't going to get anything more out of the locals.

As he drove off to Lochdubh, he noticed a cloud, a small round cloud, travelling towards the sun. The breeze through the open window felt damp against his cheek and the countryside had that waiting feeling it gets when rain is about to arrive. By the time he got back to the police station, the sky was a uniform grey, as if the clouds had sunk down rather than blowing in from the sea.

He walked Lugs and fed him and then himself. He checked on his sheep and went back indoors as the first fat raindrops began to fall. He made a pot of tea and sat down at the kitchen table to mull over the situation in Stoyre. Somehow the greyness of the day and the soft rain falling outside seemed to bring back reality to the Highlands and to his mind. He was now sure that some local had blown up the major's cottage to get rid of him. The major or some of the guests he usually invited in the summer might have offended someone, and Highland malice, as Hamish knew, ran slow and deep and took its time over getting revenge.

He carried his mug of tea through to the office and stood at the window, looking out at the rain-pocked waters of the loch. Mist was rolling down the hills opposite to hang in grey wreaths round the top of the forest trees. A small yacht sailed into view. Two figures were taking down the sails, and he could hear the chug-chug of the donkey engine.

He sat down at his desk and switched on the computer and began to type a report. The next day would be a Sunday. Hamish remembered he had promised to go to church in Stoyre with Elspeth. Might be interesting to hear one of Fergus Mackenzie's sermons and discover what it was in them that had prompted such a strong religious revival.

Jimmy Anderson arrived in the early evening. 'Blasted weather,' he said. 'Got any whisky?'

'No,' said Hamish, 'and the shop's closed. Closes early on Saturday.'

'Got anything?'

'I've got some brandy left over from Christmas.'

'That'll do.'

Hamish took down the brandy bottle from the cupboard. 'I won't join you,' he said. 'I don't like brandy much.'

'And that's why you've got it left over from Christmas. Good. All the more for me,' said Jimmy. 'Pour it out.'

Hamish poured a measure of brandy into a glass and placed it in front of him.

'Got cold in here,' complained Jimmy.

'I'll light the stove,' said Hamish. 'Any more orders?'

'No,' said Jimmy, taking a swig of brandy. 'Ah, that's better. Blair's been getting on my tits. There's bigwigs up from Scotland Yard and some bods from MI5, and Blair's been showing off by pushing me around and crawling to them.'

Hamish filled the stove with kindling and paper and struck a match. When the stove was lit, he added several slices of dark peat and a couple of logs. 'I think it was a local job,' he said.

'Well, to be sure, the dafties are all blaming it on God.'

'Did you manage to get out of them why God should be angry with Major Jennings?'

'Mrs MacBean at the general store was more forthcoming than the rest of them.'

'What did she say?' asked Hamish.

'When I asked her why God would see fit to blow up the major's cottage, she replied that God moved in mysterious ways. And believe me, that meant she was being downright talkative compared to the rest of them up in Brigadoon.'

'So long as everyone's convinced it's a terrorist attack, they'll leave the locals alone. Did the major arrive?'

'Yes, but he seemed quite unfazed. He said the cottage was insured. He said he'd had some trouble with the locals. He believes it was a piece of spite.'

'What trouble?'

'Usual trouble any incomer has up here – not getting help, plumber not turning up, no one prepared to help with the garden or building repairs, that sort of thing.'

'I'm off to the kirk tomorrow,' said Hamish. 'Maybe I'll start off by finding out why they've all gone religious.'

'Maybe you'll see the light yourself,' said Jimmy. 'Pass that bottle over.'

Chapter Four

Where we tread 'tis haunted holy ground.
— Lord Byron

Hamish's first thought when he picked up Elspeth the next day was that at least she had made the effort to dress in a more conventional manner. He had been afraid that she might have decided to turn up for church in something like hot pants. But she was wearing a long black skirt with a black sweater and had a tartan stole around her shoulders. When she climbed into the Land Rover, however, he noticed that she was still wearing her favourite clumpy boots.

'Haven't you got a pair of shoes?' he asked.

'Hamish Macbeth! Somehow you have graduated to being a grumpy husband without ever having been one. Have you seen the feet of women who have worn high heels all their lives? All bent and twisted. So just drive on and mind your own business.'

A fine drizzle smeared the windscreen. Hamish switched on the wipers, which made a grating sound. 'You need new wipers,' commented Elspeth.

'I do not,' said Hamish, who was sometimes mean about small items like windscreen wipers. 'They're chust fine when the rain's heavy.'

As if to prove his point, the rain began to pour down. 'The weather forecast's pretty good,' said Elspeth. 'It said it would get better later.'

'Do you have any idea why Major Jennings's cottage got blown up?'

'It's something to do with the villagers. I'm sure of that. There's a sort of religious mania emanating from them.'

'You mean God told them to do it?'

'Something like that,' said Elspeth vaguely. 'Oh, look, I can see a little patch of blue sky ahead.'

As they approached Stoyre, the rain abruptly ceased. Elspeth was used to the lightning-quick changes of weather in the Highlands but she still stared in wonder as the clouds rolled back and the sun blazed down on the still-black sea. Smoke rose from the cottages below them. Most villagers still had their water heated by a back boiler in the fireplace, so fires were often kept going all year round.

Up on the hill, the police tapes fluttered outside the major's cottage. The waterfront was full of cars and television vans. 'You've got competition,' remarked Hamish.

'They won't get anything out of the villagers,' said Elspeth. 'If I can't, they can't.'

'Fancy yourself as an ace reporter?'

'No, but I'm Highland and they aren't.'

Hamish parked amongst the cars. They won't get a drink here anyway,' he said. 'The pub closes on the Sabbath.'

They climbed down from the police Land Rover. There were groups of jaded press standing around. No one bothered to approach them. After their experiences trying to get something out of the villagers and failing, they probably summed up the small population as a waste of time.

Elspeth and Hamish caught up with the line of villagers making their way to the church.

'Now,' said Hamish, 'let's see what the preaching is like.'

The interior of the church was small and whitewashed. There were no religious statues, no crosses. There wasn't even an organ. A chanter, a man who struck a tuning fork on one of the front pews and sang the first note, started off the hymn singing.

They sang, 'There is a green hill far away without a city wall.'

'I used to think that meant a city that didn't have a wall,' whispered Elspeth. 'Then I learned it meant outside the city wall.'

'Shhh!' said an old lady waspishly.

The hymn was followed by two readings from the Bible, and then the minister rose to deliver his sermon. Hamish listened in surprise. Whatever had caused this religious fervour in Stoyre, it could hardly be the preachings of Fergus Mackenzie. Hamish and Elspeth were seated at the back of the church and they had to strain to hear what the minister was saying. His soft voice did not carry well. There was no passion or threat of hell-fire in his sermon. He said the villagers all knew that they were chosen by God and must live up to this privilege. He talked of Moses and the burning bush and then of the leading of the Israelites to the promised land. His soft voice and the heat of all the bodies in the church and from the sun, now blazing in through the windows, had a soporific effect on Hamish, and his head began to droop. Elspeth nudged him in the ribs. 'Pay attention.'

The service ended with the Twenty-third Psalm.

Elspeth and Hamish waited outside by the church door to see if any of the villagers said anything of interest to the minister, but all they could hear were murmurs of 'Grand service' or replies to the minister's occasional questions about health or children.

Hamish saw Mrs MacBean, who ran the general store, and taking Elspeth's arm, he fell into step beside her. 'Bad business about the major's cottage,' he remarked.

'We should not be discussing such things on the Sabbath,' said Mrs MacBean primly. 'We have our minds on higher things.' This reminded Hamish that it was a peculiarity among some Presbyterians to not even hail their best friend on a Sunday. As Mrs MacBean had said, the mind was supposed to be on higher things. They had strict observance of the Lord's Day. There would even be a member of the congregation whose duty it was to 'police' the village on a Sunday to make sure no one was doing anything sinful like watching television or hanging out their clothes.

She hurried on down the hill.

'I brought a bit of a picnic,' said Hamish to Elspeth. 'We may as well have something to eat and drink. Let's sit on the harbour wall. It should be dry by now.'

He opened the Land Rover and lifted out a basket. 'You're very domesticated,' commented Elspeth. Hamish felt a stab of irritation and wondered why even the smallest thing Elspeth said to him sounded like criticism.

Hamish had brought fruit and sandwiches and a flask of coffee. 'Now,' he said between bites of sandwich, 'what have we got?'

'Bugger all,' said Elspeth, looking dreamily over the sea.

'Think!' commanded Hamish sharply. 'Maybe the boys up the hill have found evidence of an IRA visit and so we can forget about the whole thing because whoever did it will probably be back in Ireland by now.'

'Okay, I'll think,' said Elspeth. 'At first they were afraid. Something threatened them. Then they lost that fear. Something reassured them. Let's go off on a flight of fancy. The minister talked of Moses and the burning bush. He said they were the chosen people – not the Israelites, but the people of Stoyre. They're very superstitious up here. I mean, it's not often you get weather like this right on the coast. Battered by gales all year round, poor soil to scrape a living out of, meagre fishing what with the decline in stocks and all those bloody European Union regulations.'

'We should all go and live in Brussels,' said Hamish. 'I bet they don't give a damn about rules and regulations over there.'

'Quiet! You told me to think, so I'm thinking. Maybe someone in the village has been having visions.'

'Probably the DTs.'

'Someone sees something. Can't have been the Virgin Mary. They would consider that too popish. Can't be something old and Celtic like a kelpie. That wouldn't prompt all these visits to the church. Some vision that at first frightened and then reassured. But something that told them not to talk about it.'

'Let's take it away from the supernatural,' said Hamish. 'More coffee?'

'Please.'

'Right. Say someone or some people wanted Stoyre kept sealed off. Why?'

76

'Nice little harbour for landing drugs.'

'True. But they would see real live men in a real live boat. I'll have another talk to Sean Comyn and then I'll try the Bain family again. There's Jimmy.'

Hamish waved to Jimmy Anderson, who was heading down the harbour towards them. Jimmy came up mopping his red, sweating foxy face with a large handkerchief. 'Didn't know it was going to be this warm,' he complained when he came up to them. 'Hello, Elspeth. Got anything to drink, Hamish?'

'There's a cup of coffee left in the flask.'

'Coffee! Yuk! There's not a dram to be found in this place.'

'How's it going?'

'Stone-faced locals without a word to say. Blair took over some of the interviewing and I thought he was going to have a stroke. Nobody saw anything. Nobody even got out of bed to see what the noise was.'

'Any news of any terrorist activity?'

'Nothing. You find out anything?'

'Only that something has prompted a religious fervour. The major usually brings up some friends for the fishing. Did he have anyone on the guest list that might excite the attentions of a terrorist?'

'No. And he only did some low-key work in Belfast ages ago. He's retired. Actually he's quite chipper about the whole thing. He planned to sell up and the insurance will bring him a lot more than he could have got from selling it.'

'Maybe he did it himself.'

Jimmy grinned. 'That's what Blair accused him of and they had to fly Daviot up to soothe the major down. This your day off?'

'Aye.'

'I might drop round to see you in Lochdubh on my way back. Got any whisky?'

'No,' said Hamish, 'and you finished the brandy.'

'Patel's open?'

'Not now. He only opens in the morning for the Sunday papers.'

'Damn! I'll be off, then.'

'How long will the police be around?' asked Elspeth.

'A good few days yet, and if there's any funny business going on in Stoyre, believe me, nothing's going to happen until they give up and leave. Say it's a local job – the major's cottage, I mean. It could just be spite but I don't think so. The man only came up in the summers. Now, the major was once in army intelligence. Perhaps someone didn't want any sharp-eyed outsider around, someone who might notice things the locals wouldn't.'

'Any word of Bella Comyn?'

'Nothing yet. I'd like that one caught before she messes up someone else's life.'

* * *

Once back at the police station after having dropped Elspeth off, Hamish fed his hens, some of whom were quite elderly as he never had the heart to kill any of them for the pot, walked Lugs, and settled down to watch television. He felt he'd done enough on his day off. Sean and the Bains could wait until the morning.

He had just untied and kicked off his heavy regulation boots, which he wore even when not wearing his uniform, when he heard the phone ringing in the office. He was just wondering whether to answer it or not when the answering machine clicked on and he heard the loud voice of Mrs Wellington. 'Clarry phoned from the hotel. He's been trying to get you. One of the maids says she saw Bella Comyn in Bonar Bridge today.'

Hamish rang the minister's wife and asked her, 'Where was she seen?'

'In that grocery shop just by the bridge.'

Hamish thanked her, retied his boots, and with a sigh set off on the long road to Bonar Bridge with Lugs beside him in the passenger seat.

'Now, Lugs,' said Hamish, 'I wonder just what is going on in Stoyre.' The dog turned his odd blue eyes reluctantly from the passing countryside and gave a slight sniff. 'Exactly,' agreed Hamish. 'I don't know either. And I don't like it. I've got some holidays owing. I've a good mind to go and stay there for a few days and see what I can find out. I could stay at that place Sean rented. Would you like Stoyre?'

Lugs sighed again.

'Me neither,' said Hamish, 'but something weird's going on there.'

Master and dog then drove in companionable silence to Bonar Bridge.

The sun had gone behind a bank of clouds when Hamish finally drove into Bonar Bridge.

The place looked deserted. He parked outside the grocery shop and went in. There were no customers. A woman behind the counter asked, 'Can I help you? It's Mr Macbeth, isn't it?'

'Aye,' said Hamish, stepping forward and removing his peaked cap. 'Have we met?'

'Up at the Highland Games at Braikie two years ago. My boy got stuck up a tree and you got him down.'

'I remember. It's Mrs Turner, isn't it?'

'That's right. What can I do for you?'

'I'm looking for a Bella Comyn, small, blonde, pretty. I heard she was in here today.'

'Oh, her! What's she wanted for?'

'Oh, just part of a general inquiry. Do you know where she lives?'

'Up in one of the Swedish houses on the council estate, number twenty-four Sutherland Lane.'

'She living on her own?'

'No, she's Jamie Stuart's girlfriend. They're going to get married.'

'Are they really? Who is this Jamie Stuart?'

'He's a motor mechanic. He works at a garage in Alness.'

'Thanks. I'll go and see them.'

Swedish houses are wooden two-storey houses built by the government right after World War II. Hamish cruised around the estate until he found Sutherland Lane. Number 24 seemed to be in good repair. The garden was neat and tidy. The window frames had recently been painted, as had the front door.

He rang the bell. A thin young man opened the door. 'What's up?' he asked anxiously.

'I'm here to see Bella.'

The young man stood back. 'Come in. I hope it's not bad news.' He led the way into a living room. Bella was sitting embroidering a tablecloth, the picture of pretty domesticity. When she saw Hamish, a look of pure hate flashed in her eyes, but then she smiled and said, 'Why, Hamish. How nice to see you. Tea?'

Hamish sat down and surveyed her. 'We've been looking for you, Bella.'

'What's this all about?' demanded Jamie.

'It's about that dog I killed,' said Bella. 'I told you about that. I hit it on the head to defend myself, and now the RSPCA's looking for me.'

Hamish swung round and said to Jamie, 'I hear you're getting married. Do you know she is already married?'

'We're getting married just as soon as her divorce comes through,' said Jamie.

Hamish looked at Bella. 'Have you applied for a divorce?'

'She hasn't had the courage to face that beast yet. The way he treated her!' exclaimed Jamie.

Hamish stood up. 'You'll be hearing from the RSPCA, Bella. Jamie, a word with you outside.'

Jamie walked outside into the garden and then turned and faced Hamish. 'Why the hell are you persecuting the poor girl?'

'I am here to warn you, laddie,' said Hamish. 'Listen to me, and listen to me carefully. Bella is a husband beater. If you don't believe me, you should go talk to her husband ower in Lochdubh. She's a dangerous woman and has a police record for assault.'

Jamie looked at him arrogantly. 'She told me everything, about how that Sean twisted everything to make it look as if she was the guilty one. I love her, and nothing you can say will make me change my mind.'

'She is one o' the best liars I've ever come across,' said Hamish. 'Have you any money?'

'What?'

'Are you comfortably off?'

Jamie looked at him, puzzled. 'I'm a canny man and I've a bit put by. My mother died last year and left me a good bit.'

'Then hang on to it or that one will clean you out. And do me a favour. Don't make a will.'

'I've a good mind to report you for slander!'

'Go ahead,' said Hamish wearily. He fished in his tunic pocket. 'Here's my card. If you need any help, call me.'

Jamie ripped up the card and threw the pieces on the ground, then turned on his heel and marched back into the house.

Hamish climbed back into the Land Rover and looked at Lugs. 'I've done my best,' he said. 'What else can I do?'

Back at the station, he sent a report to the Royal Society for the Prevention of Cruelty to Animals. He felt he was wasting his time. Once they had heard Bella's fictitious story about the savage dog, they would decide they had not enough to take her to court. Sean could protest for all his worth that the animal had been gentle. He hadn't been there when the dog was killed. Bella could argue that the dog had turned vicious because of the absence of its master. And the police had dropped the case.

The kitchen door opened and he heard Jimmy Anderson's voice shouting, 'Anyone home?'

Hamish went out to join him. Jimmy was holding a full bottle of whisky.

'Where did you get that on the Sabbath?' asked Hamish.

'The Tommel Castle Hotel. I told the manager to put it on your bill.'

'I don't have a bill at the hotel!'

'Well, you do now. Pour us a dram.'

'After all the whisky of mine you've drunk, you might at least pay for some.'

Jimmy gave his foxy grin. 'If it weren't for me, you wouldnae have any inside information about anything.'

Hamish lifted down two glasses from the kitchen cupboard and set them on the table. Both men sat down. Jimmy poured a large measure for himself and a small one for Hamish.

'How can cops go around arresting people for driving over the limit,' complained Hamish, 'when a detective stinks o' booze?'

'Stop grumbling, drink up, and listen. It wasnae a sophisticated bomb. It was a fertilizer bomb.'

'But the IRA use those.'

'Aye, but it does point to the locals. The blast was caused just as much by the major's Calor gas tanks exploding as from the bomb. You know the major, don't you?'

'Only ever had a few words with him. Pleasant enough man,' Hamish commented.

'All the cops and me can get out of the locals is that it was caused by the wrath of God. They say the major and his summer guests were in the way of having wild parties, full of loose harlots and drugs.'

'My my. Loose harlots! Is that exactly what they said?'

'Of course. You don't think I would put it that way. In vain did we point out that the major's friends, all upstanding middle-aged and elderly citizens, were nothing like that; they all just look stubborn and refuse to say anything else.'

'I can't understand this religious mania. I went to one of Mackenzie's sermons and there's nothing violent or rabble-rousing in them.'

'Maybe he toned it down because you were in the congregation.'

'I don't think so. I've got leave owing me. I might go up and live there for a week. If I was actually amongst them, one of them might crack and tell me something.'

'You going to clear it with Blair?'

'Not on your life. So what other news?'

'Nothing more except it's got the major out of Sutherland. He'll collect the insurance and he says he'll get somewhere down in Perthshire where folks are civilized. He thinks it's this anti-English mania.'

'Could be. By the way, I found the horrible Bella Comyn. She's living over in Bonar Bridge with a new victim. She's going to divorce Sean and marry this one.' Hamish told Jimmy more about his visit.

'We'll soon be searching the peatbogs for that one,' said Jimmy. 'I'll be off.' He stood up, screwed the top back on the whisky bottle, and made to put it in his pocket.

'Don't you dare,' said Hamish wrathfully. 'I paid for that hooch, so here it stays. And buy your own usquebae next time!'

The following day Hamish decided to try the Bain family once more. This time he saw what must surely be Harry Bain, digging at a flower bed in the front garden.

'Mr Bain?'

'Aye. What's up?'

He was a small man with rounded shoulders and long arms. His thick hair was black and curly and sat on top of his head like a wig. His eyes were light grey and narrow in his weather-beaten face.

'You've heard about the major's cottage being blown up?'

'Aye, that was a bad business.'

'What's going on in Stoyre? What's all this religious business?'

He turned away and picked up the spade which he had thrust into the earth when he had seen Hamish. 'I don't know nothing about that,' said Harry. 'We aye kept ourselves to ourselves.'

'So why did you move here?'

'Stoyre's a bit remote.'

'Lochdubh is hardly the bright lights o' the city.'

'The school's better here. The lassie wasnae learning quick enough.'

'You must have noticed something,' said Hamish impatiently. 'You're hiding something.'

'There's nothing to hide,' he snapped. 'Haven't you any criminals to catch?'

'Yes, I have. For a start, there are the criminals who blew up the major's cottage.'

'I cannae help you there. Now, can I get on wi' my work?'

Defeated, Hamish walked off. He returned to the police station and collected his dog and drove off to Strathbane. He called at police headquarters to arrange for a week's leave and met Superintendent Daviot on the stairs. 'What brings you here?' asked Daviot.

'I'm owed a few days off, sir,' said Hamish.

'At such a time? Still, I suppose with everyone from the antiterrorist squad to Blair going over what happened at Stoyre, you won't be needed. Get Sergeant Macgregor at Cnothan to cover your beat.'

'Yes, sir.'

'When will you be leaving?'

Hamish thought quickly. He should give things a couple of weeks to settle down. If he went to Stoyre right away, Blair would still be there and Blair would interfere with any investigation. 'In two weeks' time, sir.'

'Where are you going?'

'I might visit my cousin in Dornoch,' said Hamish, his hazel eyes taking on that limpid look they always got when he was lying.

'Have a nice time. How is Miss Halburton-Smythe?'

87

But Hamish did not want to discuss the once love of his life who was now set to marry someone else.

'Fine.' He touched his cap and moved up the stairs.

His business at police headquarters having been settled, Hamish went to the estate agent and rented the same cottage that Sean had stayed in. They gave him the keys, saying that no one else would want to rent anywhere in Stoyre at the moment.

On his return to Lochdubh, Hamish called on Sean Comyn to tell the crofter about his meeting with Bella. 'I hope she does ask me for a divorce,' said Sean. 'But I'm not paying her a penny.'

'I don't think you'll have to,' said Hamish. 'She wouldn't want her criminal record exposed in court. Why the deer fences?' He pointed to where a new section of deer fence stood at the beginning of a field.

'There's no money in the sheep at all,' mourned Sean. 'I'm going to try the deer.'

'Good luck to you.' Hamish turned away.

'If you hear anything more about Bella, let me know,' called Sean.

'Will do.'

When Hamish arrived at the police station, it was to find Elspeth waiting for him. 'Is this a friendly visit?' he asked. 'Or are you after news?'

'I just heard from Mrs Wellington that Bella had been sighted over at Bonar Bridge.'

'Come in and have a cup of tea and I'll tell you about it.'

Elspeth listened carefully while Hamish made a pot of tea. When they were sitting at the kitchen table, she said, 'I somehow can't see Bella just asking for a divorce without getting something out of it.'

'She can't really do anything. Like I was saying to Sean, she probably knows that her previous criminal record would come out in court.'

'So he'll be all right.' Elspeth took a sip of tea. 'That is, unless he's made a will in her favour.'

'What?'

'If he's made a will in her favour, then he should change it pronto and let her know.'

'You don't think she'd do anything to him?'

'Why not? She hammered that dog to death. She's got a new lover who'll probably swear blind she was with him the whole time if she did anything to Sean.'

'Maybe I'd better tell him to alter his will,' said Hamish slowly.

'Do it now.'

Hamish went through to the office and dialled Sean's number. There was no reply. He returned to the kitchen. 'Not there. He's changing over to deer and building fences. He's probably out in the fields.'

'Well, run over there and see him.'

'Elspeth. You're panicking. Bella's got a new patsy and he seems to have money. She'll be happy with that.'

Her gypsy eyes surveyed him. 'Don't say I didn't warn you.'

'Look, Elspeth, chust because you write that astrology column doesn't mean you haff the second sight,' said Hamish, his Highland accent becoming more sibilant in his irritation.

'In that case, you lazy copper, I'll have a word with him myself.'

'Do what you like.'

Interfering busybody, thought Hamish sourly after she had left, and then almost immediately he felt guilty. Elspeth had only been trying to help.

He worked around his croft that afternoon, enjoying being out in the sunshine and clear air. When he was in the upper field, he heard the telephone ring inside the police station. He reluctantly headed back indoors to check the answering machine. Sean's voice sounded out. 'Bella's coming to see me. She's not going to ask for anything. Just a straightforward divorce on breakdown o' marriage. She's bringing the papers over.'

Hamish remembered Elspeth's words. He got into the Land Rover and set off along the waterfront. He saw Elspeth leaving the newspaper office and jerked to a halt. 'Jump in,' he called. 'Sean's phoned. Bella's on her way to see him.'

Elspeth hopped in. 'So you do think there's some danger, after all?'

'Better to make sure there isn't.'

'Then don't drive right up to the door. Park a little way away. If she's up to anything, we want to catch her in the act. If we're not too late, that is.'

Hamish parked down at the bottom of the dirt road which led up to the croft house. There was a new Ford Metro parked outside. 'Looks as if she's here,' he said. 'She must have learned to drive. Let's hurry.'

'Look in the kitchen window first,' urged Elspeth. 'If they're just sitting there talking, we'll knock on the door.'

There was no garden. Only springy heather below the cottage windows to muffle the sounds of their approach. Hamish crouched down and peered inside the kitchen window. Sean was lolling in a chair by the fireplace, his eyes closed. An open bottle of whisky was on the table with two glasses. Bella was standing with a shotgun, loading it. She was wearing thin plastic gloves. Then she knelt down and began to try to press one of Sean's inert hands round the trigger.

Hamish darted to the door and flung it open. Mad with fright and rage, Bella turned round and Hamish and Elspeth threw themselves to the ground as the blast from the shotgun deafened them. Hamish leapt to his feet before she could fire again. He wrested the shotgun from her and got her down on the floor and handcuffed her while she screamed abuse. Hamish checked Sean's pulse. He was still alive. He guessed that Bella had drugged him and was about to fake a suicide.

By the time reinforcements had arrived from Lochdubh, Bella was crying and saying that Sean had been trying to commit suicide and she had been trying to stop him.

'Well, that's that,' said Hamish wearily when Bella had been taken away and Sean borne off in an ambulance. 'At least we've got her now. She'll be away for a long time.'

'That'll teach you to listen to me in future,' said Elspeth. 'Now I'm off to write up the story for the nationals.'

'*Sub judice*. You can't say anything until after she's charged.'

'Oh, yes I can. I just don't mention her name. I just describe everything and say a woman is helping police with their inquiries. What about buying me dinner one night?'

'I'll take you for dinner tomorrow night. The Italian's.'

Back at the police station, Hamish sat down and typed out a lengthy report. Poor Jamie Stuart. The police would have already borne him off to Strathbane in case he turned out to have been Bella's accomplice.

Chapter Five

Inspiring bold John Barleycorn!
What dangers thou canst make us scorn!
Wi' tippenny, we fear nae evil;
Wi' usquebae, we'll face the devil!
>   – Robert Burns

The next few days passed quietly for Hamish. Sergeant Macgregor over in Cnothan had sourly agreed to cover for him while he was away on 'holiday'. The bombing of the major's cottage had disappeared from even the local newspapers. Elspeth had cancelled their date for dinner, just saying she was 'on a story'. Hamish had been mildly surprised at his own disappointment.

The weather was not perfect. There had been two days of rain. But by the end of the week, the sun shone again. Purple heather blazed on the flanks of the two mountains above Lochdubh. Not a ripple disturbed the glassy water of the sea loch. It was hard to even think of violence as Hamish lounged in his deck chair in the front garden under the blue lamp with Lugs lying on his back at his feet, his paws in the air.

His peace was disturbed by Jimmy Anderson, who had come looking for the remains of that bottle of whisky. Hamish collected another deck chair, the bottle and glasses, and Jimmy sat down with a sigh of pleasure.

'How are things at Stoyre?' asked Hamish.

Jimmy held up his glass, admiring the colour of the whisky in the sunlight, before taking a hearty swig of it. 'Nothing,' said Jimmy laconically. 'Same old business. Tight-lipped locals. The powers-that-be are pretty sure it was one o' them.'

'I wonder why. I mean a fertilizer bomb probably takes a bit of knowledge of chemistry.'

'The fact is they don't think all that much was used. Bit of newspaper, bit of fertilizer, fuel and cotton, light it, chuck it inside, and run like hell. Leave the major's Calor gas tanks to do the rest.'

'Still, it takes some knowledge.'

'Anyone could get the instructions how to make it off the Internet.'

'I wouldnae think anyone in Stoyre had a computer!'

'Anyone could go to the cyber café in Strathbane.'

Hamish eyed the detective shrewdly. 'But they checked with the café and couldn't find anyone who had been accessing the information.'

'Something like that.'

'I'm thinking of taking a bit of a holiday and going and staying there,' said Hamish.

'Waste of time off, if you ask me. Does Blair know about this?'

'No! And don't breathe a word.'

'I won't.'

'So nothing's happening in Stoyre?'

'All quiet. They had a Burns reading o' Tam o' Shanter at the kirk there last night.'

'Exciting stuff.'

'Read by some woman with a reedy voice. What's tippenny?'

'Oh, the stuff that makes you fear no evil. Twopenny ale.'

'And usquebae?'

'Whisky. The water of life. Don't tell me you didn't know?'

'Never could get my tongue around the Gaelic. That bomb was probably some nasty bit of anti-Englishness. Blair suggested as much to the major and then had to back-pedal, as the good major was threatening to take the whole village to the Race Relations Board.'

'You know, there probably was never a people like the Scots to know so little about their own history. Do you know where the Scots came from, Jimmy?'

'I thought they were always here.'

'They came from Northern Ireland and proceeded to wipe out the Celts and the Picts in
one of the biggest acts o' genocide in history.
The trouble's always caused by the Low-
landers, not us. They live in a Gaelic twilight
with tartan fringes. Anyway, to get back to
Stoyre, what's the mood like? Are the folks
scared?'

'No. There's an odd atmosphere there. A sort
of suppressed excitement, like kids before
Christmas.'

'That's verra interesting. I can't wait to get
there now. But I'll keep clear until the author-
ities have gone.'

'Shouldn't be long now. If it had been a big
professional bomb, they'd have been there for
a long time. But everything now points to the
locals.'

The garden gate creaked and Elspeth walked
in. She was wearing a near-transparent Indian
blouse covered in what looked like little bits of
mirror. Her shorts were very short, showing
strong tanned legs ending in her usual clumpy
boots.

'What about having that dinner this evening?' she asked Hamish.

'All right. I'll see you at the Italian's at eight.'

Elspeth smiled at Jimmy. 'See you there,
Hamish,' she said.

'Man,' breathed Jimmy when she had left.
'You are one lucky man. What a smasher!'

'Elspeth? She's just the local reporter.'

'I know. I've met her before, remember? I didn't know she was keen on you.'

'We are chust friends,' said Hamish stiffly.

'Wish I had a friend like that,' leered Jimmy. 'She does wear weird clothes.'

'Move with the times. You're getting old-fashioned, Hamish.'

Hamish found Elspeth waiting for him when he arrived at the restaurant that evening. She was wearing a brightly coloured jacket made of diamond-cut pieces of coloured velvet over a faded black T-shirt and a long black chiffon skirt. And the boots.

He had a sudden picture of Priscilla sitting there, impeccably dressed and without a hair out of place, and felt a dark sadness. Elspeth's hair was no longer aubergine but it stood out all over her head as if she had stuck her finger in an electric socket. He noticed as he sat down that her fingernails were painted black.

Hamish had made a promise to himself never to refer to any part of Elspeth's appearance again – after all, how she looked or what she wore was none of his business – but he found himself saying sharply, 'What have you done wi' your nails? They make your hands look as if you'd shut them in a car door.'

'Sit down, shut up, and choose something to eat,' said Elspeth amiably. 'I'm starving.'

Willie Lamont, the waiter, who had been a

97

policeman until he married a relative of the restaurant owner, came up to take their order. 'What'll it be, Hamish?' he asked.

'Why don't you ask the lady first what she wants?' chided Hamish.

'Right. Michty me, lassie, your nails are black.'

'And michty me, the service in here is rotten. Do you usually make personal remarks to your customers?'

'Sorry,' mumbled Willie. 'What's it to be?'

'Caesar salad first and then lasagne.'

'I'll have a mixed salad and then the penne wi' the basil sauce. And bring us a bottle of the house wine,' said Hamish.

Willie wrote down their order and then lingered, moving from foot to foot.

'What?' demanded Hamish.

'Funny business ower at Stoyre,' said Willie. 'Know anything about it?'

'No, but I'm keeping my ear to the ground.'

'Grand. Now, how's about getting us the food?'

'Lucia wonders when you're coming to see wee Hamish, your godchild.'

'Tell her I'll be along soon.'

'He's taking his first steps and you havenae been there to see it.'

'Willie! Food!'

Elspeth watched Willie retreat to the kitchen with their orders. 'What does Lucia see in him?' she asked.

'He cleans. He's mad about cleaning. He does all the housework. That's why Lucia adores him.'

'So what's been happening about Stoyre?' asked Elspeth. 'I've just been over there.'

'You'll know more about it than I do. Find out anything?'

'No, but something bad's going on.'

'How?'

'I sense it.'

'I'm going to do something more practical about finding out,' said Hamish. He told her about his planned holiday there.

'I've some leave owing,' said Elspeth. 'I could come with you.'

'And where would you stay?'

'Wherever you're staying, of course.'

'That would antagonize that God-fearing community no end. They would say we were living in sin.'

'Well, I'll drop over and see you.'

Hamish began to feel hunted. 'Chust leave me be to get on wi' my investigation,' he said quietly.

Elspeth turned a little pink and looked relieved when Willie arrived with the wine.

'So what's been going on in Lochdubh that I don't know about?' asked Hamish to break the awkward silence which had followed his last remark.

'Maybe there's something you could do to

help,' said Elspeth. 'Do you know old Mrs Docherty?'

'Of course. I havenae seen her for a while.'

'She's all alone. She needs professional care. She's rambling in her mind and should really be in a nursing home.'

'Has she any relatives?'

'Just a daughter down in Glasgow. Mrs Wellington has written to her several times but she never replies.'

'What nursing home could she go into?'

'There's a new one just outside Braikie.'

'I'd forgotten about that one. It's called The Pines.'

'Maybe you could call on her and persuade her to go there. Mind you, it would mean selling her cottage.'

They talked together amicably and Hamish had to admit to himself afterwards that he had enjoyed the evening.

Hamish called on Mrs Docherty the following day. The front door was standing open so he put his head round it and called, 'Mrs Docherty! It's me, Hamish.'

'Come in,' called a surprisingly strong voice.

He walked into a small cluttered parlour. Mrs Docherty looked as hale and hearty as the last time he had seen her. Her grey hair was thick and her large figure was not stooped.

100

Her face was criss-crossed with a multitude of wrinkles and her faded grey eyes were alert.

'Sit down, Hamish,' she said. 'You can make us a cup of tea after you explain why you've called.'

'It's a social visit,' said Hamish awkwardly.

Her intelligent eyes surveyed him with amusement.

'Och, I heard you were getting senile,' Hamish blurted out, and then turned dark red with embarrassment.

She laughed. 'Don't look so upset. Most people weary me. I have my books and my computer to keep me amused. So when people I don't like call round, I mumble and drool. Maybe I'd better stop it or they'll be dragging me off to some nursing home.'

'I hear there's a new one outside Braikie.'

'Not all that new. It's been there for a year. I wouldn't go there even if I was on my last legs.'

'Why?'

'I think they kill people,' she sad.

'Och, come on. I'd have heard about it.'

'I had a good friend over in Braikie,' she said. 'Maisie Freeman. She got very frail and her family persuaded her to go into The Pines. It's a private nursing home, but if you sign over your house to them, they promise the best care and medical attention until the day you die. She only had her married daughter to look after her, Aileen, and Aileen is a selfish cow. Her husband's pretty well off so the loss of Maisie's house when she did die wasn't going to bother them. They just wanted rid of Maisie. She was, like I said, a bit frail but she had all her faculties. I visited her. I didn't like the staff much, very creepy and smarmy. Anyway, Maisie lasted only four weeks.'

'What happened to her?'

'She fell down a flight of steps and broke her neck. Now, the rooms are all on the ground floor and the offices upstairs. She had no reason to go upstairs.'

'Maybe she wanted to complain to the manager.'

'Then she would have sent for him. She had rheumatoid arthritis. She'd no more have tackled those stairs than she would have thought of climbing Everest.'

'What did the nursing home say?'

'They said Maisie's mind had gone and she must have wandered upstairs not knowing where she was and lost her footing. I visited her two days before her death and she was as bright as a button. But you know how it is. People think the very old are a waste of space anyway. You know what I think will happen in the future? I think they'll find a way to extend life for a very long time and keep people young-looking. The criminal element amongst the young will hate all these oldies hanging on to jobs and taking up space on the planet. Someone will start issuing dates of birth on the Internet and they'll start bumping all the oldies off.'

'I tell you what,' said Hamish. 'I'll go over there and have a talk to them.'

'I don't see how you can find anything out. I've a good bit of money put by. People don't know that. I'm tempted to check myself in there and see what happens.'

'If what you think is true, it could be dangerous.'

'Not if I pretend to be senile. I mean not all the time, because I'd need to look as if I had my wits about me some days to check in.'

'It would mean signing your cottage over to them.'

'It would be a risk and a bit of excitement for me.'

'Hold on,' said Hamish. 'I mean houses in the Highlands don't command that much money on the market. If patients started dropping like flies soon after they were admitted, there'd be an inquiry.'

'I think they'd be clever about it. I mean it's only old people on their last legs who go into nursing homes.'

'I'll go over there anyway and look around. I'll say it's a private visit. I've got an elderly relative who might be interested.'

'You could get that reporter lassie to check

the obituaries of people in Braikie who died within the last year,' she said.

'Let me have a look around first.'

'Very well. Go and make the tea.'

Hamish called in at the newspaper office after he had left Mrs Docherty's. Elspeth had a pencil stuck through her hair and was scowling at her computer. 'I'm wasted here,' she said when she saw Hamish. 'How can I put a bit of drama into the latest Mothers' Union meeting?'

'Why don't you apply for a job on one of the Glasgow papers?'

'I'll think about it. Why are you here?'

'I want a favour. Could you check up your obituary files and give me the names of old people who died in The Pines during the last year?'

'Why?'

'Can't you chust do it, lassie?'

'I'm a reporter, remember? What's happening? Someone going in for euthanasia?'

'Could be. It's an idea of Mrs Docherty's.'

'I thought she was gaga.'

'It's an act, but don't tell anyone. She uses it to get rid of people who bore her.'

'Oh, really?' said Elspeth crossly. 'She pulled that one on me. I went to do a piece on Lochdubh in the old days and she just stared at me vacantly.'

'Some people don't like reporters.'

'Okay, I'll do it if you promise to let me know if there's a story.'

Hamish drove over to Braikie that afternoon. The Pines was situated far back from the road at the end of a long drive. Hamish now remembered reading a year ago about it being built. The pine forest from which it took its name stretched all around him. Sunlight flickered down through the trees as he drove steadily towards the house. At last it came into view, a long two-storey building. He parked in front of it and entered the main door. A dark-skinned male nurse came forward to meet him. Hamish tried to guess his nationality. Indian? Pakistani?

'How can I help you?' asked the nurse.

'I've an elderly mother who might have to come here,' said Hamish. 'I wondered if I could look round.'

'Come up to the office and I'll introduce you to our manager, Mr Dupont.'

Hamish followed him up the stairs, noticing that they were uncarpeted. The nurse knocked at a frosted glass door at the top. A voice called, 'Come in.'

A small dapper man wearing a blazer with a crest rose to meet them. 'I am Mr Dupont,' he said. He had thinning brown hair and a large nose and a small rosebud of a mouth. His eyes were black. His voice had a faint accent.

'I wanted to see round the home,' said Hamish. 'My mother will soon need to go into care.'

Mr Dupont laughed. 'Strange. One does not think of policemen having mothers.'

'You know who I am?'

'You are Hamish Macbeth and you are the policeman who is based at Lochdubh.'

'This is a private matter. May I see around?'

'I will take you round myself.'

Mr Dupont came round from behind his desk. His grey trousers had knife-edge pleats and his small black shoes were polished like black glass. He dismissed the nurse and then led Hamish back down the stairs.

'You're not from here,' said Hamish. 'What brought you to the Highlands?'

'I had been managing a nursing home in Kent. The terms of employment offered here were better.'

'And is the owner from around here?'

'Mr Frazier is from the south of England as well. Property and land here are much cheaper than elsewhere in Britain. All patients have their own private rooms and expert nursing care. The ones who are not bedridden can make use of the grounds and the gym. Yes, we have a trainer to take them through gentle exercise. If I say so myself, the food is excellent and all tastes are catered for.'

He pushed open a door. 'I do not want to

disturb any patients, but this room is unoccupied at the moment.'

The room had a hospital bed, two hard chairs, one small table, and one comfortable armchair. Chintz curtains were drawn back from the window, revealing a view of that pine forest. There was a television set and a radio. The floor was thickly carpeted.

'How much do you charge?' asked Hamish.

'Two thousand pounds a month.'

'Man, I couldnae afford that!'

'Well, we have an interesting little scheme. We don't like to turn anyone away who is in need. Does your mother own her own home?'

'Yes.'

'Then all she needs to do is sign it over to us and we will guarantee to give her the best treatment until the day she dies.'

'And are all your patients under this scheme?'

He laughed. 'No, we could not afford that. Most of our patients pay or their relatives pay.'

'I wouldn't think folks up here could afford that for care.'

'But we get people from all over. That is why this site was a stroke of genius. People are very romantic about the Highlands.'

He shut the door of the room and led Hamish down a long corridor. He pushed open another door. 'This is the dining room for those who are still mobile.'

It was not a very large room, laid out with only ten tables. 'And then we come to the gym,' said Mr Dupont. He opened another door, revealing an airy room.

'I wouldn't think any of them would be fit enough for all those machines and weights,' said Hamish.

'Oh, we run a gym class for people in Braikie. Ah, here is our trainer, Jerry Andrews.'

Jerry walked in. He was a fit young man with hair of an improbable gold. He was wearing a white track suit and his tanned face was so square and so regular and his skin so smooth he looked like a plastic doll. Mr Dupont introduced him and Jerry explained in a lisping voice that he specialized in giving the elderly simple Pilates exercises and also massage.

Mr Dupont set off again rapidly on the tour, his little shiny feet twinkling in front of Hamish. 'And this,' he said, throwing open another door, 'is our pièce de résistance.'

Hamish surveyed a large swimming pool. It was empty of people, the water blue and pristine.

'Very fine,' he said. 'I'll discuss it with my mother and let you know.'

As he was escorted back to the entrance, Hamish said, 'I haven't seen any of the patients. I mean if some of them are mobile enough to use the gym and the swimming pool, why aren't they walking about?'

Mr Dupont gave a merry laugh. 'In the afternoon they all go to their rooms for a siesta.'

'I thought the old didn't sleep much. I know my mother doesn't.'

'They don't sleep much at night but they do like their nap or their quiet time in the afternoon. The old like discipline and order.'

What was that odd accent? wondered Hamish. No, not French. Maybe German. And was his name really Dupont?

Once outside, he gave himself a mental shake. Mrs Docherty was giving him unrealistic suspicions.

He drove back to Lochdubh to find Elspeth approaching the police station. 'I've got something for you,' she called out as he got down from the Land Rover.

'Come inside,' said Hamish, 'and let me have a look at what you've got.'

Elspeth sat down at the kitchen table. 'I've got four names, all from Sutherland, who died at The Pines within the last year.'

'Let me see. Mrs Hudson, Jones, Chandler, and Price. Two from Braikie and two from Cnothan. All listed in the obituaries as having died peacefully.'

'One of those at least is a lie,' said Elspeth, her eyes gleaming. She pushed forward a printout. 'There are articles about Mrs Price. She was seventy-three, not a great age. She was found dead in the swimming pool at the deep end. Daughter quoted as saying Mother couldn't swim. Subsequent inquiry. Nursing home states that Mrs Price had become confused and must have wandered into the pool. The nurse who should have made sure the door to the swimming pool room was locked when not in use was fired. Unfortunate accident. And. of course, there's Maisie Freeman.'

'Leave these articles with me,' said Hamish. 'I'll check out the other three women.'

Elspeth triumphantly, with the air of a conjuror producing a rabbit, pulled out another sheet of paper. 'I have their relatives' addresses here.'

'That's grand. I'll get on to it right away.'

'Don't I get a kiss?' She grinned at him.

Hamish flushed slightly but pretended not to hear. 'Thanks a lot, Elspeth. You'll be the very first to know if I come up with anything.'

Mrs Price's daughter, a Mrs Sarah MacPherson, lived over in Cnothan. Hamish knew he should telephone Sergeant Macgregor. But Macgregor would demand to know all about it and, being a lazy man, would shoot it down. Hamish fed Lugs, promised the dog a long walk when he got back, and set off for Cnothan, a small town he considered the dreariest and nastiest in the Highlands. Mrs MacPherson lived in a trim bungalow at the back of the church.

A small, round woman answered the door.

She was wearing an apron and her grey hair was done up in plastic rollers. 'Mrs MacPherson?'

'Yes, can I help you?'

'I am Police Constable Hamish Macbeth from Lochdubh,' said Hamish, who was not in uniform. He did not want any of the locals to report to the sergeant that a policeman had been seen in Cnothan. 'May I come in?'

'It's not bad news?'

'No, no,' said Hamish soothingly. 'Chust the wee matter.'

'Come ben.'

Once seated in a small overfurnished living room, Hamish began. 'It's about your mother.'

'About her death? I thought the police weren't going to do anything about that.'

'Some things have just come to light. Now, did she have a house she signed over to the nursing home?'

'Yes, she had a nice wee cottage, Rannoch Lodge, down by the loch. It was to come to me after she died but she said it would be better to spare me the expense of paying the fees at the nursing home.'

'How ill was she?'

'She was fair crippled with arthritis and she had brittlebone disease. It was getting difficult for her to move around without help. But she had all her faculties, whatever that damn nursing home says. She could never swim and had a mortal fear of the water.'

111

'When did you last see her?'

'It was the day afore she died.' A fat tear rolled down Mrs MacPherson's plump cheek and she brushed it away. 'She said they were giving her pills which had eased her pain. She was very chatty and she seemed to be enjoying her stay. "I'll live a grand long time and I'll get my money's worth," that's what she said.'

'I don't want anyone, Sergeant Macgregor in particular, to know I'm investigating this case again,' said Hamish. 'I don't want you to say a word about this to a soul. If the nursing home gets wind of this and if they've been up to any funny business, they'll cover their tracks.'

'I'll do anything you say, Officer, just so long as I get justice at last for my poor mother's death.'

As Hamish walked his dog along the waterfront after his return to Lochdubh, he wondered what to do. If he talked to Strathbane, Blair would come on the phone and howl at him for wasting time over a case which had already been dealt with. If he sent old Mrs Docherty to the nursing home and if anything happened to her, he would have her death on his conscience. And then what if nothing happened? What if she didn't find anything out? She would be trapped in The Pines for the rest of her life and she would have lost her cosy cottage and her independence. He took Lugs back to the police station and fed the dog a hearty meal of lamb's kidneys before making his way to Mrs Docherty's cottage.

The old lady listened carefully to his report. 'What about the other three?' she asked when he had finished. 'You've only told me about Mrs Price.'

'I decided to leave them alone at the moment. I don't want word to get back to the nursing home.'

Mrs Docherty's eyes sparkled with excitement. 'I'm going to do it. I'm going to check myself in there.'

'But you could lose your house!'

'I've always wanted to be Miss Marple. I'll put all my stuff in storage.'

'It's an awfy risk,' said Hamish, scratching his fiery hair. 'I cannae even check you in myself, for I said I was making inquiries for my mother.'

'Get that wee newspaper lassie. She can say I'm her aunt. Take a risk as well, Hamish. You'll never find out otherwise. So what if I'm there for the rest of my days? If there's nothing up with the place, I'll have people to look after me when I get really frail. If there is something, I'll find it out.'

'If you're sure . . .'

'Sure as sure.'

113

Chapter Six

Death pays all debts.
    – Eighteenth-century proverb

Elspeth was amazed at the speed with which Mrs Docherty was established at The Pines. She had taken her along the day after Hamish had spoken to her, and Mrs Docherty had signed the necessary papers and said she would move in the following day. Mrs Docherty had taken a case of books along with her clothes, her computer, and a mobile phone. She told Elspeth that as she was doing her bit, it was up to Elspeth as her supposed niece to pack up her remaining belongings and furniture and put them into storage.

Hamish had told Mrs Docherty to phone him at the first sign of trouble while he made arrangements with Angela Brodie, the doctor's wife, to look after his sheep and hens while he was in Stoyre. 'Not that I want anyone to know I'm going up there,' he cautioned her.

'Well, I think you've gone daft,' exclaimed Angela. 'If you're right and there's something going on, you are putting her life at risk.'

'I think she can take care of herself,' said Hamish crossly – cross because he was beginning to fear he had made a terrible mistake.

'On your own head be it. I've got an idea all the same. As the doctor's wife, it wouldn't look strange if I dropped in to see Mrs Docherty.'

'Oh, would you? That would be grand, Angela.'

'You don't deserve it. Mind you, I thought she was gaga.'

'She puts on an act from time to time so that people will leave her alone.'

'I'll go to see her anyway but I'll tell her I think she's made a big mistake.'

'Just as you make sure no one is listening to you. I'm not off to Stoyre for a bit yet. I'll be around.'

Mrs Docherty, once established at The Pines, was already beginning to feel she had made a big mistake. There seemed to be nothing sinister about the place. It was a bit regimented and she did not like the idea of being forced to retire to her room in the afternoon for two hours' sleep, and the other inmates, such as were still able to leave their rooms and walk about, seemed like frail ghosts.

She put on what she considered a very good act – only a few periods of lucidity and then being generally dithering and forgetful. There was, however, another new inmate, a Mr Jefferson. A man was a rare sight among these mostly senile women patients. On her first day she had been encouraged to go to the recreation room. The less mobile patients were pushed in in wheelchairs and lined up in front of a large television set and left. Mrs Docherty found this sight very depressing. The sun was shining outside and she longed to escape into the pine woods for a breath of fresh air.

But she could not wander outside, for, since the staff thought her wits were addled, she was sure they would come after her. She went back to her room and opened the window. The window was low, and as her bedroom was at ground level, she was able to step outside with only a little creaking and groaning. She took a deep breath of pine-scented air and walked across the grass with faltering steps, just in case anyone should see her, until she was in amongst the pines. She found a fallen log some little way into the woods and slowly sat down to consider her situation. She had really thought that it would be all right. If nothing was going on, she would have her books and computer to keep her amused. But she had not allowed for the depressing effect so many frail, elderly, and nearly mindless old people would have on her. To be surrounded by so much living death, she feared, might make her lose her own wits. If only she could get the papers back, the ones she had signed giving the nursing home her cottage, along with the deeds to her house. Suddenly she could feel the hairs rise on the back of her neck. She had a feeling of being watched. Mrs Docherty turned around slowly.

The other new inmate, Mr Jefferson, was standing there, leaning on his stick and surveying her. When he saw her looking at him, he came up and sat down next to her. 'Grand day,' he said.

Mrs Docherty pinned a vacant look on her face.

'It's quite an act,' he said amiably. His accent was faintly Cockney. 'But my room is next to yours. I was leaning out of my window and I saw you climbing out of yours. What's your game?'

Mrs Docherty drooled a little and made bleating sounds. 'They'll come looking for us in a minute,' he said. 'They do that. It's a sort of well-padded prison. Do you want to know why I'm in here?'

Curiosity made Mrs Docherty drop her act. 'Because you're old?'

'I'm only eighty-eight,' he said crossly. 'It all started when I was up in court for the last time.'

'What for?'

'Theft.'

'Are you a burglar?'

'Forcibly retired. I went under various names. The last was Colonel Fforbes-Peters.' His accent changed to upper-class. 'I was good at ingratiating myself with the horsy set. Got invited for weekends. Lifted a bit of Spode here, a bit of silver there, often some jewellery. But I got caught.' He reverted to his usual accent. 'Now, my son is a barrister, thanks to all the money I got from my illegal life. He's not like me. He's pompous and strict and has a social-climbing wife. He managed to get a pet psychiatrist to diagnose me as suffering from mild kleptomania. He told me he would arrange this if I would bugger off to a nursing home of my choice and never darken his career again. So here I am. What's with the act?'

Mrs Docherty gave a resigned shrug and told him all about her suspicions about the nursing home. She ended with 'I feel I've made an awful mistake.'

'I don't think so. I smell villainy. It takes one to know one.'

He was a small, spry man with brown hair and a small brown moustache; both were probably dyed, thought Mrs Docherty. He had large ill-fitting false teeth and his ears stuck out from his head. He suddenly cocked that head to one side. 'Listen. They're coming for us.'

'These woods are large. Chances are they won't find us.'

119

'The dogs will.'

'Dogs!'

'Shhh. Do your dumb act and I'll say I saw you wandering off and followed you. And,' he added hurriedly, 'don't take any pills. It's my belief half of them in there aren't as daft as they look. I think they're tranquillized up to their old eyeballs.'

'I flushed them down the loo. Do you think . . .?'

Mrs Docherty broke off as the trainer, Jerry Andrews, appeared through the trees with two bloodhounds straining at the leash.

'Up you get, Mother,' said Mr Jefferson, putting on his 'posh' voice. 'Shouldn't go wandering off.' He beamed at the trainer. 'Here we are. Saw her tottering off and thought I'd better go after her.'

Jerry's plastic-looking face was impassive. 'We don't like patients wandering in the grounds. They could get hurt. Bring her along and follow me.'

Mrs Docherty began to feel frightened and was glad of Mr Jefferson's strong grip on her arm. She babbled incoherently as she was led back to the house.

'Don't go to your rooms,' ordered Jerry. 'Take Mrs Docherty into the recreation room and I'll let you know when her room is ready.'

Mrs Docherty, once in the recreation room, slumped down in an armchair.

'What's your name?' whispered Mr Jefferson.

'Mrs Docherty.'

'Your first name?'

'Annie.'

'Okay, Annie. I'm Charlie. We'd better pretend to go to sleep. Makes us look like no threat at all.'

Mrs Docherty did fall asleep, tired from the walk and the fright of seeing Jerry with the dogs. She at last awoke to find a nurse bending over her.

'Come on, Annie,' said the nurse, a powerful-looking woman. 'Rest time.'

I've just had a nap, thought Mrs Docherty crossly. But, dithering and muttering incoherent complaints, she allowed herself to be led back to her room.

Mrs Docherty was a tall woman, but the nurse manoeuvred her on to the bed with ease. She held out a glass of water and two white pills. 'Take your vitamins, dear.'

Mrs Docherty held the pills in her mouth until the nurse had left and then rose and spat them out in the washstand basin in the corner of the room. It was only when turning round that she realized bars had been fixed across her window. She fought down a surge of panic and went to try the door to her room. It was locked.

Suddenly feeling very old and weak, she sat down on the bed and placed her hands firmly on her knees to try to stop them from shaking.

The door handle began to turn slowly and she let out a whimper of fright. Charlie Jefferson slid in. 'How did you get the door open?' gasped Annie.

He dangled a ring of skeleton keys in front of her. 'So they've barred your window,' he said. 'That's good.'

'What's good about it?'

'They *are* up to something. Chasing people with dogs. Barring the window.'

'I wish I could get those papers back, the ones I signed, giving them my cottage.'

He pulled a half bottle of whisky out of his pocket. There were two glasses on the wash-stand. He poured two measures of whisky and handed one to Mrs Docherty. 'Have a dram, as you say in these foreign parts.'

They sat side by side on the bed, sipping whisky.

'I've a proposition to put to you,' he said.

Emboldened by the whisky, Mrs Docherty grinned. 'This is so sudden.'

'Listen. If I get those papers back for you, can I come and live with you?'

'What!'

'Here. Have another drink. How old are you?'

'A year older than you.'

'Right. We could look after each other. I wouldn't get in your way.'

'I like being on my own!'

'Think about it.'

'I'll think about it. We're both getting to the age when we'll soon need help. But, I mean, I don't even know you and you're a crook.'

'An ex-crook.'

'There's another thing,' said Mrs Docherty. 'If there's something going on here, if they're bumping people off, then I should try to get some evidence. Let me put it this way: if you help me to get evidence, I'll seriously consider you moving in with me.'

'You're on. What I need to do is to get up to those offices and go through the files, find out who else signed their house over and keep an eye on them.'

'Don't get caught. They may have infrared alarms or something.'

'I doubt it. Who have they ever had to fear? God, someone's coming.'

They sat, rigid. Footsteps came along the corridor, hesitated outside the door, and then went on.

'I'd better go,' he whispered. He deftly screwed the cap back on the bottle. He rinsed out both glasses and put them back on the washstand, and then put an arm through the bars and opened the window. 'Get the smell of whisky out,' he said. 'Close it when I've gone.'

He slid silently out of the room and then she heard the click of the lock.

Mrs Docherty checked her watch. Still half an hour to go until the rest hour was over. She closed the window, forced the pills she had spat out down the plughole, and took out her mobile phone and rang the police station at Lochdubh.

Hamish Macbeth listened in alarm as she told him about Mr Jefferson and the happenings of the day.

'I should never ha' agreed to it,' he mourned. 'I want you out o' there – fast!'

'Not without my cottage.'

'I'll send Elspeth up to see you.'

'Won't do much good. I think they'll watch me closely for a bit. I have to keep up my gaga act.'

'I'm sending her anyway.'

Elspeth was now as worried as Hamish. She had taken down the For Sale sign outside Mrs Docherty's cottage and had hidden it in the back garden. When she got to The Pines, she was shown into the recreation room. A nurse was on duty, listening to every word, so Elspeth had to keep up the act of being concerned for her 'aunt', while poor Mrs Docherty pretended not to understand anything she said.

At last in desperation, she asked the nurse, 'May I take Auntie for a walk?'

'I'm afraid we cannot allow that,' said the nurse smoothly. 'Your aunt was found wandering in the grounds. We do not want any harm to come to her.'

'But I would take care of her!'

'No, I am afraid that is not possible.'

So Elspeth left feeling every bit as frustrated and guilty as Hamish Macbeth.

When Angela Brodie called half an hour after Elspeth's visit, she was unable to get a word of sense out of Mrs Docherty either.

That night, Mrs Docherty wondered how Charlie Jefferson was getting on. She had to admit it was reassuring to have an ally, for the very silence of the place was scary and her door had been locked again. The nurse had given her pills but had not waited this time to see whether she had taken them, so Mrs Docherty put them in her handbag, wrapped in a tissue, planning to give them to Elspeth on her next visit so that the girl could get them analyzed. She had been told they were vitamin pills but Mrs Docherty was sure that they were at least sleeping pills. That would account for the night-time silence of the nursing home.

The nights never really get dark in the north of Scotland and grey light filtered through the drawn curtains. She pulled them back and then sat in an armchair by the window to wait for Charlie.

She was just beginning to nod off towards four in the morning when she heard the click of the lock and sat up straight. Mr Jefferson slid round the door and then locked it behind him.

'There's enough light in here. If we switch on the light, they might see it. I wouldn't put it past them to have someone patrolling the grounds.'

'What have you got?' she asked eagerly.

'Well, I can get your deeds back anytime and the papers you signed. But we'll leave that for the moment. We've got two names at the moment, apart from you. There's Mrs Hague and Mrs Prescott. I've actually spoken to Mrs Prescott. She's got all her wits. She had a big house in Perthshire, worth a lot. I think she's the one to watch.'

'What does she look like?'

'Black hair, very thin, dyed. Very small and stooped. She was wearing a cotton dress with big red roses on it.'

'I know the one. She's mobile. Do you know, the gym and the swimming pool are never mentioned? We're supposed to get a massage as well.'

'They run the gym classes and water aerobics for outsiders,' said Mr Jefferson. 'Can't be bothered wasting time on us old fogies.'

'I wonder who signed the death certificate for Mrs Price.'

'Hamish said there was something about it in the papers. There's supposed to be a doctor here. I can't remember his name. Anyway, let's stick close to Mrs Prescott.'

'Easy for you. I'm supposed to be gaga,

126

remember? If I start talking to her, they'll get suspicious.'

'Let's try anyway.'

In the recreation room next morning, Mr Jefferson sat down next to Mrs Prescott. 'I get awfully tired of nothing but television, don't you?' he began.

'They don't seem to offer anything else. It's nothing but pills, which make me feel when I wake up that I've got a hangover,' she complained.

'Why did you choose here?'

'I was running out of money. The house was too big for me to manage any more. I heard about their offer of care for the rest of my life if I signed over my house. Seemed like a good idea. I was beginning to dread all the bills. Last winter was hard and my heating bill was enormous. It's nice not to have to worry about paying for food or care.'

She broke off as her body was racked with a sudden spasm of coughing. When she had recovered, she said ruefully, 'I've got emphysema. Comes from a lifetime of smoking. I still crave cigarettes. They caught me smoking out of the window yesterday and I got a rollicking. The doctor says he can give me an injection which will stop my craving.'

'What doctor?'

'Dr Nash. He's the resident doctor.'

'It's odd. I've heard of people getting acupuncture, or nicotine patches, or hypnotism. I've never heard of an injection.'

'Well, they're the experts. They should know.'

'And when are you getting this injection?'

'At three o'clock. In the surgery.'

'Where's that?'

'It's along that corridor between the gym and the swimming pool.'

Mr Jefferson chewed his false teeth nervously. If he told her not to go, she would ask why. And if there was nothing sinister about that injection, then he would have no chance of finding out anything at all.

The rest period started at two o'clock. Once they had all been escorted along to their rooms, he waited for half an hour and then visited Mrs Docherty. She listened while he told her about the injection.

'What can we do?' she asked.

'I've already been all round the building. I know now where the surgery is. If we go out of my window and walk round without being seen, we can look in the window of the surgery. They've stopped locking you in. Must have decided you're harmless.'

Mrs Docherty looked at him curiously. 'Don't you worry about your own safety?'

'You forget. My stuffy barrister son checked me in and he's paying. They can't get a house out of me. Let's go.'

As they crept out, into Mr Jefferson's room and out of his window, Mrs Docherty could feel her heart beating with excitement and hoped she wouldn't drop dead from it before they found out what was really going on. They had to crawl on their hands and knees past all the windows. 'I'm too old for this,' she panted at one point.

'It's all right,' he hissed. 'We're here at last. It's just coming up to three o'clock.'

They peered in at the bottom of the window. A man in a white coat who must be Dr Nash was talking to the Indian-looking nurse. Mrs Docherty and Mr Jefferson heard the murmur of voices but could not make out what was being said. Then Mrs Prescott was led in by another nurse. There was some conversation and then she was laid down on a bed. Talking all the while, Dr Nash lifted a syringe. The Indian-looking nurse rolled up the sleeve of Mrs Prescott's cotton dress. The syringe was inserted. Dr Nash went on talking. Mrs Prescott's eyes closed. The two nurses and the doctor stood watching her. Then Dr Nash felt her pulse and nodded and all three left the room.

'I think she's dead,' whispered Mrs Docherty. 'What'll we do?'

'We wait until dinnertime and I'll ask where she is. If she's dead, you phone that policeman and get a police pathologist over to do a proper autopsy.'

'The police will want to interview us,' said Mrs Docherty as they began to crawl back, 'and this lot may kill us.'

'So we'll get the hell out of here tonight and the police can interview us at our place. I'll get your deeds. They won't interview us until after the autopsy.'

Back in her room, Mrs Docherty was so exhausted that she slept nearly until dinner-time. When she awoke, it all seemed like a bad dream. Surely they had let their imaginations run away with them. Mrs Prescott would be sitting there as usual.

Mrs Docherty's knees ached terribly after all the crawling. She washed and changed because the dress she had been wearing was all grass stains. It was only on her way to the dining room that she realized they might be getting suspicious of her. Gaga old ladies did not normally change their clothes or appear promptly for meals.

Her heart sank as soon as she entered the dining room. Mrs Prescott's place was empty. Mr Jefferson was shaking out his napkin. 'Where's Mrs Prescott?' he asked the waitress.

'Oh, sir, she took a turn and she's dead.'

'Elsie!' shouted a nurse from the door. 'No gossiping with the patients!'

Mrs Docherty shuffled the food around on her plate. She could not eat. The evening seemed endless. She had to wait until dinner

130

was over, wait until the evening's television was over, and wait until the nurse took her to her room. Her eyes fell on the pile of books beside her bed. How could she be so stupid as to bring books and a computer? Maybe they thought Elspeth had brought them. She remembered that Elspeth had told them that her 'aunt' occasionally had lucid days.

She added the pills to the ones she had already saved and then took out her mobile phone and called Hamish Macbeth. He listened carefully and then said urgently, 'Don't say I connived at getting you to go there. Just sit tight.'

'We're getting out of here tonight.'

'How?'

She told him about Mr Jefferson.

'If Strathbane ever finds out I've encouraged burglary, I'll be finished. Make sure he doesn't leave any fingerprints.'

'I'm sure he won't. Tell Elspeth to get my stuff out of storage tomorrow.'

Hamish sat for a moment, frowning, after Mrs Docherty had rung off. Then he phoned Superintendent Daviot at home and explained the whole thing.

'We'll send a police pathologist and a squad right away. Are you sure this Mrs Docherty isn't making the whole thing up?'

Hamish patiently told him again about the deal where patients could sign over their houses to the nursing home and about how five had died and Mrs Prescott made a sixth.

'This is terrible. I'd better come myself as well.'

'See you there, sir,' said Hamish, then prayed that his suspicions would be proved correct.

Mrs Docherty had a suitcase packed. She felt she had waited so long that something might have happened to Mr Jefferson. Then she heard a slight noise outside her window and looked out. Mr Jefferson was just getting out of a long, low sports car.

'Go into my room,' he whispered, 'and out the window.'

Her heart was thudding like a drum as she carried her suitcase into his room and then her books and computer and handed them through the open window.

'Hurry up!' he urged.

She climbed out and got into the car, closing the door quietly behind her.

'Now I've got to hot-wire this thing,' he muttered.

'How did you get it here?'

'It's on a slope. I just released the brake and it rolled down.'

Suddenly a square of light lit up the car. The Indian-looking nurse appeared at Mrs Docherty's window.

'Come *on*,' hissed Mr Jefferson desperately.

The car sprang into life with a roar. He reversed up the hill just as the main door burst open and the trainer with his dogs rushed out.

Mrs Docherty clung on desperately as Mr Jefferson sent the car hurtling around the bends of the drive.

'Did you get my deeds and the papers I signed?' she shouted above the roar of the engine.

'Yes! Hang on. I'd forgotten about those electronically controlled gates.'

'They're closing. We'll never escape!'

'Hang on, Annie. Here we go!'

He jammed his foot down on the accelerator, and as the car hurtled through the closing gates, they heard the terrible sound of tearing metal from either side.

'Done it!' he said, screeching round the road. 'The bastard's car's taken a beating and it serves the murdering prick right!'

'Whose car?'

'Dr Nash.'

Annie Docherty began to laugh.

Hamish Macbeth had to delay his visit to Stoyre. It turned out Mrs Prescott had died of an overdose of morphine. Other bodies were

133

being exhumed. Detective Chief Inspector Blair was in hospital with a liver complaint, which made it easier for Hamish to cover up for Mr Jefferson. Mr Jefferson told police that they both feared for their lives: that the offices had been unlocked and he had taken back Mrs Docherty's papers. Yes, he had a criminal record but he was truly reformed and, he pointed out, if it had not been for himself and Mrs Docherty, the police would not have found out anything.

Mr Dupont turned out to be Heinrich Bergen, wanted by the Hamburg police for a similar scam in Germany.

The paperwork involved kept Hamish at his computer for hours at a time. He felt it was fortunate that Annie Docherty and Charlie Jefferson were getting all the credit for the detective work so that he didn't need to worry about promotion to Strathbane.

Elspeth had sent a story to the nationals. Mrs Docherty and Mr Jefferson were being hailed as the modern Miss Marple and Hercule Poirot. And then the fuss died away as the first cold, dark nights settled in and Hamish turned his mind back to Stoyre.

As he moved into the holiday home on the waterfront of Stoyre at the end of August, Hamish could sense, rather than see, curious eyes watching him. Lugs let out a grumble of discontent as he prowled suspiciously around.

'Aye, I know what you mean,' said Hamish. The air inside smelled damp, dusty, even though the place had obviously been recently cleaned. He carried his suitcase upstairs to the bedroom and returned to the living room and crouched down by the fireplace. He had requested fuel because the nights were getting cold. There was a basket of peat, a basket of logs and some kindling in a large box beside the fireplace. He picked up a copy of the *Highland Times* from the table. It was an old issue. He crumpled up pages of it and arranged them in the hearth, set the kindling and struck a match, then sat back on his heels to watch the blaze. Smoke billowed out from the fireplace. Cursing, he ran and opened the door. He waited until the fire had died down and then gingerly put his hand up the chimney. It had been blocked off with wads of newspaper. He pulled them down along with a fall of soot.

Still cursing, he cleaned up the mess and set the fire again. This time it went off with a roar. He heaped on peat and logs. He got a vacuum cleaner out of a cupboard under the stairs and plugged it in. He switched it on. Nothing happened. Of course, he was supposed to pay for every little bit of electricity. He fished a fifty-pence piece out of his pocket and put it in a meter over the front door. Now the vacuum worked. He cleaned the soot that had fallen on the carpet, switched off the vacuum cleaner, and went upstairs to wash and unpack.

He went through to the bathroom. There was no bath, only a shower. Hamish Macbeth did not like showers. He liked to wallow. But, he considered, as he was so filthy with soot, the shower for the moment was a better idea. It was once he was under the shower that he discovered there was no soap in the dish. But he had taken a bottle of shampoo into the shower with him, so he used that to wash his hair and clean himself all over.

He towelled himself down and changed into clean clothes and then he unpacked. The wardrobe was just a recess with a dingy curtain over it and only three wire hangers dangling from a rail. Lugs was sitting at the entrance to the bedroom door, curiously surveying his master.

'It iss a disgrace, that iss what it iss, Lugs,' said Hamish, the sibilance of his accent betraying that he was rapidly losing his temper. 'How can they expect the tourists when they treat them like this?'

There was a chest of drawers of the yellow soapbox variety. The drawers were difficult to open. He arranged as much as he could in the drawers, hung up his one good suit and his uniform, and left the rest in the suitcase, which he kicked under the bed.

He sat down on the bed. It felt hard. It was covered in thin blankets and a slippery quilt.

'Well, now, Lugs, it will just have to do. Let's see if the shop is still open.'

Followed by Lugs, he walked out of the house and along to the general store. He could hear people talking inside, but when he walked in, there was silence.

He shrugged and carried a wire basket around the shelves, selecting various items. He had brought a box of groceries with him but he needed fresh milk and bacon and bread as well as soap.

He carried the basket up to the counter, where Mrs MacBean began to take the groceries out of the basket and ring them up on an old-fashioned till.

He paid for them. The groceries lay on the counter.

'Haven't you a bag?' asked Hamish.

'Bags are three pence.'

Hamish sighed. 'I'll have two, then.'

'What are you doing here?' asked Mrs MacBean.

'I'm on holiday.'

'From Lochdubh?'

'Aye, why not?'

She looked up at him, her eyes showing an internal war between a longing for gossip and a desire to keep quiet. Curiosity won.

'You were on that case o' the nursing home at Braikie?'

'Aye, bad business that.'

'It is the bad enough business getting old,' she said, leaning on the counter, 'without folks trying to kill you.'

'It is that,' said Hamish amiably. 'They're right wicked people. But it was old Mrs Docherty who was the brave one. She . . .'

Her face suddenly closed down. 'If that's all, Mr Macbeth, I have to take inventory of the stock.'

Hamish turned slowly round. The shop, which was a sort of mini-supermarket, consisted of two small lanes of groceries and two cold cabinets and one freezer. A doorway at the back of the shop was concealed by a curtain. The curtain moved slightly and then was still.

He turned back to Mrs MacBean. Her old eyes were like grey glass. No expression. He picked up his groceries and walked out.

It was a misty day. Everything was still except for the slight plash of waves on the shingly beach. He walked back to the cottage, opened the door, and set about making a late breakfast.

The cottage was dark, so he switched on the overhead light, which consisted of two bulbs concealed in a china bowl hung on wires.

He stacked away the groceries he had brought with him along with the ones from the shop after leaving out the bacon and eggs. Lugs gave a low growl.

Hamish gave a click of impatience. 'I've forgotten dog food. Wait here.'

He went out and ran along to the shop. As he opened the door, he could hear Mrs MacBean saying, 'He says he's on holiday . . .' and then she saw him and fell silent. There were five people in the shop. They began to leave, eyes on the ground, shuffling past him without looking at him.

Hamish collected six cans of dog food and a bottle of whisky, paid for them, and left. He returned to the cottage, fed Lugs, and switched on the electric cooker.

The lights immediately went out. Cursing, he put another fifty pence in the meter and the lights came on again.

'The rats have got that meter rigged,' he said to Lugs. He made himself breakfast and then called the estate agent and reported a 'faulty' meter, 'for I am sure you wouldn't be cheating the customers.'

Alarmed, the estate agent said he would have an electrician call immediately. There was one in Stoyre.

Hamish had just discovered to his fury that even the hot-water tank had a coin box attached when there came a knock at the door.

He opened it and looked down at a small gnome of a man carrying a tool bag.

'I am Hughie McGarry,' he said. 'The mannie in Strathbane says that as you are only here for the week, I've tae bypass the meter.'

'That's great,' said Hamish. 'Come in.'

'It'll take a bit of time. If you wass to just maybe go for a wee walk and keep out of my way, it would be for the better.'

'All right,' said Hamish, reflecting that there was nothing in his luggage worth stealing. He banked up the fire, put Lugs on a leash, and headed for the door. 'How long will you be?'

'About an hour.'

'And you live here?'

'Aye, up the hill a bit near the kirk.'

The gnomelike man picked up a chair and placed it under the meter. 'I'll chust be having a look at this.'

Although the mist was beginning to roll back and the sun shone down, McGarry was dressed in several layers of clothes, which all smelled strongly of peat smoke. His wrinkled face was grimy and his eyes had odd red glints in them. He pulled a lever beside the box. 'I'll just switch the electric off at the mains. Why do you not be going away?'

Hamish walked along the waterfront. He said 'Hello' and 'Grand day' to various villagers, who responded politely with 'Aye, so it is,' but there was an odd atmosphere of watching and waiting.

Above the village, the last remnants of the mist were trailing off up the mountain flanks. A heron sailed lazily overhead. It was one of those forgotten villages of the Highlands, reflected Hamish. Quite amazing in beauty

140

and yet so far off the beaten track that few outsiders ever discovered it. The air smelled clean and fresh and new. He suddenly wished with all his heart that there was nothing sinister going on in Stoyre. But there was still the question of who had blown up the major's cottage. It stood on the hillside, a blackened shell.

He began to consider seriously for the first time that he might have put himself in danger. Whoever had gone to the lengths of bombing the major's cottage might decide to attack him. He returned and got into the Land Rover and with Lugs beside him drove to Braikie and bought two smoke alarms. When he returned to Stoyre, it was to find that McGarry had finished his work and left, leaving the door open. Hamish prowled around, inspecting everything. He cautiously switched on the light but there was no sinister flash, no explosion.

He built up the fire, although the day was quite warm outside, to disperse the remaining chill. He affixed the smoke alarms, one downstairs on the living room ceiling and another at the top of the stairs above the small landing.

There was a fire extinguisher in the kitchen. He placed it by the front door.

After an early dinner, he felt he should take the evening off and read. He had bought the bottle of whisky at the local store just in case Jimmy dropped over to pay him a visit. He poured himself a glass, picked up a book, and began to read. Lugs stretched out in front of the fire with a contented sigh.

Earlier in the day, Elspeth went to Mrs Docherty's cottage to see how the two local celebrities were getting along.

'Very well, my dear,' said Mrs Docherty. 'We did enjoy our bit of fame.'

'It's not over yet,' said Elspeth. 'You'll have your day in court. What's it like living with Mr Jefferson?'

'At first I thought it might be a bit claustrophobic, but it's worked out quite well. We have our separate rooms and he likes going off and pottering about the village.'

'Aren't you worried he might be tempted to return to his criminal activities?'

'He's a bit long in the tooth to want to face up to any more time in prison. I think he'll be all right. Where's Macbeth? There's a note on the police station door referring all calls to Cnothan.'

Elspeth hesitated. But there could be no harm in telling this elderly lady where Hamish was. 'As long as you don't tell anyone . . .'

'No, I won't.'

'Well, do you remember that business at Stoyre where some major's holiday cottage got blown up?'

'Yes, of course. It was in all the papers.'

'He's gone there on holiday. Officially on

holiday. Some cottage on the waterfront is where he is. But he wants to nose around and see if he can find anything out.'

After Elspeth had left, Mrs Docherty hailed Mr Jefferson, when he arrived, with 'That policeman, Hamish, has gone to Stoyre on holiday.'

'Really? The place where they blew up that cottage?'

'That's the one. He's actually going to stay there to see if he can find anything out.'

'He might have told us. I mean, didn't we solve that nursing home business for him?'

'We could always go over there this evening and see him.'

'I'll drive,' said Mr Jefferson quickly. Mrs Docherty was famous for cruising along at around twenty miles an hour.

In the holiday cottage, the smoke alarm on the upstairs landing started to shrill. Lugs rose from the hearthrug and began to bark. His master lay asleep in the armchair. Lugs seized one trouser leg and pulled. But Hamish did not awake. Lugs put back his head and began to howl.

'It looks as if everyone left,' said Mr Jefferson, parking on the waterfront. 'The place is deserted.'

Mrs Docherty climbed stiffly out of the car. 'I hear a dog howling,' she said.

143

'Over there,' cried Mr Jefferson. 'There's smoke coming out of the top windows of that cottage.'

He ran towards the door of the cottage, with Mrs Docherty hurrying after him as best she could. He hammered on the door. He tried the handle. The door was locked. He took out his skeleton keys and unlocked it. Lugs ran to meet him as the door opened, barking wildly. Mr Jefferson put a handkerchief over his face and ran up the stairs and into the bedroom. Flames were licking along the skirting board. He nipped down the stairs again and threw the switch beside the meter, cutting off the electricity and plunging the cottage into darkness. Then he went back upstairs with the fire extinguisher and aimed it at the flames until they were extinguished. The window was open a few inches. He opened it wide and let the acrid smoke billow out.

Coughing and wheezing, he went downstairs. In the glow of the firelight, he could see Mrs Docherty slapping Hamish's face.

'Is he dead?' he asked.

'No, just out cold. What caused the fire?'

'Faulty wiring, I think. I've cut off the electricity. Let's call the police.'

'No, let's try to get Hamish awake. If the police come back to Stoyre, it'll set back his investigation. He might not like that. Is there anything we can use as an emetic?'

Mrs Docherty searched the cupboards.

'Nothing but salt. That would do but we'd best get him awake first. Get him on his feet.'

The elderly couple heaved and pushed, with only the result of sending Hamish toppling over on to the floor.

'They may have poisoned him,' panted Mr Jefferson. 'I'll bring the car round to the door. We'll try to get him in the back and take him to Dr Brodie.'

'He's drugged, I'm sure, but his pulse is strong. Okay, get the car.'

Fortunately for them, Hamish regained brief consciousness, enough for them to get him out the door and into the car, where they thrust him into the backseat. Lugs jumped in after his master. Mr Jefferson relocked the door and set off, driving at breakneck speed.

Dr Brodie opened the door and stared in bewilderment at the elderly couple who were both talking at once about fire and drugs and Hamish. At last he made out what they were saying and went out to the car. Hamish blinked at him groggily.

'Come on, lad,' said the doctor, easing him out of the car. 'Let's get you inside.'

His wife, Angela, came out to help.

Hamish was laid down on the living room carpet. Dr Brodie shone a light in his eyes. 'Yes, it's a fair guess he's been drugged. Better call Strathbane.'

'I think you should ask Hamish first what he wants to do,' said Mrs Docherty. 'It's an undercover operation,' she added importantly.

'Oh, very well. We'll walk him up and down a bit. Angela, you take one side and I'll take the other.'

Slowly Hamish recovered until he was able to sit and drink black coffee.

'It was the whisky, I'm sure of it,' he said. 'I bought a bottle at the store. A man called McGarry called round to fix the electric meter. He may have doctored the whisky and done something to the wiring. Did you bring that bottle of whisky with you?'

'There was no whisky that I could see and no glass,' said Mrs Docherty. 'I looked in case you'd taken pills or something.'

'Whatever is going on in Stoyre which prompted someone to try to kill a policeman must be pretty criminal,' said Hamish. 'Did you phone Strathbane?'

'No, we were waiting to see what you wanted to do.'

'I cannae keep quiet about it,' said Hamish. 'Let me phone Daviot.'

They waited while he phoned. They could hear Hamish telling his chief about what happened and then outraged squawks coming down the line.

Then Hamish interrupted with 'This is serious, sir. I have an idea. May I come and discuss it with you?'

When he rang off, he said, 'Can I borrow your car, Angela? I'm going to talk to Daviot.'

'You're still in no fit state to drive,' said the doctor.

'That's all right,' said Mr Jefferson happily. 'We'll drive him, won't we, Annie?'

'Of course we will.'

Angela smiled. 'You'd best come with me to the bathroom and wash your face, Mr Jefferson. You're all black with smoke.'

Despite feeling groggy, Hamish could only wonder at the energy of the old couple as Mr Jefferson with Mrs Docherty beside him and Lugs and Hamish in the backseat drove off at speed in the direction of Strathbane. 'Are we going to his home?' asked Mr Jefferson, braking violently as a deer appeared in the middle of the road. 'Good thing I didn't hit that,' he said amiably as the deer leapt off into the night. 'Could have written off the car.'

'And us,' said Hamish, who felt he had endured enough shocks. 'No, he's meeting me at police headquarters. How did you guess it was the wiring and know to switch off the electricity?'

There was a silence. An owl flitted across in front of them and for a brief time there was only the sound of the engine. Then Mr Jefferson said reluctantly, 'I may as well tell you, being a reformed character, I once pulled that trick – not to try to kill anyone, mind, but

147

to clear a house I was staying in so that I could lift a few trinkets during the confusion.'

'I never thought I would be grateful to someone wi' criminal experience,' said Hamish. 'You saved my life. How did you know I was at Stoyre?'

'Your girlfriend told us,' said Mrs Docherty.

'She iss not my girlfriend,' said Hamish testily, and leant back and closed his eyes.

Chapter Seven

Man is the only animal that laughs and weeps; for he is the only animal that is struck with the difference between what things are, and what they ought to be.
– William Hazlitt

'I hope you have some definite facts to report,' said Daviot. 'It's two in the morning.'

Hamish told him of the attempt on his life.

'And you didn't even phone? I'll get the boys over there, fast!'

'Wait a wee minute, sir. If you do that, the locals will obstruct you as before. There's no evidence of that drugged whisky. They'll all gang up together and swear I was drunk. I'm sure that electrician knew his job, just as I'm sure no money has been spent on that cottage in keeping it in order in years. The wiring will appear to have been faulty, and if an electrician checks through the house, I'm sure he'll find some of the wiring really is faulty.'

'So what do you suggest?'

'I suggest you get an undercover squad of workmen to go over to Stoyre and check everything and help me clean up. I want the locks repaired and a burglar alarm put in. Don't tell the estate agent anything about it at the moment. I'll return there tomorrow with the workmen and go on as if nothing happened. That will scare whoever's trying to get me. I think they'll lie low for a bit. Whatever is going on there, it must be something big, something that involves the whole village. There are lots of handy inlets and bays north of Stoyre and the only way to them is along a dirt road leading north from the village. I'd like to take a look in case anyone's landing anything illegal.'

Daviot studied Hamish, wishing, not for the first time, that the man were more like a regular policeman. Every time he looked at Hamish Macbeth, with his long, lanky figure, pleasant face and flaming red hair, he saw a maverick. But Strathbane police had hit the headlines with the solving of the insurance fraud and the hospital business, and both investigations had been successful because of Hamish.

'All right,' he said reluctantly. 'You've got the rest of the week. If you don't come up with anything, it'll be a waste of money. Are you recovered from the drugs?'

'Pretty much.'

'How did you get here?'

'That elderly couple, Docherty and Jefferson, who saved my life, gave me a lift.'

'Keep them out of this one. Promise?'

'I'll do that,' said Hamish.

They discussed arrangements and then Hamish went up to the canteen, where he found Mr Jefferson feeding Lugs sugar buns.

'You'll ruin his teeth,' howled Hamish. He looked at the bowl on the floor. 'And you've been giving him coffee.'

'The poor wee dog needed a treat,' said Mrs Docherty. 'So, are they sending men over there?'

Hamish hesitated. Detective Harry MacNab was at the next table and obviously straining his ears to hear what they were saying.

'Let's go,' he said.

On the drive back he was pestered with questions until he said wearily, 'All right. I'll tell you. But you've got to keep away from Stoyre.' He described his plan.

'We could help you,' said Mr Jefferson.

'No, you've done enough. You are not to go near Stoyre. Do I have your promise?'

They both gave him a reluctant 'yes'.

'Did they ever find out what was in those pills they gave us at the nursing home?' asked Mrs Docherty, changing the subject.

'Betterdorm. Sleeping pills.'

'What's Betterdorm?' asked Mrs Docherty.

'Betterdorm is a brand name. The drug is a central nervous system depressant similar to barbiturates. The effect on the body is a reduction in the heart and breathing rate and blood pressure. Small doses create a feeling of euphoria. Larger doses can bring about depression, irrational behaviour, poor reflexes and slurred speech. It's a grand way of making old folks seem senile.'

'Maybe that's what's behind all this in Stoyre,' said Mr Jefferson. 'Maybe someone's landing drugs and all this religious business is a cover-up.'

'Forget Stoyre,' snapped Hamish. 'Chust drop me off and don't go near the place again.'

The next day, Hamish looked out of the window of the house on the waterfront. Behind him, workmen were cleaning off the smoke damage and checking the wiring. One was putting in a burglar alarm and a locksmith was changing the locks. What did they make of it all?

'They' were the villagers. They stood in groups a little way away from the front of the house, watching and whispering. Through the open window, the hissing and murmuring of their voices reached Hamish's ears, sounding like the waves on the beach.

He felt a superstitious shudder run through his body. It was like being trapped in some science fiction film where the aliens had taken over the population.

And then a small noisy sports car roared along the waterfront and jerked to a stop outside the house. Elspeth climbed out. She was wearing a scarlet ankle-length cardigan over a white shirt blouse and brief shorts. Hamish felt ridiculously pleased to see her. It was as if her very arrival had broken some sort of spell. The villagers began to move off.

'Come in,' said Hamish. 'What brings you?'

'I came to see what you were up to,' said Elspeth. 'Why all these workmen?'

'Had a bit of faulty wiring.'

'Oh, yeah? So what's the reason for the new burglar alarm and the new locks?'

'Walk across to the harbour wall with me. Come on, Lugs.'

'What's up with Lugs?' asked Elspeth. 'He looks right miserable.'

'His coat was all smoke. I had to put him in the shower this morning. He'll perk up when he gets the sun on his back.'

They leant on the harbour wall. 'At least there aren't any gales,' said Hamish. 'I think that's why the cottage was so cold and damp when I moved in. I'll bet on a stormy day the waves crash over this wall and go right up to the door.'

Elspeth bent down and patted Lugs. He shrugged as if to push her off and moved slightly away, looking up at her out of his strange blue eyes.

'Your dog is jealous of me.'

'Havers. He was never jealous of Priscilla.'

Damn that bloody woman, thought Elspeth. Aloud she said, 'So tell me the truth. What's really going on?'

'You've to say nothing, mind, and nothing in print. If I get something, you'll be the first to know.'

So he told her about being drugged, then the fire and how he was rescued.

Her eyes shone with excitement. 'So they were prepared to kill a policeman to keep whatever they're hiding quiet!'

'It looks like that.'

'So why aren't Strathbane rounding everyone up in the village?'

'I persuaded the boss to leave me be. They won't try anything more for a bit.'

'Exactly,' said Elspeth impatiently. 'They'll lie low until you leave.'

'When the workmen are finished, I'm going to walk up the coast a bit and have a look.'

'I'd come with you but I've got a story over in Cnothan.'

'What about?'

'It's a cake-baking competition, so help me.'

'You won't last long up here with all these fiddling stories.'

'If I stick around you, I'll get something big. I feel it in my bones.'

'You can do something for me.'

'Like what?'

'See if you can get me admiralty charts for the bit of coast to the north of here. See if there are any caves. Somewhere a boat could be hidden.'

Elspeth was just returning to the newspaper office in the late afternoon when she saw old Mrs Docherty standing looking out over the loch.

'Where's your partner?' she asked when she had crossed the road to join her.

'Oh, him. I'm sick of him.'

'Already? What's the matter?'

'He wants us to get married.'

'And you don't want to?'

Mrs Docherty heaved a sigh. 'I wish he'd leave me alone. He doesn't know I made a will out in his favour. I'm not leaving anything to that daughter of mine. She hasn't been near me in years. I mean he thinks if he marries me, he'll be secure. He hasn't any money of his own.'

'If you're leaving him the money anyway, why not marry him?'

'The truth is, I wouldn't mind being on my own again. It upsets me, having someone around. I've got this pain in my arm. Maybe that's what's making me crotchety.'

155

Hope it's not angina, thought Elspeth. 'When did you last have a check-up?'

'Not in years. I don't hold with doctors and hospitals.'

'Dr Brodie's all right. Might be wise to talk to him about that pain.'

'I'll think about it.'

When Mrs Docherty opened the door of her cottage, she choked on the cigarette smoke which was hanging in the living room in grey wreaths. 'I told you not to smoke in my house,' she said wrathfully.

Mr Jefferson stubbed out his cigarette and opened the window. 'You're turning into a nag, Annie. You should be grateful to me. If it hadn't been for me, you wouldn't have a cottage.'

'I'd have discovered enough for the police to work on without you.'

'So you say.'

Mrs Docherty suddenly felt she could not stay in the same room as him. He would have to go. Hamish Macbeth! He would know what to do.

'Where are you going?' asked Mr Jefferson as she made for the door.

'Out,' she snapped.

As Mrs Docherty cruised along the waterfront at twenty miles an hour, she saw Elspeth again and stopped. 'I'm off to see Hamish Macbeth,' she said. 'He'll know what to do about getting rid of Charlie Jefferson.'

'You might not find him at home. He was going to walk north out of Stoyre and search the bays and inlets.'

'It'll be dark soon. I'd better get a move on.' She drove off.

It took her a long time to get to Stoyre because she always drove very slowly. She parked on the waterfront and rang the new doorbell outside Hamish's cottage. But he did not answer.

She decided to walk north out of the village so that she might meet him on the road home. It was a clear, starry night. She followed the grass-grown track until she began to feel tired. She realized it was time to turn around. She had the whole distance to walk back. She sat down on a rock to rest for a moment.

Mrs Docherty was just about to get to her feet when a frightening apparition rose in front of her. It was a horrible cloaked figure, so tall it blotted out the stars.

She knew it was the Grim Reaper. She let out an animal scream of pure terror and clutched her heart.

Hamish Macbeth was sitting in a corner of the pub in Stoyre, his dog at his feet. There was a

157

large space all around him. The locals were all seated as far away from him as they could get. Let them get rattled, thought Hamish, and something might happen.

His mobile phone rang. It was Elspeth.

'I'm a bit worried, Hamish. Have you seen Mrs Docherty?'

'No, I'm in the pub being sent to Coventry.'

'She's fed up with Charlie Jefferson even though she's left him everything in her will, and wants to live on her own again. She took off for Stoyre some time ago to ask you for your help. Trouble is, I told her you were going to search north of the village and she may have gone that way.'

'I didn't go,' said Hamish. 'The workmen took all day. I'd better go and look for her.'

The minute he left the Fisherman's Arms, he saw Mrs Docherty's small car parked outside his cottage. He set off rapidly out of the village. The wind was rising and a thin veil of clouds was streaming across the moon and dimming the stars.

He hurried along with Lugs racing at his heels. He took out his torch and shone it in front of him.

He had just crested a hill when he saw her lying there. He felt for a pulse but there was none. He shone his torch on her face. It was a death mask of horror.

He took out his phone and called Strathbane

and then took off his jacket and placed it gently over Mrs Docherty's contorted face.

The next few days were a nightmare. The autopsy determined that Mrs Docherty had died of a heart attack. Daviot said enough was enough. Hamish's covert operation wasn't working. And if Hamish thought there was something odd going on to the north of the village, then it was time a whole squad was sent up to comb the area. He dismissed Hamish's plea that something had frightened the old woman to death. The police pathologist said she had been suffering from angina and she could have dropped dead at any moment. Enough money had been spent on that cottage. Daviot had discussed the matter with Detective Chief Inspector Blair, who had pointed out – wisely – that it was a waste of police funds. Hamish was to go back to his beat. The estate agent would be billed for some of the repairs. It had probably been faulty wiring, after all.

He, Daviot, had received a report from Scotland Yard that the major had been in debt when his cottage had blown up and it had been insured well above its value. The fear was the major had arranged the blast himself, although nothing could be proved.

But Hamish had one more task to do before he left Stoyre. While vanloads of police arrived in Stoyre and set out to comb the coast, he made his way up to the church, where he knew a service was going on.

He walked down the aisle and up to the pulpit, elbowing the startled minister aside. He glared down at the congregation and said, 'You killed her. I know you killed her because you are aiding and abetting the wickedness that is going on here. You have her death on your hands. Something or someone frightened that blameless woman to death. You and your damned religious services. I hope you all rot in hell!'

And with that he strode out of the church.

Macbeth was in a foul mood for the rest of that day. He felt he should call on poor Mr Jefferson but decided to leave it until the evening. He was sure there was something sinister going on in Stoyre. Mrs Docherty may have had a weak heart but he was sure she had been frightened to death by someone or something.

After he had typed up a long report, he sent it to Strathbane, made himself and Lugs some food, and then wearily decided to call on Mr Jefferson. The old man opened the door to him, his eyes red with weeping. 'Come in, Hamish,' he said. 'I don't know whether I'm crying because my son says I've got to go into another old folks home or because I miss her dreadfully. I only knew her for a little bit but she didn't make me feel lonely. Sit down.'

'You obviously haven't heard about the will,' said Hamish.

'What will?'

'Mrs Docherty's. She told Elspeth before she died that she had left everything to you. So if you want to go on living here, you can. You'd better have a look and see if you can find the name of her solicitors.'

'Would you mind having a look, Hamish? I can't touch her things or I'll start crying again.'

Hamish searched the cottage until he came across a black metal box at the top of Annie Docherty's wardrobe. In it were papers, birth certificate, marriage certificate, and two wills. One left everything to her daughter, but to his relief, there was a copy of the new one, testifying that Mr Jefferson had been left everything. He took it through to him and said, 'You'll find the name of the solicitors there. Give them a ring in the morning. The daughter's been informed.'

'I suppose she'll be coming up for the funeral.'

'I'm afraid not.'

'Why's that?'

'She's a hard creature. When I told her that her mother was dead, she said calmly it was only to be expected. She then asked me how much she could expect to get from the sale of the cottage. I told her everything had been left to you and she shouted that you could pay for the funeral and no, she would not be attending.'

'I've arranged everything anyway,' said Mr Jefferson. 'I just went ahead because I knew she was on bad terms with her daughter. I'm surprised the solicitors didn't phone me.'

'It's too early yet and like all their kind, they'll probably be sending you a letter, second-class post. But at least you'll be able to send them the expenses for the funeral.'

'Will you be there?'

'Man, this is the Highlands. The whole of Lochdubh will be there. It's at two o'clock tomorrow, isn't it?'

'Yes, the body was released yesterday. Archie Maclean said it would be nice to lay her out here in the old tradition but I couldn't bear that. I want to remember her the way she was when she was alive.'

Archie Maclean, thought Hamish suddenly. I wonder whether he's been able to find out anything about Stoyre from Harry Bain.

'I was shocked to learn she was actually ninety-two when she died,' said Mr Jefferson. 'She told me she was younger.'

'She probably didn't feel like ninety-two,' said Hamish. 'She was full of life.'

'I feel guilty about her death.'

'Why?'

'I should have done all the investigating at the nursing home myself. I shouldn't have

162

got her to crawl on her hands and knees all the way round to the surgery that day. I fear the strain of it all killed her.'

Hamish decided not to rattle him at the moment by telling him about his suspicion that she had been frightened to death.

He said instead, 'People aye feel guilty and angry when someone dies. But the autopsy shows that she was ready to pop off anytime. You'll begin to feel better once the funeral is over.'

'Do you think it would be sacrilegious to have a smoke? Annie couldn't bear me smoking in the house.'

'It's fine. She'd want you to be comfortable.'

'I wanted to marry her, you know. Did she say anything to you about me?'

Hamish's eyes took on that limpid look they always got when he was about to lie. 'She said you were the finest gentleman she ever met.'

He lit a cigarette with shaking fingers. 'Thanks, Hamish. I was very fond of her.'

'I believe you were,' said Hamish quietly. 'I'll see you at the funeral.' He stood up. He turned in the doorway. 'By the way, have you made the catering arrangements?'

'What?' Mr Jefferson gazed at Hamish uncomprehendingly through a haze of cigarette smoke.

'The wake, man. They'll all be round here after the funeral. Oh, never mind. I'll see to it.

Just get some whisky in from Patel's and some sweet sherry for the ladies.'

Hamish left and called on Mrs Wellington, Angela Brodie and the Currie sisters to beg help with the catering. He hit a stumbling block with the Currie sisters.

'She was living in sin, living in sin,' said Jessie.

'At her age? She was doing nothing of the kind. Only someone with a truly dirty mind could think that,' said Hamish. 'If neither of you are prepared to help, I'd better be on my way to find some *proper* Christians.'

'There's no need to take on so,' said Nessie. 'We'll start baking.'

It was a calm day of hazy sunshine when Mrs Annie Docherty was laid to rest. The whole village was at the churchyard. Mr Patel had closed his shop and the fishing boats bobbed lazily at anchor in the loch below the church. Hamish knew the funeral parlour would have done their best to rearrange Mrs Docherty's features into an appearance of calm. But as the coffin was lowered, he felt he could see that anguished, frightened face staring up at him through the coffin lid, and, while the others bent their heads in prayer, he stood there and vowed vengeance. He had been told to leave Stoyre alone. He had been told that enough money and manpower had been wasted on the place. The fact that the major might well have blown up his own home had soured Strathbane. But somehow Hamish would carry on the investigations on his own.

After the service was over, they all walked to the church hall. Mrs Wellington had phoned Mr Jefferson the night before to say that the cottage would be too small to hold all the people. The wake started quietly as the trays with glasses of whisky circulated and people told stories about Mrs Docherty and how she had come to the village some thirty years before. Then the minister made a little speech about what a grand lady she had been, and to Hamish's horror, Mrs Wellington began to sing 'Amazing Grace' while the pianist desperately tried to follow her tuneless voice. After that, the party became noisy, and to Mr Jefferson's amazement, the village band consisting of drums, fiddle and accordion arrived and began to play.

'How long will this go on for?' he asked Hamish.

'All night. It used to go on for weeks.' He saw Jimmy Anderson walking in and went to join him. 'Didn't expect to see you.'

'Just thought I'd pay my respects.'

'You can smell free whisky miles off,' said Hamish cynically. 'Get yourself a glass and let's step outside.'

When they were standing outside the church hall, Hamish said, 'So Stoyre is finished?'

'Seems that way.'

'Jimmy, that old woman died of fright.'

'I'm with you there. But they combed that coast all around and found nothing. Cost a lot of money and Daviot is still growling about what it cost to replace the wiring in that holiday cottage and to install new locks and a burglar alarm. As usual, it's a matter of money.'

'If I do find anything, it'll be terrible trying to get them interested again.'

'Do you really think something bad is going on there?'

'Of course. And Major Jennings may be in financial difficulties but I'm willing to bet he didn't blow that cottage up himself or get anyone to do it for him.'

Jimmy finished his whisky. 'If I hear anything, you'll be the first to know. Best get back inside.'

Hamish made his way to where Archie Maclean was helping himself to food from the buffet. 'Did you find out anything from Harry Bain?' he asked.

'Nothing about Stoyre,' said Archie. 'But, och, he is one frightened wee mannie. He jumps at shadows. He believes in the fairies.'

'What! Wee glittery folk wi' wings?'

'No, the other kind. Dark wee men.'

'Does he now? I wish he would speak to me.'

'Bad business about Mrs Docherty. She was a grand old lady. Always good for a crack.'

'You mean, she didnae pull her senile act on you?'

'No, she liked me. Are you sure that Jefferson creature didnae bump her off? He gets everything she owned.'

'Who told you that?'

'Oh, word gets around.'

'No, he had nothing to do with it, and if you hear anyone say so, try to scotch that rumour. This has been hard enough on the man.'

'Here's your girlfriend,' said Archie.

'She's not my girlfriend,' said Hamish crossly, and turned round expecting to see Elspeth. But it was Mary Bisset who stood looking up at him.

'You never did take me for that dinner, Hamish,' she said. She was slightly drunk.

'Your ma practically called me a dirty old man.'

'Oh, that's Ma for you. I never listen to her. You and me should get it together.'

She was pressing her bosom against him. Her eyelashes, heavily coated with mascara, batted at him. He backed away. 'Och, you are one bonnie lassie,' he said desperately, 'but you shouldnae go on like that or my girlfriend'll get mad.'

Mary pouted. 'I didnae know you had a girlfriend.'

'Hamish!'

'Elspeth,' said Hamish with relief. 'I wondered where you'd got to? Feel like a breath o' fresh air?' He took her arm.

'I've just arrived . . .' she started to say, but he hustled her towards the door.

'What's this all about?' asked Elspeth when they were outside.

'It's about Mary Bisset. She was coming on to me and I was feart that any moment her mother would be after me with the rolling pin.'

Elspeth laughed. 'We'll walk a bit until she cools down.'

Hamish looked down at her. In the light shining from the windows of the church hall, he could see she was wearing a grey floaty sort of dress decorated with a few tiny sequins which glittered as she moved like stars behind a veil of cloud. Her hair was piled on top of her head. She was wearing high-heeled sandals. He began to feel uncomfortable and wished she were wearing some of her outrageous clothes along with her usual clumpy boots.

'What's up?' she asked.

He cursed her sixth sense. 'I am not used to seeing you look so attractive,' he blurted out.

'Well, that's a backhanded compliment if ever there was one. When's your day off?'

'Saturday. Here, I don't want to mislead you . . .'

'Relax, copper. I wasn't going to suggest a day of sin. What about a trip to Stoyre?'

'Why? The case is closed.'

168

She stopped and looked up at him. 'You know and I know there's something badly wrong there. We'll take a picnic. We'll put on our hiking boots and look along the coast ourselves.'

'What can we find that a whole squad of detectives and policemen couldn't?'

'I've got those admiralty charts for a start.'

'And?'

'There's so many inlets and bays, they can't have covered them all. I also got ordnance survey maps. That track north of the village, if you follow it along to where the land rises and the cliffs begin and the track peters out, there are caves down there. Done any rock climbing?'

'Some.'

'I've done a lot. It might be worth going down the cliffs and having a look at one of these caves.'

'You've got ropes and things?'

'Yes. You'll need proper climbing boots. We could have our picnic in Stoyre and then walk along. It would be a bit much to carry the picnic stuff and the climbing equipment.'

'All right,' said Hamish.

'We'll need to leave Lugs behind. He might try to go down the cliff after us.'

'He's a sensible dog,' said Hamish. 'He'll pine if I leave him behind.'

'I could cope with another woman,' said Elspeth half to herself. 'But a dog!'

169

'What?'

'I said, leave Lugs with Angela. He likes her and he can chase her cats all day long.'

'Then we'll do it. Best get back to the party.'

They turned round and began to walk to the church hall. Mary Bisset was standing outside. Elspeth put an arm around Hamish's waist and leant her head on the side of his arm. 'Darling,' she said loudly, 'no one can kiss quite like you.'

Mary flounced back into the hall.

'Now, that's torn it,' complained Hamish. 'It'll be all over the village tomorrow.'

Sometime during the wake, Hamish had switched over to drinking mineral water. He wished that Jimmy Anderson had done the same. The detective was sleeping it off in the one cell in the police station. The following morning, Hamish had tried to wake him, but Jimmy had only groaned, muttered it was his day off, and gone back to sleep.

It was Jimmy who had done the damage, thought Hamish. He had got very drunk and had told the Currie sisters in confidence that Mrs Docherty had died of fright. Nessie had told Mrs Wellington, and Mrs Wellington had repeated what Nessie had said in her loud, booming voice at one point when the hall was quiet. Hamish had tried to stop the gossip but to no avail. He could only be thankful that Mr

Jefferson had left to go to bed. He only hoped he wouldn't hear about it from someone, for, if he did, Hamish was sure he would decide to go to Stoyre to investigate for himself.

He left a note for Jimmy telling him to make himself some breakfast and then he set off on his rounds. Although he could have legitimately gone to Stoyre because the village was on his beat, he decided to leave the place alone until Saturday. He cruised down into the village of Drim and called on Jock, who ran the general store. 'Everything quiet?' he asked.

'Dead quiet. We arenae getting the tourists this year.'

'And does that surprise you? The way you folk treat strangers is a disgrace.'

'We aye like keeping ourselves to ourselves.'

'Meaning you never try to be friendly to tourists and then you wonder why they don't come back.'

'There were some strange folk in a boat.'

'Really? What kind of a boat?'

'A big powerful cruiser. They came in for supplies. Foreigners they were.'

Hamish took out his notebook. 'Description?'

'Och, I was never the one for noticing people. Foreigners all look the same to me.'

Anyone else might have wondered whether the shopkeeper was being racist and was referring to Japanese or Chinese, but Hamish knew

171

that Jock even considered the English to look all alike.

'Try,' he said patiently.

Jock turned round. 'Ailsa!' he shouted.

His wife came out from the back shop. 'Those foreign men,' said Jock, 'Macbeth here wants to know what they looked like.'

'Oh, them. Two of them came in but there were others on the boat. One was tall with blond hair and a thin face and the other was small and dark. They spoke together in some foreign tongue.'

'Did you get the name of the boat?'

'I did.'

'So what was it?'

'Blessed if I can remember.'

'Jock?'

'Don't ask me. I cannae remember yesterday.'

Hamish sighed and closed his notebook. He knocked on doors around the village. The best bit of information he got was from an elderly lady who said she liked watching the birds on the loch through her binoculars. She said that she remembered it at the time as odd. There were boards over the side hiding the name, and when they had cruised off down the loch, there was something hanging over the back which obscured the name as well and it hadn't been flying a flag. So how had Ailsa managed to see the name? He went back to the shop but this time Ailsa said that maybe she had just imagined seeing the name.

I wonder if there's a connection with Stoyre, thought Hamish. Maybe it's drugs, after all.

He drove off and called at various other villages, checking on old people, stopping here and there for a chat, and returned to the police station in the early evening. Jimmy had gone, leaving his dirty breakfast plate and cup on the kitchen table. Lugs, who had accompanied Hamish, started rattling his food bowl noisily.

Hamish cooked food for the dog and then fried a trout for himself. He had just finished eating when Lugs put a paw on his knee and looked accusingly up into his face.

'What is it?' asked Hamish. 'You're not getting any more food.' He bent down to pat the dog's head. Lugs jerked away. Hamish looked down at him, puzzled.

The kitchen door opened and Elspeth called, 'All right if I come in? I've got the maps and things.'

Lugs gave a low growl and slumped off into a corner and lay down, turning his back on them.

If that dog were human, I would swear he was jealous, thought Hamish, looking at his dog in amazement. And yet Lugs had not been jealous of Priscilla. Maybe because the beast knew there was no hope there, thought Hamish cynically. So why should he think there's anything going on between me and Elspeth?

'If you've finished brooding over your dog, Hamish,' said Elspeth sharply, 'we could take a look at these maps.'

'Oh, sure. Wait until I clear the table.' Hamish collected his dirty plate and cutlery and threw them in the sink. 'Right, let's see what we've got.'

Together they pored over the maps. 'There are some caves below the cliffs,' said Hamish.

'But the cliffs are steep there. Wouldn't the land swell make it tricky for a boat to get in there?'

'Maybe not at low tide.'

'Still, it would be tricky. The weather's been fairly calm this summer. Think what it would be like at the foot of these cliffs in the middle of a storm.'

'We can have a look. I'll go into Strathbane tomorrow and buy climbing boots.'

Hamish felt quite sulky when they set out on Saturday in Elspeth's sports car. The climbing boots had cost what he considered an evil lot of money. Hamish did not like what he considered unnecessary expense and he usually wore his police regulation boots even when he was out of uniform. And Lugs had had to be carried to Angela because he had dug his paws in and refused to move.

But the day was fine with that bracing chill in the air that always heralded the arrival of

174

the early Highland autumn. 'Isn't it a glorious day?' said Elspeth.

'We'd better stop before we get to Stoyre and have our picnic. Don't want to draw attention to ourselves.'

Elspeth pulled off the road outside Stoyre and they spread the picnic out on the blazing heather on a hill which overlooked the village.

'No wine?' said Elspeth.

'No wine,' snapped Hamish. 'We'll need all our wits about us for the climb. God knows this is costing me enough.'

'I could have brought the picnic,' said Elspeth. 'I didn't know your bank balance was so perilous that a few sandwiches and coffee would be considered such an expense.'

'It's not the food, lassie. It's the boots.'

Elspeth looked, puzzled, at Hamish's large black regulation boots. 'I thought you got those free along with your uniform.'

'Not these! The climbing boots.'

'Oh, I didn't think. You can't earn much as a copper. Couldn't you have borrowed a pair?'

'I tried. No luck.'

'I tell you what: if we do find out anything big and I sell a story to the nationals, I'll pay for the boots.'

Hamish suddenly smiled at her. 'I'm being churlish,' he said. 'If we do find anything, it'll be worth every penny.'

They ate in companionable silence. Then Hamish said, 'It might be an idea to leave the car here and circumvent the village. If we go by way of the foothills round the back of the village, they might see us at a fair distance and just put us down as hikers.'

'Okay,' said Elspeth, beginning to put plates and cups back into the basket. 'Let's set out and find out what's in these caves.'

They walked in a large circle until they came down to where the grassy track leading north out of the village petered out.

On they went until they reached the top of the cliffs. They could hear the waves pounding below and the screech of sea birds, diving and wheeling over their heads. Hamish took out the maps and spread them on a flat rock, a remnant of the Ice Age which jutted out of the purple heather.

'About a mile on,' he said at last, rolling up the maps. 'We'll start our descent there. It's low tide and there should be a bit of a beach. No point in ending up with nothing but the sea below us.'

They walked on in single file, Elspeth's small sturdy figure leading the way. Her legs were strong and tanned and she carried her rucksack with ease. She was wearing shorts and a red-and-white-checked gingham shirt. At last Hamish called a halt. 'I think this is the spot.'

* * *

Charlie Jefferson was walking along the water-front when he met Mrs Wellington. 'You look well,' said the minister's wife. 'The rest of the village seems to have one monumental hang-over. I hope you are bearing up.'

'Yes, I'm fine,' he said sadly. 'At least it wasn't murder.'

A look crossed her face, and his eyes sharpened, 'That's odd,' he said.

'What are you talking about?'

'I said at least it wasn't murder, and you got a funny look on your face.'

'No one likes the subject of murder,' said Mrs Wellington, and she hurried off.

He stood watching her. Then Angela came towards him with Lugs on a leash.

'Where's Hamish?' asked Mr Jefferson.

'He's gone out for the day somewhere,' said Angela. 'I'm looking after Lugs.'

'Where's he gone?'

'I don't know,' said Angela, and Mr Jefferson guessed she was lying. She said goodbye to him and walked on.

His curiosity sharpened, Mr Jefferson went into the general store. He walked quickly behind a rack of groceries and stood there. If there was any gossip, someone would tell Mr Patel. Then he heard a man's voice saying, 'That detective fellow was really drunk, and do you know what he was saying?'

'I left early,' came Mr Patel's reply.

'He was after saying that poor auld Mrs Docherty was frightened to death.'

'Never!'

'I saw Macbeth heading off with that reporter lassie. Maybe he'll find something.'

Mr Jefferson hurried up to the counter. He recognized Mungo Patterson, a forestry worker.

'What was that you were saying about Annie being frightened to death?' he demanded.

'I neffer said a word,' lied Mungo. 'I was chust saying that the prices these days would frighten a man to death.'

Mr Jefferson clicked his false teeth in disgust and walked out. He would drive over to Stoyre. He was sure Hamish was there.

Hamish and Elspeth stood on a beach of shingle and watched, mesmerized, the huge Atlantic waves rearing up and crashing at their feet. 'Let's look around,' shouted Hamish above the roar. 'I think we might have come down at the wrong place. Can't see any caves.'

'There's a cleft in the rock over there,' said Elspeth. 'Might lead somewhere.'

'We'd better hurry. The tide has turned.'

They left the beach and clambered over the seaweed-slippery rocks. 'Even if it leads some-where,' shouted Hamish, 'it won't help us. Can't get a boat in there.'

Elspeth entered the cleft in the rock with Hamish after her. They found themselves in a large cave. They both took out torches and flashed them around. 'Nothing,' said Hamish. 'We'd better climb back up and try further along.'

'Wait!' said Elspeth. 'It goes further back. It might lead somewhere.'

She set off and Hamish reluctantly followed. 'It goes round the corner here at the end,' she shouted back. They walked on down a natural passage hollowed out over the centuries by the pounding of the waves.

'I think we'd better turn back,' said Hamish. 'We'll be caught by the tide if we wait much longer.'

'Just a bit further.'

They turned another bend and heard the sound of the waves growing louder. The passage suddenly opened out into another cave, and in front of the open mouth of the cave, the waves rolled up a narrow beach.

'Someone's been here.' Elspeth stooped down and picked up a Coke can.

'Could be the place,' said Hamish. 'When the tide's up, you could ride a boat in here. Tricky, but it could be done.'

He walked to the mouth of the cave and looked out. 'There are outcrops of rock on either side of the cave. Forms a sort of natural harbour. That's why the waves aren't so fierce here.'

'Hamish!' called Elspeth. 'Come here and look.'

He went back into the cave to join her. She was holding up a bunch of seaweed. 'It's plastic,' she said triumphantly, 'and it was covering that.'

His eyes followed her pointing finger. Revealed was a mooring post painted black.

'This is new,' said Hamish, his eyes gleaming. 'We'd better get out of here and get back up that cliff and decide what to do.'

Mr Jefferson's old legs were getting tired. He decided to go along the cliffs a little further and then turn back while he still had any energy left. He marched on, thinking, I'm doing this for you, Annie. Stay with me.

At last he felt too tired to go any further and sank down into the heather.

He lay on his back and looked up at the sky and at the wheeling birds. Maybe just a nap to recharge his batteries. He closed his eyes.

Then, abruptly, he opened them again. Nearby, there was a scraping sound. He might not have heard it had he been upright, but lying as he was, buried in the heather, he could hear the sound as it travelled along the ground. He cautiously raised his head. Along the cliff top a man was crouched over something, scraping away. He was wearing a black anorak with the hood up, shielding his face.

Mr Jefferson sank down in the heather, his heart beating hard. There was something

180

sinister about that figure. He lay there, listening, until the scraping stopped. Then he heard footsteps approaching him, passing him, and going on in the direction of the village. He waited ten minutes and eased himself up. Then he cautiously got to his feet and looked about. No one in sight.

He walked to where he had seen the man crouched down. A climbing rope had been tied round a rock, and Mr Jefferson saw that just where the rope vanished over the cliff edge, it had been scraped and frayed until only a few strands were left.

Frightened, he looked this way and that. Whoever was down there – and it could be Macbeth and Elspeth – someone had planned that the rope would snap. He pulled at the rope until he was past the frayed bit and began to wrap it securely round the rock.

Then he went to the cliff edge and lay on his stomach and tried to look down. But the edge jutted out, obscuring his view of what was directly below him.

He tried shouting but he knew helplessly that the tumult of waves, the wind, and the cries of sea birds were drowning his voice.

'Something's wrong,' said Hamish. 'That rope was a few feet longer.'

'Hamish, I'm sure it's all right. We'll need to chance it.'

A huge wave swept over the shingle and crashed around her ankles. 'Hurry!' she screamed.

'You go first,' said Hamish. 'I thought you had the professional climbing equipment, not chust one damn rope.'

'It's a good rope,' shouted Elspeth. 'And the cliff is only about thirty feet high.'

She seized the rope and began to climb. Hamish waited until she had disappeared over the top of the cliff and then grabbed the rope and lifted his feet just as a huge breaker swept under him.

When he finally scrambled over the top of the cliff, it was to find Elspeth and Mr Jefferson sitting together in the heather.

'This is no place for you,' said Hamish angrily. 'What brought you? How did you find us?'

Hurriedly, before Mr Jefferson could speak, Elspeth told Hamish about the frayed rope. Hamish bent down and examined it. 'What did the man look like?'

'I couldn't see his face,' said Mr Jefferson. 'He was wearing a black anorak with the hood covering his head.'

'Let's get out of here,' said Hamish, untying the rope. 'We'll walk back through the village and be damned to them. The damage is done. How did you manage to find us?' he asked again.

Mr Jefferson told him about hearing that

Mrs Docherty had died of fright and how he had assumed they had gone north from the village and had walked until he had seen the man fraying the rope.

They walked back slowly, letting the now exhausted Mr Jefferson stop and rest from time to time. When they entered the village, no one was about. No curtains twitched as they passed.

'Meet up with us at the police station,' said Hamish to Mr Jefferson.

'Aren't you going to phone Strathbane?'

'That's what I want to discuss with both of you.'

Once they were all in the kitchen of the police station, Hamish said, 'It's like this. If I phone Strathbane, they'll send men out. They'll find the mooring in the cave but they won't find anything else. Whoever the villains are, they'll lie low until the police disappear again. And they've terrified the villagers into silence.'

'They've done something other than terrify them,' said Elspeth. 'They don't seem in the least terrified. They're all in the grip of some spiritual experience. I wonder what it is. Do you think someone is trying to land a large consignment of drugs?'

Hamish sat quietly for a moment. 'They've no need to frighten or manipulate a whole village into silence. There are plenty of secret landing places in the north of Scotland, and that cave will take a very experienced boatman to pilot a boat in there.'

'A wreck?' said Mr Jefferson.

'Now, there's an idea,' said Hamish slowly. 'What's the law on wrecks?'

'I've got my laptop in the car,' said Elspeth. 'I'll get it and look up wrecks.'

She went out to her car and returned with her laptop and switched it on. 'Let me see. Ah, here we are. Wrecks. It says here: "The Protection of Wrecks Act 1973 confers powers on the Secretary of State with respect to any site in United Kingdom waters which is or may prove to be the site of a vessel lying wrecked on or in the sea bed which ought to be protected from unauthorized interference on account of the historical, archaeological or artistic importance of the vessel or of any objects contained or formerly contained in it which may be lying in or near the wreck." There!'

'So how would someone go about getting permission?' asked Hamish.

'From the Secretary of State, but it says here only to persons who appear to him "to be competent and properly equipped to carry out salvage operations in a manner appropriate to the historical, archaeological or artistic importance." Even if anyone gets permission, then anything they find must be reported to the receiver of wrecks, who must advertise that the wreck has been found in order to inform potential claimants of the find.'

'Well, that's a start,' said Hamish. 'I'll get on to the secretary of state's office to see if anyone has applied for permission to salvage anything up here. If not, I'll get a list of wrecks and take it from there. Mr Jefferson, it was grand you came along at the right time but don't go near Stoyre again. Promise?'

'I promise,' said Mr Jefferson, and crossed his fingers behind his back.

When Elspeth and Mr Jefferson had left, Hamish walked over to Angela's to fetch Lugs. 'Come in and sit down,' said Angela after Lugs had exhausted himself by barking and leaping around Hamish. 'Lugs has been quite depressed. He hasn't even bothered my cats. Coffee?'

'That would be grand. I'll just be taking it black,' added Hamish quickly, noticing that one of the cats had its head in the milk jug.

'So what's going on?' asked Angela. 'Or are you dating that pretty reporter?'

'No, I am not. Is she pretty?'

'If you haven't noticed, you're the only one who hasn't. Mary Bisset is telling everyone that the pair of you are an item.'

'I only told her that to keep her away from me.'

'So what were the pair of you doing?'

'Nosing around Stoyre.'

'Find anything?' she asked, placing a mug of coffee in front of him. He removed a cat hair from the edge of the mug and wondered if Angela would notice if he didn't drink it.

'Not a thing,' said Hamish. Although he usually confided in Angela, he didn't want anyone else from Lochdubh taking it into their heads to play detective. 'Apart from Harry Bain, is there anyone else in Lochdubh who once lived in Stoyre?'

'There's old Mr Gorrie out on the Drim road.'

'I'll be having a word with him.'

'Why?'

'Just curious about something.'

'Like what?'

'Dinnae nag me, Angela. I don't feel like talking at the moment.'

Hamish drove out the following morning to see Mr Gorrie. He supposed Mr Gorrie was pretty old. But it was hard to tell in the Highlands, where whisky and the often ferocious weather made people look older than they were.

Mr Gorrie answered the door. His face was seamed and cracked and criss-crossed with many wrinkles. But he still had a straight back, although his head had shrunk down on to his shoulders. He smelled strongly of peat smoke and cigarette smoke.

'Come in, Hamish,' he said. 'It's been a while since you've called.'

Hamish felt guilty. He usually made a point of calling on all the old people on his beat who lived alone to make sure they were all right. Somehow he had forgotten about Mr Gorrie.

Hamish did not want to launch immediately into inquiries about Stoyre, so they chatted about the weather and the fall in sheep prices. At last Hamish said as casually as he could, 'You used to live in Stoyre, didn't you?'

'Aye, when my Jeannie was still alive, bless her. We had a bit cottage on the waterfront. But after two huge storms which had the waves battering right at our door, Jeannie said she didn't want to be near the sea any more, and I had retired from the fishing, so we got the cottage here. Poor Jeannie. She's been dead this twenty years. There was a long while when all I wanted to do was join her, but the good Lord wouldn't be having it so here I am. I still drive but it's getting to be a fair nuisance. Every time I've got to renew my licence I have to send in a long doctor's report to say I'm fit.'

'Do you keep in touch with anyone in Stoyre?'

'No, I've no family there and I only drive into Drim now to get groceries.'

'When you lived in Stoyre, did you hear anything about a shipwreck near there?'

'No, not a one. Wait a bit, though. Away back at the beginning of the war . . .'

187

'World War II?'

'Aye, that's the one. I mind the days when you talked about the war and everyone knew which one you were talking about. After I was demobbed and came back, my father told me two Germans were found on the beach near the harbour. One was dead and the other didn't live long. The one that lived a bit wouldn't say whether he was off a ship or what.'

'And when would this be?'

'I can't remember exactly, but it was sometime at the beginning of the war.'

Hamish sighed. He would need to wait for a report from the Secretary of State's office. He had put in his request that morning before he had left to visit Mr Gorrie. He hoped the government office would send the reports directly to him as requested and not send them to Strathbane.

He realized with a start that Mr Gorrie was talking. '. . . like Napoleon,' he said.

'I'm sorry,' said Hamish. 'I suddenly thought of something else. What about Napoleon?'

'Russia. I hate to think what would have happened if Russia had stayed allied to Germany. But they didn't, and it was Hitler deciding to attack Russia that weakened him. Napoleon did the same, see? Lost thousands of men. Man, there's nothing in the world can fight a battle better than a Russian winter.'

They talked for some time about general

things and Hamish promised to call on him more regularly.

You might end up like that, he told himself. One day you might be old and living on your own. He remembered his rosy dreams of marrying Priscilla and starting a family. And now Priscilla would be marrying someone else. Why? he wondered. She was never much interested in sex. Maybe her fiancé had lit some spark in her that he had been unable to do.

His mind turned back to Stoyre. All those years ago, two sailors had been washed ashore, one dead and one dying. They must have come from somewhere, some vessel.

Well, there was nothing he could do but wait for that report.

Chapter Eight

From ghoulies and ghosties and long-leggety
  beasties
And things that go bump in the night,
Good Lord deliver us!
                              – Old Scottish prayer

Two days later Hamish received a long fax from the Secretary of State's office. He grabbed it out of the fax machine and read it eagerly, then threw it down in disgust. 'Nothing!' he said to Lugs. 'Not a thing. No record of a wreck near Stoyre at any time in history. Now what?'

If there had been a report of some wreck containing a possibly valuable cargo, then he could have reopened the case with Strathbane.

He phoned Elspeth and told her about the report. 'What now?' she asked.

'I don't know,' said Hamish, feeling helpless. 'I swear something or someone frightened poor Annie Docherty to death. It would have been dark when she got there. I wonder if they would try to frighten me.'

'They've tried to kill you twice before. They might not bother leaping out of the bushes and saying boo, or whatever it was they did to Mrs Docherty. I think you ought to tell Strathbane about that cave and the new mooring.'

'And what happens when they find there is no mooring? They may have moved on. Then if I do get some proof, the police will be reluctant to do anything about it.'

Mr Jefferson sat in Annie's cottage and stared blindly through a haze of cigarette smoke. There must be something he could do. If something had prompted this odd spiritual revival in Stoyre, then there might be a clue in the manse. He could wait until they were all in the church and break into the manse.

He phoned Hamish Macbeth. 'What's the name of the man who runs the pub in Stoyre?'

'Andy Crummack. Why?'

'That's the name. I might have run into him before.'

'Look here, Mr Jefferson, I think Stoyre is a very dangerous place. You are not to go there.'

'Of course not,' said Mr Jefferson. 'I gave you my promise, didn't I?'

He said goodbye and rang off and then looked up the number of the Fisherman's Arms in the phone book and dialled. A man answered and Mr Jefferson asked, 'Is that Andy Crummack?'

'Yes, who are you?'

'Just a tourist. I wanted to have a look at your church. When is the next service?'

'Tomorrow at eleven.'

Mr Jefferson thanked him and rang off. If they were prepared to give the time of the service to an outsider, then nothing was going on inside the church itself that they were worried about anyone finding out about.

He would arrive in Stoyre in the morning, just when he was sure they were all in the church, and get into the manse and see what he could find out. He owed it to Annie.

Mr Jefferson set out the following morning, feeling excited and rejuvenated to be doing something at last. He timed his arrival in the village to ten minutes past eleven. The place looked deserted. He hurried up to the manse and went round to the kitchen door at the back. He tried the door and found it was open. He walked inside and went through the kitchen, looking for the minister's study. He came to a locked door and took out his skeleton keys and opened it. Eagerly he hurried in and went straight to the desk. He began to riffle through the papers.

Sermons and parish business, nothing of interest. He slid open the drawers on the right. Nothing of interest there either: just reams of paper, bank statements and old sermons. He opened the desk drawers on the left. In the top drawer was a print of a painting. He turned it over. On the back it said: 'Josephe, Bishop of Sarras and son of Joseph of Arimathea, promises to entrust the Holy Grail when he dies to Alain, who kneels in prayer. From *History of the Holy Grail*, French manuscript, early 14th century.'

Was this anything? he wondered. Was this the reason for the religious revival in Stoyre? Had the superstitious locals been persuaded that someone was going to give them the Holy Grail?

He heard a slight movement behind him and turned round too late. A bag was thrown over his head and his arms were pinned to his sides.

For the next two days, Hamish had to leave speculations about Stoyre alone. A seven-year-old child, Tommy Gilchrist, had gone missing from his home in Braikie. Police combed Braikie and the area around it. Detective Chief Inspector Blair was in charge of the investigation, and when not holding press conferences, he was making sure that Hamish did not go anywhere near the parents. He wanted the glory of solving this case all to himself.

Hamish had to rely on snatched conversations with Jimmy Anderson to get news of the background. 'They seem pretty simple folk,' said Jimmy. 'Ian and Morag Gilchrist had the child late. To my mind, maybe they were a bit strict with the boy. I saw his room. No posters or games or anything you might expect.'

'What about relatives?' asked Hamish.

'An aunt and uncle in Strathbane, nothing there.'

'Any of his clothes missing?'

'The things he was wearing to school when he disappeared, that's all.'

'Any food or money missing from the house?'

'I don't think anyone asked them that. Why?'

'The wee lad might have done a runner,' said Hamish.

'It's getting on two days. I think maybe he's had an accident. Oh, here's Daviot. Run off and knock on some more doors.'

'Macbeth!' called Daviot. At the same time as Hamish approached his boss, the squat and sweating figure of Blair came hurrying up. 'We don't seem to be getting anywhere,' said Daviot.

'We're doing our best,' growled Blair. 'Go about your duties, Macbeth '

'Wait a minute,' said Daviot. 'Have you had a word with the parents?' he asked Hamish.

'No.'

'No, what?' barked Blair.

'No, sir.'

'I think perhaps you should talk to them.'

'I don't see . . .' began Blair wrathfully, but the superintendent held up his hand. 'Macbeth knows the people here. He might get something out of the parents that you've missed. Get along and see them.'

Hamish went speedily off to where the Gilchrists lived on a council estate on the edge of town. He explained to the policeman on guard at the door that he had been ordered to speak to the parents.

He removed his hat and sat down in a chair facing the parents, who were sitting side by side on a sofa, and studied them. They were middle-aged and remarkably alike with their round, chubby figures and round, impassive faces. Mrs Gilchrist's rather doughy face showed no traces of weeping. Hamish was uneasily reminded of the villagers of Stoyre. There was a secrecy here, he thought, his Highland radar sharpening – and righteousness.

'Just a few questions,' he said soothingly. 'You say the boy set out for school as usual but the teachers report he never got there.'

'That's right,' said Mr Gilchrist, his voice grating and rusty, like the voice of a man who did not speak much.

'Had Tommy been unhappy?'

'He had no reason to be unhappy,' said Mrs Gilchrist. 'We give him everything.'

'I notice in the reports there is nothing from his school friends. Did he have a particular friend?'

They looked at each other. Then Mr Gilchrist said, 'Not that we know of.'

'But you must be friendly with some of the parents. Mrs Gilchrist?'

'We keep ourselves to ourselves.'

'May I see the boy's room?'

Mrs Gilchrist rose heavily and moved to the door. Hamish followed her. She walked upstairs and pushed open a door.

Jimmy never said it was as bad as this, thought Hamish.

The room had a narrow bed, a thin tall wardrobe, a hard chair and a desk. There was a bedside table with a copy of the Bible on it. Hamish stood very still, sensing the air around him.

'Let's go downstairs again,' he said. 'Just a few more questions.'

He sat down again and faced Mrs Gilchrist as she sank down on to the sofa. 'Did Tommy go the kirk?'

'Aye,' said Mr Gilchrist proudly. 'Every Sabbath without fail. He goes with us to the kirk in the morning and then Bible class in the afternoon and Bible reading in the evening.'

'That's an awfy lot of religion for a wee boy.'

'There's never enough religion,' said Mr Gilchrist, his eyes burning.

'Do you mind? I'll just have a look outside at your back garden.'

They said nothing, just sat and stared at him. Hamish went through the kitchen at the back, opened the door and banged it shut with himself on the inside. He slid open various drawers until he found one with a number of keys in it. He selected a small silver one. As quietly as a cat, he tiptoed back to where he had seen a padlocked cupboard under the stairs when he had come down from Tommy's room. He slid the key into the padlock and opened the door. Two terrified eyes stared up at him. Tommy Gilchrist was bound and gagged.

Hamish rushed to the front door and flung it open and shouted, 'He's here!'

Then he ran back in and lifted the boy out as police erupted into the house and crowded round him. The boy began to cry. Hamish untied him and removed the gag and, lifting him gently in his arms, carried him outside. From the living room came the angry voice of Jimmy Anderson charging the parents with cruelty and neglect.

'We've rung for an ambulance,' said the policewoman. 'Poor wee man. His parents must be monsters.'

'I think they're religious fanatics,' said Hamish grimly. 'But, hush, no more talking in front of the boy.'

Camera flashes were going off in Hamish's face. The press had arrived. Hamish turned to the policewoman and whispered, 'He's fouled himself bad. They didn't even let him get to the toilet. Get in there and get pyjamas and clean clothes.'

The ambulance didn't take long to arrive,

but it seemed like an age to Hamish. He lifted the boy tenderly inside. The policewoman, carrying a small suitcase with Tommy's clothes, got in and Hamish handed her the boy.

Blair, seated in the local pub at the bar and cradling a large whisky, was just saying to the barman, 'It's a waste o' police time, if you ask me. He's probably fallen off a rock or into a tarn up on the moors.'

Then he heard the sound of a siren speeding past the pub. He gulped down his drink and rushed out. The first thing he saw was the crowd outside the Gilchrists' house and Mr and Mrs Gilchrist being led out to a police car.

He grabbed hold of Jimmy Anderson after brutally shoving his way to the front of the crowd. 'What's happened?'

'Hamish found Tommy tied up in a cupboard under the stairs. Man, we didnae even think to search the house.' Jimmy added maliciously, 'Ye should ha' been here. The press got some right fine pictures of Macbeth carrying the wee boy.'

'What prompted those parents to do such a dreadful thing?' Hamish asked Jimmy when they were sitting that evening in the police station in Lochdubh.

'They found a copy o' *Playboy* magazine under his mattress. They said the devil had got into him and it was up to them to starve it out of him.'

'They're the devils. What's going to happen to the boy?'

'The aunt and uncle are at the hospital, Mr and Mrs Clair. They're regular folks and seem right fond of the boy. I hope they get the care of him. Daviot's had us all on the carpet. Why didn't we search the house? Well, for God's sake, how did you think of that? I mean, when a child goes missing and the parents have reported it, you don't think to search their house.'

'I saw the boy's room. The mother hadn't been crying. I saw the Bible by the bed. But why did they report him missing?'

'They didn't. There's a young schoolteacher who teaches Tommy. When he didn't show, she went round to the house. The parents said he had set out for school and that was that. So she began to ask questions around the town and then she phoned the police.'

'Can I come in?' called Elspeth, opening the kitchen door.

Before Hamish could reply, she walked in and sat down with them. 'You're the hero of the hour,' she said to Hamish. 'You'll get that promotion yet, like it or not. But I've another mystery for you.'

'Like what?'

'No one's seen Mr Jefferson about the place and the car's missing. I've just been up to his cottage. The door was locked, but I found a window at the back and climbed in.'

'Breaking and entering,' teased Jimmy. 'We should arrest you.'

'Listen, I found a note on the kitchen table. It's handwritten. It says, "I've gone down south for a bit. See you soon, Charlie."'

'Got it there?'

'Here.' She pulled it out of her pocket and handed it over.

'Is that his handwriting?'

'I wouldn't know,' said Elspeth. 'And why leave a note like that in a locked cottage?'

'I don't like this. It's something to do with Stoyre. I'm going over there now. See if I can spot his car.'

'I'll come with you!'

'No, I'll go on my own. I'll be less conspicuous that way.'

In vain did Elspeth protest. Hamish set off with Lugs.

It was a clear, starry night with a hint of frost in the air. Hamish left the Land Rover on the waterfront and proceeded to walk all round the village but could see no sight of Mr Jefferson's car.

'We'll just walk out to the north,' he muttered to Lugs. 'The silly auld fool might have gone that way again.'

201

Master and dog set off out of the village. They were just reaching the crest of a hill where the track petered out when suddenly a huge cloaked figure rose up in front of Hamish. At first he was frozen with superstitious terror, but then he looked down at his dog. Lugs was sitting there placidly in the moonlight, glad of the rest after all the walking. Hamish took a deep breath. 'Come on, boy,' he said, and walked straight through the apparition and out the other side. He turned and looked back and it was gone.

He hurried back to the Land Rover and drove as fast as he could to Lochdubh. He knew now what had killed Annie. He rushed into the office and his hand wavered over the phone. Instead of phoning Strathbane, he phoned Elspeth and told her what had happened. 'It's a hologram,' she said excitedly. 'Have you seen one before?'

'Never.'

'Oh, they sometimes have one in castles or museums of some historical figure.'

'Do you know anyone who could make one?'

'I think so. I've got a former boyfriend, bit of a geek, lives in Strathbane. You'd better phone headquarters.'

'Not yet. I've got to show these gullible villagers how they've been tricked. Can you get your friend up here tomorrow with his equipment? Would it take long to make one?'

'I'll need to ask him. I think he was experimenting with them at one time. I know a hologram is light-wave interference pattern recorded on photographic film that can produce a three-dimensional image when illuminated properly. What do you want a hologram of?'

'Jesus Christ.'

'Is that an oath or a request?'

'A request. What's this boyfriend's name?'

'Ex. Graham Southey.'

'After you've spoken to him, get him to phone me.'

Hamish paced up and down, and when the phone rang, he seized it. It was Graham. Hamish filled him in on the background and then asked, 'Can you do it?'

'I'll bring the stuff up tomorrow,' said Graham. 'This is very exciting. But remember, the room hasn't got to have too much air movement or too much ventilation noise or other kinds of vibration. There should be a uniform stable temperature.'

'I think that'll be all right.'

'I'll work all night and be over tomorrow.'

Hamish thanked him and rang off. Now he would see if he could produce something at last to break the uncanny silence of Stoyre.

Mr Jefferson sat bound to a chair in the cellar of the manse. He was not gagged and he had screamed and yelled until he was exhausted. At mealtimes, two masked men untied him and waited until he had eaten, then they marched him over to a bucket with a lavatory seat on top of it and stood patiently while he tried to perform like a child being potty-trained, and then they tied him up again. He was unusually fit for his age but he was beginning to feel weak and frail. The villagers of Lochdubh had been very solicitous about his well-being since Annie had died and he was sure they would have been calling at his cottage and having not found him there, would have alerted Macbeth. If this was the manse, then what kind of minister was this? At least they hadn't beaten him up. The food, although he had been able to eat little of it so great was his fright, had been tasty and nourishing. He tugged futilely at his bonds. He sensed that the manse above him was empty. His greatest fear was that they – whoever *they* were – would kill him eventually.

The villagers of Stoyre gathered uneasily in the church. Blinds of old blackout material dating from World War II covered the windows.

Fergus Mackenzie, the minister, stood up and addressed them. 'Mr Macbeth here, for some reason, believes we have been tricked and is about to demonstrate how.'

'Rubbish,' shouted an angry woman. There

was a move towards the door. But Hamish had made sure they were all locked in.

Graham was standing at a table at the back of the church with his equipment. Hamish had expected him to be a weedy-looking nerd with thick glasses but Graham was tall and handsome with blond hair.

Hamish nodded to him. The church filled with the sound of celestial music, swelling and rising, and suddenly a hologram of Jesus Christ appeared before the startled eyes of the congregation, who began to fall to their knees. The eyes of the Christ were compassionate and his arms were spread out over the kneeling villagers.

The music died away. Hamish's usually soft voice was harsh as he shouted, 'So that's how it's done. Someone has made you believe you saw a vision. All this is, is a simple hologram. Go and join Graham at the back of the church and he'll show you how it's done.'

Elspeth began to tug up the blinds one at a time and shafts of sunlight lit the church as everyone gathered around Graham, who gave them a succinct lecture on how a hologram was made. There was a gasp and the sound of someone falling. Mrs Mackenzie, the minister's wife, had fainted dead away. Several men carried her to a pew.

'So now I want you to come forward,' said Hamish when Graham's lecture was finished, 'and tell me how they tricked you.'

People stood shuffling their feet, their heads hanging.

'I'll tell you,' said Fergus Mackenzie. 'It was a dark day a few months ago and I was just about to start my sermon when God appeared before us.'

'How did you know it was God?' asked Hamish.

'It was like in the religious illustrations in the Bible.'

'Long hair, long flowing beard, and open-toed sandals?'

'Don't be blasphemous, Officer.'

'Get on with it,' shouted Hamish. 'An old woman has been frightened to death with one o' your visions.'

'There was music and then we heard this unearthly voice. God told us that men working in His cause were going to raise the Holy Grail from the depths of the sea. It would be a long and arduous task and we had to make sure no one from inside or outside the village spoke of this, or His wrath would descend on us and we would all burn in hell fire.'

'And have you seen these men? Where are they?'

'They have a boat out to the north in Scorie Bay. You must not blame us, Officer. We are simple people.'

'And did God tell you to blow up the major's cottage?'

'We had another vision . . .'

'What was it this time?'

'It was the angel Gabriel. He told us that the major was a sinful man and that the Grail could not be brought into the village church if he was present.'

'So who did the dirty deed?'

The minister hung his head. 'We are all responsible.'

'I'll deal with that later. You've all to keep your mouths shut and go about your business as usual. I don't want these men alerted. Now,' said Hamish, 'what have you done with an elderly gentleman called Charlie Jefferson?'

Mr Jefferson heard footsteps clattering down the cellar stairs. He could feel a wave of fear engulfing him. What if they had come to finish him off?

The door opened and Hamish Macbeth walked in, followed by Elspeth and Graham. Mr Jefferson's eyes suddenly blurred with tears and he choked out, 'I thought you would never come.'

Hamish took out a clasp knife, opened it, and cut Mr Jefferson's bonds. Elspeth knelt down and massaged his ankles. Hamish handed Mr Jefferson a flask of brandy and he took a hearty swig. 'Anyone got any cigarettes?'

Graham took out a packet and lit one and handed it to him.

'So what happened?' asked Mr Jefferson.

'First, you'd better tell me how you got here,' said Hamish.

'I learned that Annie had been frightened to death. I thought I'd come over and have a look in the manse while they were all in church. I mean, that minister had such a grip on the whole village, I thought there might be something here. I was just looking in his desk when I got a bag thrown over my head and then I was frogmarched down here.'

'Mr Jefferson, I can hardly charge the minister with kidnapping you because Strathbane knows your record and will ask nasty questions about why you were breaking and entering. I will take you back to Lochdubh, and I want you to stay there until this business is cleared up.'

'I don't want to stay in Lochdubh any more,' said Mr Jefferson, his eyes filling with tears again. 'It's not the same without Annie. Do you think she'd mind if I sold her cottage and moved back down to London? It's too violent up here.'

'I don't think she would mind at all,' said Hamish. 'Let's get you home. Elspeth will drive you. Your car's in the minister's garage. Leave it for the moment. You're not fit to drive. I'll get someone to bring it over.'

'I'll drive it now,' said Graham. 'I left mine at the police station.'

'Thanks for all your help, Graham. Now let me deal with the minister.'

When they had left, Hamish joined the minister in the manse kitchen. 'You will need to excuse my wife,' Mr Mackenzie said heavily. 'She's gone to lie down. This has been a terrible strain on her. She was frightened that old gentleman would die. I think we were all turned mad.'

Hamish looked at him curiously. 'This is a whole new century. How can people be so isolated from the real world with television and all?'

'We don't have the television in Stoyre. The mountains block off reception and they are not going to bother about a little place like this. We have a very strong belief in God.'

'And damn little common sense,' said Hamish. 'Now, I do not trust you enough yet to confide in you. But you are all to sit tight or I will book the whole village for murder and kidnap. Do you understand me?'

He nodded his head.

'If you do this, I will let you off for the kidnapping of Mr Jefferson.'

'I will do what you say.'

'Have you seen these men diving in Scorie Bay?'

'We were instructed to keep clear of it. But I think they hide their boat somewhere during

209

the day and dive at night. You must forgive us. We thought it was the will of God.'

'You ought to try Christianity or Judaism for a change,' said Hamish sarcastically, 'and stop going on as if you're members of a weird cult. Do you know how the myth of the Holy Grail started? It dates back, just like the beliefs of the people of Stoyre, to the old Celtic legends of magic drinking vessels.' A vision of Annie Docherty's contorted face rose before him and he added savagely, 'Chust grow up, man. Grow up!'

When he left the manse, he thought, Now for Strathbane. I've some explaining to do.

Back in Lochdubh, Hamish tried to leave Lugs with Elspeth, but the normally good-natured dog growled and bared his teeth, and so Hamish had to beg Angela for her help again. Then he drove to police headquarters and marched up to Chief Superintendent Daviot's office, only to find his way barred by Daviot's secretary, Helen.

'You are *not* to go in there,' she said, standing in front of the door. 'He is busy and is not to be disturbed.'

Hamish lifted her aside and marched straight in. Daviot was seated in an armchair in front of a small television set watching a Rangers versus Celtic football match. He struggled to his feet and demanded wrathfully, 'How dare you burst in here? I asked not to be disturbed.'

'You won't mind when you hear what I've got to say,' said Hamish amiably.

'Very well. You may sit down. It had better be good.'

Hamish patiently began at the beginning, telling about the hologram that had been operated to frighten him and Annie Docherty and about his demonstration to the villagers of Stoyre. He did not, however, say anything about Mr Jefferson.

'So,' he finished, 'they're diving on Scorie Bay at night and that's when we should catch them.'

'We should get on to the Secretary of State's office and find out what they are diving for.'

'I've already done that,' said Hamish patiently. 'There's no record of any wreck there.'

'We could have got started on this sooner if you hadn't decided to keep all this information to yourself!'

'Until I'd managed to get the villagers and the minister to open up,' said Hamish, 'you would have found nothing. You'd have sent a squad along there in daylight and found nothing.'

'Goal!' shouted a voice from the television set.

Mr Daviot twisted round and looked at it and sighed. 'Very well. I'll see to it and keep you posted.'

'No,' said Hamish.

'I *beg* your pardon, Macbeth?'

'I mean sir, I want to be there when the squad goes in. This is my case.'

'It's too big for you. Oh, very well. I'll try to get the men rounded up and we'll go there, say, at midnight and meet you in Stoyre and then we'll all go along.'

'I know where they moor the boat,' said Hamish. 'It's in a cave and the only access to it is down the cliffs, and you can't get in at high tide. You'll need expert climbers.'

'We'll have boats *and* climbers,' said Daviot, his eyes straying longingly towards the television set.

'But you will let me know it's on for tonight?'

'Yes, yes.'

Hamish waited impatiently all day. The phone rang several times but it was only locals phoning up for a chat, and Hamish had to restrain himself from shouting at them to get off the line.

At last at five o'clock, Jimmy Anderson rang. 'It's off for tonight, Hamish,' he said.

'Why on earth . . .?'

'Haven't you been listening to the weather forecast?'

'Man, I've been sitting by the phone all day waiting for news. What's up with the weather?'

'Hurricane-force winds are due to hit the

coast this evening. It's batten down the hatches and wait for tomorrow and hope it dies down. They won't be out in this weather.'

Hamish rang off and sat brooding. If there was a wreck and that wreck contained something so valuable for these men to take such risks, then greed might prompt them to ignore the weather forecast.

He got out the maps Elspeth had given him and located Scorie Bay. It was further to the north than the cave, a wide basin. So they weren't diving in the little natural harbour beside the cave where they moored their boat. He felt anxious and restless. What if they had been bringing up stuff from some wreck and storing it? What if there was only one last dive? Perhaps when the squad arrived, say tomorrow, they would have gone. Perhaps they had an informant in the village who would have tipped them off that the villagers now understood how the visions had been created. That might panic them into ignoring the weather. Perhaps hurry and greed had made them forget to tune in to the shipping forecast.

He decided he simply had to go out to Stoyre and see for himself. It was taking a risk. If he was seen by any of the men, they might pack up and leave and then there would be nothing to find by the time the police arrived.

He fed Lugs and then set out for Stoyre in the police Land Rover. There was a strong wind blowing. But in Sutherland, people, including Hamish, were used to ferocious winds.

He parked the car in the shelter of a disused quarry outside Stoyre. He feared if he parked it on the waterfront, salt spray might damage the engine. He climbed out of the Land Rover and began to head through the village and out to the north. The full fury of the rising wind struck him and he reeled against its force like a drunken man. It tore and boomed in the heavens like the wrath of the God that the villagers of Stoyre believed in. The air was alive with stinging spray from the waves crashing on the shore.

Bending his head, he forged on up to the top of the cliffs. It felt as if the whole world were in tumult. The weight of the large and powerful light he was carrying in a knapsack on his back strained at his shoulders.

One enormous roaring gust sent him sprawling in the heather at the side of the track and he lay there, gasping. He could not take out the map because he knew it would be ripped out of his hands. He staggered to his feet and forged on, using a torch to light his way. At last he recognized the rock round which he had tied the rope. Not far to go now.

It was as bad as walking in a fog, he thought. The air was thick with spray. The noise was tremendous. He felt as tired and beaten as if he had been in a fight. His eyes were stinging with salt. The wind was shrieking now, like a demon.

He gained the top of the cliffs. Below him, if he had guessed correctly, was Scorie Bay.

His torch showed a small track, like a rabbit track leading downwards. There had been a beach shown on the map.

Hamish slid off his knapsack and dragged it to the very edge of the cliffs beside the track. He doubted whether the beach would still be there.

He undid the straps of the knapsack and took out the large light, set it up, and switched it on. Its powerful beam shone down on waves like mountains. No one would be out on a sea like that.

He tilted the powerful light on its stand and pointed it left and right.

And then it shone on a boat, a cruiser. It had just crested a giant black wave. The skipper at the wheel shielded his eyes from the light and soundlessly cried out something. The boat disappeared down a trough. Hamish waited. He thought of Annie Docherty's twisted, frightened face and could feel no pity for the men on board.

The boat rose again. The skipper was still shouting. He could see other men, about four of them. The boat was held on the top of the wave for what seemed like an eternity. It balanced on the crest, a toy on the ferocity of the ocean. It slid sideways down into the next trough and disappeared.

Wiping the salt from his eyes, Hamish kept the beam steady. No boat rose on the next wave. Then the beam picked out the yellow of oilskins and the white of a life jacket. A man was trying to swim to safety, and yet there was no way Hamish could get down the cliffs to see if he could help. He knew the wind would pluck him off the path and throw him into the sea.

The man struggled on the top of a wave and was lifted up and carried towards the cliffs. His mouth opened in a soundless scream as he was borne inexorably forward. Hamish briefly shut his eyes. When he opened them again, there was nothing on the heaving, roaring sea. Then after a few minutes the light picked out bits of wreckage.

He switched off the light and with a struggle got it back into the knapsack, which he wedged between two rocks.

Doubled up against the wind, he headed back towards Stoyre.

It seemed to take hours. One powerful gust threw him down against a rock and he yelped in pain, then lay there for a few moments to get his breath and summon up enough energy to get him down to the village to shelter.

As he gained the hill above the village, a small moon soared out from behind black ragged clouds.

Hamish stared down in dismay and then sank to his knees.

Huge waves were crashing over the village, pounding over the houses, and spreading out up towards the church.

Drowned Stoyre.

Chapter Nine

*Lord, Lord! Methought what pain it was to
     drown;*
What dreadful noise of water in mine ears!
What sights of ugly death within mine eyes!
Methought I saw a thousand fearful wracks;
A thousand men the fishes gnaw'd upon;
*Wedges of gold, great anchors, heaps of
     pearl . . .*

– William Shakespeare

Hamish blinked salt spray from his eyes. There
was a faint flicker of light from the church on
the rise above the village. By a circuitous route,
he began to stumble towards it while above
him the heavens roared and screamed and the
very ground beneath his feet seemed to shake
with the ferocity of the storm.

He gained the church door. There was a
small door let into the main doors, and he
seized the handle and pushed it open and then
turned around and forced it shut against the
strength of the wind.

Then he gazed around the church. All the villagers, their pets, and even their hens seemed to be there. They sat silently in the pews. Against the wall of the church was a large pile of belongings. He took out his mobile phone but could get no reception at all. His clothes were soaking. He went up to the altar to where the minister was checking through a list of names. 'I've got to get through to headquarters,' said Hamish.

'All the phones are down,' said Fergus Mackenzie. He raised his voice. 'Mrs Tyle? Where is Mrs Tyle?'

'She chust wouldnae come with us,' called a tearful voice. 'And she's there with her wee granddaughter who iss visiting her from Oban.'

'Where does she live?' asked Hamish.

'The waterfront.'

'The waves are going right over those houses,' said Hamish. He stood up and shouted. 'I'm going out there to see if I can get to Mrs Tyle. I'll need a strong rope and some of you men.'

'You'll never get near the place,' called Andy Crummack.

'We can try. For God's sake, find me a rope.'

A length of stout bell rope was produced from the vestry. Hamish coiled it up and carried it to the church door. Andy and two other men came with him.

'We'll get down as far as we can,' said

Hamish. 'I'll tie this round my waist. Pull me back in if it looks hopeless.'

They opened the door and went out into the night. Hamish thought rapidly. Great waves were crashing over the row of small two-storey fisherman's cottages on the waterfront and then sweeping up the back gardens and up towards the church. He tied the rope round his waist. 'Hold the rope steady so that the undertow doesn't send me flying into the cottages. Which is Mrs Tyle's?'

'Third from the end,' roared Andy.

Hamish waited for the waves to retreat and counted the interval before they returned. Then he set off. He waited until more huge waves had crashed over the cottage and then began to run. The undertow from the retreating waves was very strong, and he fell twice and had to be pulled upright by the men holding the rope. He saw a metal clothes pole at the end of the garden and seized it just as the waves crashed over again. He hung on tightly, holding his breath until the waves retreated, and made a dash for Mrs Tyle's cottage. The back door was open. He stumbled towards it, pulled forward by the undertow. He grabbed the banisters at the bottom of the stairs as the waves hit again, pouring through the broken windows at the front of the cottage. Again he held his breath and felt his muscles straining. The waves retreated just as the banister collapsed under his clutching fingers. The rope tugged at his waist. He untied it. He dashed the salt spray from his eyes and ran up the stairs. Mrs Tyle and her granddaughter might just be in a back room.

At the top of the stairs. he tripped over a body. He felt with his fingers. It appeared to be a woman. His groping fingers found the neck. No pulse. The smash of the waves hit the house again but with less ferocity this time. He pushed open a door at the back. A whimper came from somewhere near the ceiling.

'Where are you?' he shouted.

'Up here,' quavered a child's voice. A sliver of moonlight shone into the room. There was a tall old-fashioned wardrobe. He saw the gleam of a pair of small eyes at the top.

'I'm here to rescue you,' he shouted. 'Give me your hand.'

He felt a small hand clutching his and gave a tug. 'Jump! I'll catch you.' He held the child to his chest and ran for the stairs just as another wave hit the cottage, and the ceiling above where the child had been lying crashed in.

'He's a goner,' shouted Andy Crummack as they reeled in the rope. The men retreated up to the ground in front of the church and sat down, staring at the tumult of water and waves lit by a small moon.

They were too dazed and shocked to go back into the shelter of the church, although the wind tore at their clothes and they were all wet to the skin with flying spray. Another enormous black wave crashed down over the cottages and Andy tugged off his cap and bent his head, salt tears mingling with the salt water on his face.

'There's something!' cried one of the men. 'I see something.'

The wave retreated and the tall figure of Hamish came stumbling out of the kitchen door holding a child in his arms.

They ran towards him, tumbling and slipping in the water until they reached him. They caught hold of him and with strong arms around him, helped him up to dry land and into the church.

'Get this child some dry clothes,' shouted Hamish, 'and then get her something hot to drink. What's her name?'

'Annie,' said one of the women.

At least I've saved one Annie, thought Hamish. He said gently to the child, 'You're safe now.'

'Where's Grannie?' she asked.

'She'll be along later,' lied Hamish. 'Go on. You'll feel better when you're dry.'

Fergus Mackenzie approached him. 'I moved my clothes into the church. I have laid out dry clothes and a towel for you.'

Hamish followed him into the vestry.

'I assume Mrs Tyle is dead?' the minister said.

Hamish nodded and began to strip off his clothes.

'She was a stubborn woman,' Fergus said sadly. 'She would not leave.'

Andy Crummack walked in and handed Hamish a half-pint bottle of whisky. 'Have a swig o' that.'

'I will have no drinking in God's house,' said the minister severely.

Hamish ignored him and took a gulp of whisky and handed the bottle back to Andy. Then he rubbed himself down and put on the underwear, jeans and sweater that the minister had laid out for him, along with thick socks and a pair of carpet slippers.

Hamish saw a battered armchair in a corner of the vestry. 'I'll just sit down for a moment,' he said. 'I'm mortal tired.'

He sank down into the armchair. His eyes closed and he fell immediately into an exhausted sleep. Andy went out into the church and came back with two blankets, which he draped over Hamish.

He turned to the minister. 'I suppose you'll be saying this storm is God's punishment.'

'I don't know anything any more,' said the minister, and began to cry.

Hamish awoke with a start. He looked at his watch and shook it but it had stopped. He had bought it from a booth at a Highland Games fair for two pounds. It was an imitation diver's watch. The salesman had said it was waterproof and shockproof. I should ha' known better, thought Hamish.

He went out of the vestry. The church was empty except for a few hens and two cats sleeping on one of the pews.

He went out into the sunshine. Now only a stiff breeze was blowing and the sky was pale blue with little fluffy clouds. The sea had retreated but waves were still crashing over the harbour wall. People were moving about inspecting the damage.

Hamish felt stiff and sore as he walked across the sodden grass and up towards where he had left the Land Rover. It had been sheltered from the ferocity of the wind by the steep walls of the quarry. He switched on his radio and called police headquarters and gave a report. He was instructed by Daviot to wait until the Air Sea Rescue Patrol arrived. The coastguard would be informed. It might take some time because there had been disasters all along the coast.

'If you don't mind, sir,' said Hamish, 'I'll just go back to Lochdubh and get my uniform and make sure there's no damage to the police station. It'll take everyone a while to get here.'

'Very well. But don't be too long about it.'

No 'Congratulations,' thought Hamish. No 'Go home and get some rest.' He drove off in the direction of Lochdubh, glad that the landscape was mostly treeless or, he was sure, the road would have been blocked.

He hoped that Lochdubh had fared better than Stoyre. At least Lochdubh was not right on the Atlantic but down at the end of a sea loch.

Hamish finally drove over the humpback bridge into the village. He saw Mrs Wellington and stopped the Land Rover and leant out of the window. 'Much damage?'

'Tiles off roofs and no electricity,' she said. 'But we've been very lucky. The forest opposite has taken the brunt of it.'

Hamish looked across the loch and saw that a number of pine trees had been uprooted. 'I'd best check the station,' he said.

He drove on and parked at the police station. He clucked in dismay. The roof had blown off the hen house and the living room window had been smashed.

Wearily he got out of the Land Rover and got out his tools. He had been planning to have a short nap but he would need to do some temporary repairs. A familiar bark made him turn round as he was working on the roof of the hen house. Angela stood there with Lugs.

'I was getting worried,' she said. 'When you didn't come home last night, I took Lugs. I had to stop Elspeth going off into the storm to look for you.'

Hamish climbed down the ladder and patted Lugs. 'I'll need to ask you to look after the dog a bit longer, Angela.' He told her briefly what had been happening. 'Do me a favour, Angela, and go and tell the Bains what's been going on. That wee girl of theirs might have been having nightmares.'

'Do you have to go back? You look exhausted.'

'I want to be there at the end. I want to see if any of those men have survived and find out what they were looking for. I couldn't have got near Scorie Bay this morning. The waves are still mountainous.'

After she had left, pulling a reluctant Lugs along with her, Hamish boarded up the broken window in the living room, shaved, and changed into his uniform, and set off again. As he drove past the newspaper offices, he felt he should tell Elspeth about what he had found but decided to leave it until later.

As he drove fast towards Stoyre, he caught up with a long convoy of police vehicles.

Out to sea, two Air Sea Rescue Patrol helicopters were swooping and diving.

Feeling energized now that so much professional help was at hand, Hamish fell in beside the convoy as it drove down into Stoyre.

As Hamish climbed down on to the waterfront, Blair approached him, his face red with anger. 'You've delayed things by keeping all this to yourself,' he roared. 'We could have got them.'

'In the middle o' a hurricane?' marvelled Hamish.

The detective chief inspector opened his mouth to blast Hamish further but shut it quickly as Daviot came up to them. 'Glad you're here, Hamish,' he said, the use of Hamish's first name being a sign he was really pleased with him. 'You'd better guide the men along the cliffs to Scorie Bay. It will be low tide in half an hour and the sea is calming. We might be able to get down there.'

'At least there are no press around to clutter the place up,' observed Hamish.

'Everyone has had strict instructions. There will be no leak to the media until this is over.'

Hamish noticed the carefully blank look on the detective chief inspector's face and wondered if Blair had tipped them off.

He fell into step beside Jimmy Anderson and they led the men in climbing gear up out of the village. People were standing outside their ruined houses, just staring. They seemed to be in a state of shock. Smashed fishing boats lurched up and down in the harbour.

The fine weather made the storm of the night before seem like some dark nightmare. If it weren't for the ruined houses in the village, it would be hard to believe that anything had happened at all.

'Not doing any scaling down the cliffs your-self?' asked Jimmy.

'Not unless I have to,' said Hamish. 'All I want to do is get this day over and sleep.'

'They must be a damn silly lot of sheep to have believed in those holograms,' said Jimmy, who had heard the story.

'All we like sheep are gone astray,' quoted Hamish. 'Don't be too hard on them. Life in Stoyre is difficult. Particularly in winter, they're really cut off from the rest of the world. They can't get television reception here unless they're on digital, and I doubt if any of them would consider affording the money for a tele-vision set and a digie box. I tell you, Jimmy, sometimes on dark stormy nights I get pretty superstitious myself.'

'I don't know how you stick it in Lochdubh but it may not be for long now.'

'What do you mean?'

'You cannae go on avoiding promotion after a coup like this.'

'I'll think o' something,' said Hamish.

'Can you remember exactly where Scorie Bay is?'

'I left my knapsack above it, wedged between two rocks. It'll act as a marker.'

'I thought that reporter girlfriend of yours would be here.'

'She's not my girlfriend.' Hamish felt a pang of conscience. But as soon as he could, he would phone her.

They walked on. The stiff wind that had been blowing when they arrived had settled down to a gentle breeze.

'Much damage anywhere else in Britain?' asked Hamish. 'I havenae heard the news.'

'Just right up here in the north. We took the brunt of it. I always think it's odd that in such a small country there should be such a difference in the weather between north and south.'

'This is it,' said Hamish. 'There's my knapsack.'

He led the climbers forward. 'You should be able to get down that little path but you might need the gear for later. There's a cave I want you to look at.'

Four men started off down the path. 'I've brought my flask,' said Jimmy. 'We could sit here and have a dram before Blair catches up with us.'

'No thanks, Jimmy. I think I'll go down after them.'

Jimmy noticed that Hamish was wearing climbing boots with his uniform. 'You look like a demented gnome in those,' he said. 'So you planned to go down, after all?'

'This bit's easy. I might leave the bit leading down to the cave to them. '

'I'll wait here,' said Jimmy, sitting on a rock and taking out his flask.

Hamish picked his way down the steep path. It was precipitous and he had to hang on to clumps of gorse to stop himself from falling.

At last he gained the beach, just a sliver of pebbled shore. The men were bending over a body lying half in and half out of the water.

One signalled to a hovering helicopter. 'Before you haul him up,' said Hamish, 'let me have a look.'

He bent over the man. He was fair-haired with hatchet features. 'Help me off with his life jacket,' said Hamish. 'It won't do him any good now.'

'He's heavy,' said one of the men.

'Is he now?' Hamish knelt down beside the dead body and unzipped a pocket at the front of the oilskins. He lifted out two gold bars.

'That's probably what helped to kill him,' he said, sitting back on his heels. 'Greed.'

Behind them came a crashing sound and stream of oaths as Blair made his descent down the final part of the path on his bottom. Behind him came Daviot, as surefooted as a goat in his city shoes.

'What have you got, Hamish?' asked Daviot.

'You had no right to touch that body before your senior officers arrived,' yelled Blair. 'You're nothing but a village bobby.'

'Now, Blair, that's enough,' said Daviot with a smile. 'He won't be a village bobby for long after this.'

Hamish's heart sank but he said, 'This man was carrying two bars of gold.'

'Indeed!' Daviot crouched down beside the body. 'I suppose they must be from some wreck. Any stamp on them?'

'None, sir.'

Daviot said to one of the men, 'Search him for papers. The police photographer should be up there with the pathologist. Get them down here, Hamish, and then we'll get the body lifted off. And then get back down here yourself. The divers will be arriving soon and I want you to point out to them where you last saw the boat.'

'Very good, sir,' said Hamish, and saluted, anxious to keep relations between himself and Daviot as distant as possible, thinking all the time of the threat of promotion.

As he wearily climbed up again, he longed for sleep. He found the police photographer and the pathologist approaching and said he would lead them down the path. 'The press have arrived in Stoyre,' grumbled the pathologist. 'The police are keeping them back in the village.'

Hamish thought again of Elspeth and groaned inwardly.

Elspeth switched on the television set in the newspaper office to see if there was anything of interest on Strathbane Television news. Power was still cut off to Lochdubh but the newspaper offices had a generator.

'One of the worst-hit areas in the northern Highlands was at the village of Stoyre in Sutherland,' said the announcer. 'We are going over to our reporter on the spot, Callum Sinclair.'

A bearded man in an anorak appeared on the screen. 'I am standing among the ruins of the waterfront of this village which has been destroyed by last night's hurricane.' In the infuriating way of television reporting, he filled the screen, allowing only a glimpse of the village behind him.

'But there is an added drama here,' he went on. 'There is a huge police presence along the cliffs to the north. It seems that foreign divers have been terrorizing the people of Stoyre . . .'

Elspeth switched off the set and ran out to her car. When she got hold of Hamish Macbeth, she'd kill him!

Hamish was waiting patiently on the beach for the boat with the divers to arrive. If only Daviot and Blair had not been present, he would gladly have lain down on the shingle and gone to sleep.

At last a boat with divers rounded the headland. Hamish signalled to them the spot where he had last seen the boat. The pathologist and the photographer having finished their work, Daviot signalled to the helicopter to take up the dead man.

'I'd best take the climbers along to that cave,' said Hamish.

He followed the climbers back up the path.

'It's along here,' he said to the leading man. 'You'll find a cleft in the rock, and if you go into it and follow the passage round, you'll find where they moored their boat.'

'We'll rope you up,' said the man. 'You'd best go down first and lead us.'

Wearily Hamish led the way over the cliff, sighing with relief when he reached the beach. He waited for the others and then said, 'The tide is on the turn. We'll need to be quick.'

He led them through the cleft and round the passage until it opened out into the large cave he had explored with Elspeth. Oh, Elspeth, he thought gloomily. You are never going to forgive me.

The first thing they saw, piled on a ledge of rock beside the mooring post, was a pile of gold bars. 'Man, will you look at that!' said one. 'Must be a fortune there.'

A wave crashed towards the cave. 'We'd best get out of here while we can,' said Hamish.

'I've got a camera,' said one of the climbers. Hamish waited impatiently while he took pictures of the gold and then they all started back.

Hamish's arms ached and his head swam with fatigue. When he gained the top of the cliff, he sincerely hoped he would never have to go down there again.

He reported the find to Daviot and then asked, 'Have they found any more bodies?'

'One more at the outside of Scorie Bay. He had gold on him as well. You've done very well, Hamish. I think we should all go back to the village and make some sort of press statement.'

'I'll do that,' said Blair eagerly.

'No, this is Hamish's show. Just a brief statement saying foreign divers were searching a wreck illegally. It is feared all died in the storm. Strathbane will issue a further bulletin later in the day, something like that, and then I think you may go home.'

Hamish had been about to refuse facing the press, but at the magic words that he could go home he decided he could face anything.

As they walked back to the ruined village, they were surrounded by television crews, reporters and press photographers.

Daviot introduced Hamish as the constable who had solved the mystery of Stoyre. Hamish gave a brief statement, as instructed. He was just saying, 'No more questions,' when Andy Crummack shouted, 'They should know how ye saved wee Annie's life.'

'What's this?' cried several voices, and cameras and tape recorders and boom microphones all swung in Andy's direction.

Andy gave a graphic description of how Hamish had risked his life in the storm to save Annie.

Blair ground his teeth as camera flashes exploded in Hamish's tired face. 'I think that's all,' said Daviot. 'You may go, Hamish. Well done.'

Hamish suddenly took off and, with all his remaining energy, sprinted to his Land Rover. But before he could get there, a furious figure caught his sleeve. 'Bastard,' she hissed.

'Och, Elspeth,' said Hamish. 'I hadnae the time. You work for a weekly anyway.'

'I cover for some of the nationals as well. I never want to speak to you again.'

Hamish saw the press gaining on him, jumped into the Land Rover, and drove off. He promised himself he would make it up to Elspeth. He would give her more background on the case than any other reporter would get. And she knew about the holograms.

Once back in Lochdubh, he called on Angela to enlist her help, saying he planned to sleep as long as possible. 'Just leave Lugs in the kitchen this evening,' he said, 'but don't tell anyone I'm there. I'm not going to answer the door or the phone.'

Once inside the police station, he ate a sandwich and then undressed and with a long sigh of relief got into bed and fell down into a deep and dreamless sleep. Outside the police station that day, press gathered, press banged on the door, and the phone went constantly, but Hamish didn't hear any of it. By evening, the news that Strathbane was about to issue a report sent them all hurrying off.

Angela, seeing that the coast was clear, unlocked the kitchen door of the police station and let Lugs inside. The dog rushed through to the bedroom and jumped on the bed, barking loudly. Hamish woke up and patted his dog.

He rose and dressed and was just looking through the fridge and kitchen cupboards when Jimmy Anderson turned up, announcing his arrival by shouting through the letter box. Hamish let him in. Jimmy was carrying a bottle of whisky and a large steak pie.

'The whisky's from Andy Crummack and the pie is from the minister's wife.'

'I'll pop it in the oven. What's been happening? Any more bodies?'

'Aye, four more. German. But listen to this. The divers have found the wreck of a German submarine. They found some papers sealed in oilskin. Seems the gold was bound for Russia, when Russia had that Non-Aggression Pact with Germany and got a bit of Poland and the Baltic States in return. I don't know what'll happen to the gold but that's up to the receiver of wrecks. I suppose it belongs to the German government. Still, it's up to the powers-that-be to sort things out.'

'How did the submarine get wrecked?'

'Straight into a big underground rock in Scorie Bay.'

'But couldn't they have escaped? The water's not deep.'

'One man got to shore and then died, so the locals say, them that are old enough to remember. For some reason the others stayed too long. And it happened in the middle of winter, so the water must have been freezing. It depends on the Germans whether the skeletons are left down there as a sort of war grave or brought up for burial.'

'They must have been heading up the coast of Britain to go round the top and over to Russia that way,' said Hamish. 'But why come in so near to the shore?'

'Maybe they lost their bearings. Who knows? Oh, well, who cares anyway?' said Jimmy callously. 'Won't that pie be ready by now?'

'Give it time. It's a stove, not a microwave.'

'Why don't you get a microwave, you old-fashioned thing?'

'Never got round to it.'

Jimmy grinned. 'Blair's real sore at you for getting all the limelight. He'll push Daviot to promote you. Maybe even get you sent down to Glasgow.'

'I'll think of something.'

'The only thing that's going to rescue you this time from promotion is death or a nervous breakdown.'

Hamish got to his feet. 'I'll check that pie now. If I had a nervous breakdown, they might pension me off and I wouldnae like that either.'

'Maybe just a wee nervous breakdown.'

'I'd need to get a certificate from Dr Brodie, and he's an honest man and he wouldn't be taken in by an act.'

'You could put it to him this way. If they take you out of Lochdubh, they may just close down the police station here. They've closed down village police stations all over the country. Tell him it's his duty to the village to certify you temporarily daft.'

'I'll maybe give it a try. Pie's ready.'

Hamish divided it up. He placed a large section on a plate for Jimmy, a small slice for himself, and a small slice for Lugs.

'You're never feeding good pie to that dog!' exclaimed Jimmy. 'Have you never heard of dog food?'

'Lugs likes people food,' said Hamish defensively. 'Besides, he's been left on his own a lot recently. He deserves a treat.'

'Ach, get yourself a woman.'

Lugs let out a menacing growl.

'It's all right. He was only joshing,' said Hamish quickly, and Lugs bent his head and began to eat.

'Talking about women . . . this is delicious,' said Jimmy. 'Aye, on the subject of women, what about that pretty reporter lassie?'

'If she ever speaks to me again, it'll be a miracle,' said Hamish. 'She found the chap to set up the hologram. She found me the maps. She went down the cliff with me to that cave. I should have taken time to tell her about the search today.'

'Buy her some roses.'

'In Lochdubh?'

'There's a grand florist's in Strathbane.'

Hamish looked at him. 'I tell you what: if I give you the money, could you send a bunch of roses to her?'

'Will do. What's the message?'

'Just say, "I'm sorry, Hamish." That should do it.'

The following day, Jimmy went to the florist's. Next door to the shop was a newsagent's with papers with black headlines about the find of the gold and in some, in a smaller box on the front, headlines trumpeting BRAVE PC RESCUES CHILD. Jimmy went into the florist's and ordered a dozen red roses to be sent to Elspeth at the newspaper office in Loch-dubh. 'What message?' asked the assistant.

'I'll write it for you,' said Jimmy.

He chewed the end of the pen. Hamish's message was too blunt. The man needed some romance in his life. In block capitals, he printed: 'I am very sorry. All my fondest love. Your Hamish.'

The next day, Hamish got out of the police station by way of the kitchen window at the back after having lifted his dog out. The press were hammering on the door at the front. He made his way up the hill through the field where his sheep grazed and by a circuitous route went round the back of the village, down the lane next to the Currie sisters' cottage, and so to Dr Brodie's surgery.

The surgery was full and Hamish began to feel more hopeful. He knew half the layabouts were there for certificates about their fictitious bad backs, and if Dr Brodie could go along with them, he could go along with his supposed nervous breakdown.

He read the romance stories in several old numbers of the *People's Friend* to pass the time. Forestry workers and people who worked in offices in Strathbane filed in clutching their backs and came out walking upright and with smiles on their faces.

At last it was his turn.

'Sit down, Hamish,' said Dr Brodie. 'What's up with you? I can't remember the last time you were ill. Have you seen the papers? You're being hailed as a hero.'

'In a way, that's why I'm here,' said Hamish. 'It's like this: I know they're going to offer me a promotion, which means moving to Strathbane or, worse, maybe even Glasgow.'

'Maybe it's time you moved on. But what's this got to do with me?'

'I want you to certify that I am having a nervous breakdown.'

'I can't do that. That would be an outright lie.'

'So what about all the certificates you've been writing out for bad backs?'

'That's different. Some do have bad backs. Some have psychosomatic bad backs because they hate their work but can't afford to be unemployed. A couple of days off every so often keeps them employed.'

'Then to ease your conscience, look at it this way: if they move me, they'll probably close down the police station in Lochdubh.'

'You can't get me with that,' said Dr Brodie. 'Look at all the cases you've solved recently.'

'They'll argue that Sergeant Macgregor, who's a lazy hound, could well cover the extra area with help from Strathbane, and the reason they'll do it is because Blair is so anxious to get me into the anonymity of a large police force, he'll back any proposal to move me. You won't have a policeman in Lochdubh.'

'Maybe. But if I lie and say you've had a nervous breakdown, they might get a trained psychiatrist to look you over.'

'I could handle that. I could just sit there and look vacant.'

'Then they might not notice the difference from your usual self. Okay, let's handle it this way. You've done a lot recently, no one can deny that. Let's say you are suffering from a mild depression and exhaustion. I will recommend rest and a break from your duties. That's the best I can do. And if I were you, I would take a holiday and clear off. I will send a report to Strathbane along with a certificate.'

'Grand. I owe you. There's one more thing.'

'Go on.'

'Could you phone the wife and ask her to stroll along to those pressmen outside the police station and tell them all if they want to find me, I'll be down in Strathbane at police headquarters?'

'I'll do that.' Dr Brodie picked up the phone and rang his wife. When he rang off, he said, 'She's on her way to the police station now. Wait here and she'll ring back when the coast is clear. You are my last patient, aren't you?'

'Very last one.'

'Are you leaving today?'

'I'd better do that. But I'll go to Stoyre first.'

'You'll find press there as well.'

'Not if I leave it until later. There's nowhere for them to drink in Stoyre now the pub's wrecked and nowhere to settle down for the night.'

Dr Brodie studied the lanky red-haired policeman. 'It's odd to know a truly unambitious man.'

'You're one yourself,' said Hamish defensively. 'You could have a large practice in the city but you stay here.'

'That's different. I have a loyalty to my patients.'

'And I have a loyalty to the people of Lochdubh,' said Hamish gently.

'Well, let's hope my explanation about your ill health works.'

The phone rang. 'It's Angela,' said the doctor. He listened to what his wife had to say and then rang off. 'She's got rid of the press for you. What will you do for transport? If you are officially on holiday, you can't drive around in the police Land Rover.'

Hamish smiled. 'I took it when the balance of my mind was disturbed. Besides, I don't think they'll come looking round the police station.'

He left and hesitated outside the newspaper offices and then noticed the florist's van driving up. Better leave seeing Elspeth until later, much later.

Back at the police station, he packed a rucksack and typed out a notice referring all calls to Sergeant Macgregor at Cnothan. He then opened a cupboard and got out a tent and camping equipment. 'Going to live rough, Lugs,' he said. 'No phone calls. No one to bother us.'

He loaded up the Land Rover and waited for evening. From time to time, someone knocked at the door but he did not answer it. It might, of course, be Elspeth but he would phone her after he had been to Stoyre.

Stoyre was in darkness when he drove down into it. The electricity had not yet been restored to the ruined village. He parked the Land Rover and with Lugs at his heels walked up to the manse and knocked on the door.

Fergus Mackenzie answered and smiled when he saw Hamish. 'Come in. What brings you?'

Hamish followed him through to a living room where his wife was sitting bent over a piece of embroidery by the light of an oil lamp.

'Sit down,' said the minister. 'Would you be so good as to make us some tea, dear? Or maybe you would like something stronger?'

'Nothing for me,' said Hamish. 'I wanted to ask you how things were. Everyone got insurance?'

'No, a lot of them never bothered. The fishing boats are wrecked but at least they were insured. This village has turned bitter. The newspapers all got the story about how we were tricked with holograms. They won't speak to the press now.'

'I thought something like that might have happened. I want you to get on to Strathbane Television . . .'

'I know you've done a lot for us. But everyone feels they have suffered enough ridicule at the hands of the press.'

'I'll speak to them. Any way of rounding them up and getting them into the kirk?'

'I could ring the bell. That would bring them.'

'Do that,' said Hamish, 'and I'll speak to them.'

They walked together to the small stone church and Hamish rang the bell. The villagers began to straggle up the hill towards the church. Hamish waited until they were all in the pews. Then he stood up and addressed them.

'I know the press have made you all look like fools but a lot of you are in sore need of money. You can make the media work for you. You've done nothing to excite the sympathy of the great British public. Do you want to be crippled by money worries for the rest of your days, or do you want help?'

'We could all do wi' a bit o' help,' shouted Andy Crummack.

'Then the minister will get Strathbane Television along here tomorrow and we'll set the stage. The minister will hold a brief service down at the harbour . . .'

'We're sick o' religion!' shouted a woman.

'You're sick o' false gods,' reproved Hamish. 'Now, while the minister is giving his brief – and I mean *brief* – service, some of you must be crying. You've got to look really pathetic.'

'Shouldn't be hard,' said Andy, and several people laughed.

'Now, I need a pretty lassie with a good voice.'

'That's Elsie Queen,' shouted a woman. 'That's my Elsie. She's won medals at the Mod.'

The Mod is the annual Gaelic singing festival.

'Is she here? Bring her forward.'

A slim teenager was pushed up to the front by a small aggressive woman whom Hamish judged to be the girl's mother. Elsie was tall and slim with a long white Modigliani-type face and long straight white-blonde hair. Her eyes had the slightly oriental cast you see in some Highland faces.

'Have you got a white dress?' asked Hamish.

'I've got a grand one I wore at the Mod,' said Elsie.

'Good. Now, all gather round and this is what you've all got to do.'

Sharon Judge had not been working as a reporter for Strathbane Television for very long. She wondered as the television van drove towards Stoyre if she would ever get a real break. Stoyre had been covered. She had heard that the locals had clammed up again. There would be nothing to film and it would be a wasted day.

The minister had said something about a service. The cameraman would film it, she would do her report, and the whole thing would be scrapped. She was often amazed at the wasted money spent on stories which were destined never to appear on the screen.

Sharon knew she was not aggressive enough – or sexy enough. She was cursed with a friendly open face under a mop of curls. Men teased her and said she looked like a schoolgirl but she was not the sort of girl they made passes at. Her glamorous friend Elena said that she was the kind of girl men liked to marry but Sharon found that to be little consolation.

The soundman, who was driving, stopped the van down at the harbour. 'Here we go,' he said. 'After I set up, ten minutes should be enough.'

They all climbed out. Villagers were gathering at the harbour. They were all dressed in black apart from a fey-looking girl who was wearing a long white gown. A piper was standing by the harbour wall in full Highland dress.

'Hey, this might be good,' said the cameraman, brightening.

'I'll wait until the service is over and do some interviews,' said Sharon.

The cameraman, Jerry Mathieson, looked at her sympathetically. He knew she was always landed with lousy jobs. He had a fondness for her. She wasn't like the other hardbitten women at the television station. He had volunteered to go on this job with her in the hope of getting to know her better.

'I think we might be on a winner,' he said. 'Maybe if I get some good shots of the service, you can do a voice-over.'

Sharon began to feel a surge of excitement as

the black-clothed villagers gathered on the harbour in front of the dazzling blue of the sea. The pretty girl in white was having a tartan sash arranged over one shoulder by a small woman. The sash was pinned in place by a magnificent cairngorm brooch.

The minister took his place in front of the congregation and raised his hands.

'We are gathered here together,' he said, 'in memory of Mrs Tyle, who was drowned in the storm. May she rest in peace. We are also gathered here to draw comfort from each other in our suffering. You have ruined homes and ruined boats. You must wonder how you are going to cope with the dark days ahead . . .'

'Look at those faces in the front row,' Jerry whispered to Sharon. 'Marvellous.'

Arranged by Hamish Macbeth, the craggiest and therefore most photogenic of the villagers had been placed in front of the minister.

'And so,' the minister was going on, 'you may feel forgotten by the world in your suffering. You may feel that this is a judgement on us for having been so tricked by a bunch of evil men. But I am asking you to have hope. There are good people in the world, and I am sure there are people who will help us. May the Lord bless you all.'

The congregation fell silent. Then Elsie Queen began to sing a Gaelic lament. Her pure clear voice soared up the hills. Several of the women began to cry openly and some of the men had tears running down their faces. Sharon felt a lump in her throat.

When Elsie's voice finally died away, the piper tuned up and they all sang the Twenty-third Psalm. The cameraman could feel his excitement building. Those wonderful faces, and that girl in white contrasting with the black clothes of the rest, and the tall piper, all set against the harbour, would make tremendous pictures.

After the singing, there was a short prayer.

Sharon stepped forward to do some interviews, expecting to be rebuffed, but people talked to her movingly about their losses, about their shock, and about their shame at having been tricked by what turned out to be holograms.

When they finally packed up and drove towards Strathbane, Jerry said, 'We'll get this one on the six o'clock news. You're perfect for this, Sharon. Feel like a drink with me afterwards to celebrate?'

'Are you sure we've got something to celebrate?'

'Sure as sure.'

She smiled at him. 'I'd like that very much.'

'I don't know if my eyes were deceiving me,' said the soundman, negotiating the big van round the hairpin bends, 'but I thought I saw that tall copper, the one who saved the wee girl, at the back of the congregation, but when I looked again, he had gone.'

'Red-haired, isn't he?' asked Jerry.

'Yes, and taller than most.'

'I interviewed a tall man with red hair,' said Sharon, 'but he was one of the villagers.'

'Can't have been the copper.'

Elspeth switched on the six o'clock news to see if there were any further reports from the police in Strathbane about the wreck. Instead she found herself looking at the pretty face of Sharon Judge introducing the service at Stoyre. Elspeth had to admit it was very moving and was furious at having missed it. As it went on, she began to feel there was something staged about it. Then at one point the camera panned over the faces of the congregation and she got a glimpse of Hamish Macbeth's face. Then he ducked down and was lost to view.

When it was over, she sat back in her chair, feeling angry. That service would bring the cheques rolling in from all over. The villagers could never have arranged something as photogenic as that all by themselves. But Hamish Macbeth could have thought of it. So he wanted to advertise their plight and yet he had not even bothered to tell her.

The roses he had sent her were in a vase on her desk.

She picked them up and threw them in the wastepaper basket.

Chapter Ten

GUILDENSTERN: *The very substance of the ambitious is merely the shadow of a dream.*
HAMLET: *A dream itself is but a shadow.*
ROSENCRANTZ: *Truly, and I hold ambition of so airy and light a quality that it is but a shadow's shadow.*
— William Shakespeare

'So we are all agreed, gentlemen,' said Superintendent Daviot, looking down the table at the high-ranking police officers, 'Hamish Macbeth will be transferred to Glasgow to begin training for the CID?'

There were murmurs of assent.

'What will happen to the police station at Lochdubh?' asked Blair, who was delighted to find himself in such exalted company and wanted to make his presence felt.

There was a buzz of discussion and then the chief constable said, 'Is it really necessary to keep that station open? We need to prioritize.

Sergeant Macgregor at Cnothan could well cover Macbeth's beat.'

A sharp-eyed detective chief inspector from Glasgow said, 'Wait a bit. We've been looking at all the cases Macbeth has solved and only recently at that. There was the insurance fraud in Strathbane for a start . . .'

'That was Strathbane and that's not on Macbeth's patch,' said Blair.

'So why did it take a Highland constable from another area to solve it?'

'Macbeth pursued the investigations because he discovered the fraud while inspecting a burglary in Braikie,' said Daviot.

'We'd have got on to it,' protested Blair. 'We didn't really need Macbeth.'

'Oh, really?' said the Glaswegian. 'But there had been previous frauds and all to do with that wine and whisky importer and you weren't able to discover anything then.'

Daviot flashed Blair a warning look. 'Normally,' he said soothingly, 'Macbeth does not lead a very demanding existence, and we have been meeting here because we feel his talents are being wasted in a Highland village.'

A constable entered and handed an envelope to Helen, Daviot's secretary, who had been taking the minutes. She opened it and said, 'Sir, I think you should read this.'

She handed it to Daviot, who studied the contents of the envelope, his face darkening.

'I am afraid, gentlemen,' he said, 'that this is

a letter and a medical certificate from a certain Dr Brodie in Lochdubh. He says Macbeth is suffering from depression and exhaustion and has recommended two weeks' leave.'

'What!' howled Blair. 'That man is a born liar.'

'If he is prone to exhaustion,' said one, 'I feel he will not be up to the rigours of crime in the city.'

'He's faking,' growled Blair, his face red with fury. 'That doctor's a friend of his.'

'Helen, get Dr Brodie on the phone.'

Helen left the room and came back a few moments later. 'I have the number. Will I get him for you, sir?'

'No, give me the phone.' Helen placed a phone in front of him and told him the number.

The others waited. They could hear Daviot asking questions and then he listened in silence as the doctor spoke. Finally he thanked him and said goodbye.

'Macbeth,' he said heavily, 'has gone off somewhere, no one knows where. His final message was that he would be back on duty in two weeks' time.'

'This is rubbish . . .' started Blair.

Daviot turned cold eyes on him. 'Would you please wait outside?'

His face flaming, Blair left. He paced up and down outside. Oh, please, he prayed to the God he didn't believe in, send Hamish Macbeth to Glasgow, or the Outer Hebrides, or anywhere but Lochdubh.

255

He waited a long time. At last the door opened and they all filed out. Blair waited impatiently and then approached Daviot. 'Well?' he demanded.

'Well, what?'

'Well, sir, what's happened?'

'We have decided to leave Macbeth where he is for the moment. He should have reported to us. We cannot suspend him from duty, as he is such a hero. He always was a bit of a maverick. Perhaps it would be safer to leave him where he is. No!' He held up his hand to stifle the outburst that he could see was just about to erupt from Blair. 'You should know when to keep your mouth shut. There was no need for you to have attended the meeting. The least you could have done was to keep quiet and not make an exhibition of yourself. Dr Brodie is a fine man. I was over in Lochdubh once with my wife, and our poodle, Snuffy, fell ill. The local vet was on holiday so we took poor Snuffy to Dr Brodie. He was kindness itself. He kept Snuffy overnight at the surgery for observation and the dog was right as rain the next day. We must respect the opinion of such a man. You may go.'

Blair went off to get well and truly drunk.

Hamish, camped on a hillside, heard his mobile phone ring and answered it. It was Dr Brodie. 'That friend of yours, Jimmy Anderson, called. You're off the hook, so enjoy your holiday.'

'Thanks a lot.'

'You should be thanking your boss's dog. That animal fell sick once and I looked after it and gave it back to him, cured, the next day. He thinks I'm a genius.'

'What was up with it?'

'I did a bit of detective work myself and found the Daviots had been at the Italian restaurant where Willie Lamont, it turned out, had said he would look after the animal in the kitchen and fed the brute to bursting point. All I did was let the beast sleep it off. So what are you doing now?'

'Camping. Just me and Lugs. Peace and quiet. Have you seen anything of Elspeth?'

'The reporter? No. Why? She's never ill.'

'I phoned her a couple of times and she just hung up on me.'

'You always were unlucky in love,' said the doctor, and roared with heartless laughter.

Hamish walked the rest of the day and then went back to a camping spot next to a river where he had parked the Land Rover that morning. He set up his tent, got out his camping stove, and started to fry sausages. 'This is the life, eh, Lugs?' he said, turning sausages in the pan.

Lugs wagged his tail and lolled his tongue and gazed eagerly at the sausages.

The sun was setting behind the mountains, going down in a blaze of glory. Hamish felt content. Worries about Priscilla's marriage and worries about Elspeth were firmly put to the very back of his mind. For two whole weeks, he was free from responsibility. He had seen no one all day except two hillwalkers in the distance.

After supper, he read for a while by the light of a gas lamp and then decided to turn in. He gave himself a perfunctory wash and settled down in his sleeping bag, still dressed in sweater and trousers because it was a cold night. Lugs snuggled down at his side and soon both were fast asleep.

Hamish awoke with a start in the middle of the night, all his senses suddenly alert. He automatically felt for Lugs's rough coat and, not finding the dog, struggled out of his sleeping bag. He lit the gas lamp. No dog.

And then he froze. The tent flap opened and a man crawled in. He was holding a pistol. 'Don't make a move,' he said. He had several days' growth of beard. He was wearing an anorak over black trousers that Hamish noticed bore white marks of salt. He was small and wiry with a long thin face and black eyes which glittered dangerously in the light of the camping lamp.

'My dog?' asked Hamish through dry lips. 'What have you done with my dog?'

'Quiet, isn't he?' sneered the man.

That accent! 'You're German,' said Hamish. 'You were with the diving team.'

'And I recognize you from the newspapers,' the German said. His voice was light and his English perfect. 'So this is the policeman who wrecked all our plans.'

'How did you make it to shore?'

'Because I didn't weight myself down with gold bars like the rest. Now, you are going to make me something to eat. I have you covered.'

Keep him talking, thought Hamish. The tent was low, so he had to move doubled up. 'I'd be better to take the stove outside,' he said.

'No. Here!'

Hamish pumped up the stove and lit it and put the frying pan on top of it. 'I have bacon and eggs,' he said.

'That'll do.'

'And then what?' asked Hamish.

'Then I will kill you and take your police vehicle.'

Hamish looked at the gun. 'We're not very up on guns in the Highlands,' he said, his voice soft and amiable as if entertaining a friend. 'What kind is it?'

259

The man laughed. 'You're brave. It'll be a pity to kill you. This, my friend, is an HS 2000 semi-automatic pistol, made in Croatia. It's the best of its kind anywhere.'

The fat was hot. Hamish laid in two rashers of bacon. This man may kill me but I'll try to at least damage him first, he thought. He knew that the landscape for miles around was empty of habitation, and who was going to come by in the middle of the night?

And then he heard voices. He could hardly believe his ears. Then a woman saying loudly, 'Shine your torch. It's a dog. He's wounded.'

The man swore. 'Move outside and join them. Fast!'

Hamish switched off the stove and moved forward through the tent flap, carrying the gas lamp with him. The light shone down on Lugs. The dog was lying still, a nasty-looking wound on his head. Hamish could feel rage boiling up inside him. Two figures were crouched down beside Lugs. A man and a woman. They were probably the hillwalkers he had seen earlier.

The man was shining a torch on Lugs. 'What happened here?' he asked.

'Get to your feet,' ordered the German, 'and put your hands on your head.'

Startled, they rose up, and stood staring at the gun.

'You join them,' the German said to Hamish. 'Back against the Land Rover. It looks as if I'll have to kill all of you,' he said.

260

'Don't you want to eat first?'

He grinned. 'You're a cool one. I can cook for myself.'

'Did you hit that dog?' asked the woman, tears starting to her eyes.

'Had to silence it. Lured it out of the tent with a bit of cheese. I've been stalking this man all day.'

'Shoot him but let us go,' cried the woman. 'We won't say anything.'

'What were you doing walking the hills in the middle of the night?' asked Hamish.

'We're on our honeymoon,' she said. 'We thought it would be so romantic to walk under the stars.'

'I am Hamish Macbeth, police constable of Lochdubh. What are your names?'

'I'm Peter and this is Linda,' said the man.

'For Gott's sake,' said the German, his accent thickening. 'Let us get this over with.'

He raised the pistol.

'Do you mind if I turn my back?' asked Hamish. 'I neffer did like to look death in the face.'

'Oh, very well. All of you turn round. Against the Land Rover.'

'Do ye mind if I say a wee prayer?'

'You are crazy,' he said. 'Make it short.'

Hamish quietly slid one long arm through the open window of the Land Rover and his fingers grasped what he hoped to find.

261

'Get on with it!' shouted the German. 'I don't know why I am even bothering with this nonsense!'

'For what you are about to receive,' said Hamish gently, 'may the Lord make me truly grateful.'

In one fluid movement, he seized the shotgun he had loaded earlier, meaning to shoot a rabbit for the pot, dropped to the ground, rolled over, and blasted the German in the chest.

Linda began to scream. 'Shut up!' shouted Hamish. 'Let me think.' He had to get Lugs to a vet. He would have to explain why he had taken the Land Rover on holiday with him. Worse, he would have to explain why he had a loaded shotgun in the front seat of the vehicle, which was unlocked and had a window open.

He knelt down by the German. There was no pulse.

Ignoring Linda, who was now sobbing, and Peter, who was being sick, he got into the Land Rover and switched on the radio. Desperately he radioed Strathbane, asking for a helicopter, explaining roughly what had happened. He gave them as exact a location as he could and said he would light a bonfire.

He then turned and said to Peter, 'You're going to have to help me find wood and heather to make a fire. Pull yourself together, man.'

Hamish then bent down beside Lugs. The dog had a bleeding wound on his head. Lugs was still breathing . . . just.

He got his sleeping bag from the tent and covered the dog and then went to help find stuff for the bonfire. 'There's nothing but heather,' panted Peter, rushing back with an armful.

'That'll do. We need piles of it.'

Linda had slumped down beside the Land Rover, her eyes closed. Hamish jerked her to her feet. 'You're in shock, so you cannae go to sleep now. Get moving and help with the fire.'

'Can't you cover that man up?' She shuddered and looked at the dead body of the German.

Hamish went into the tent and came out with a rug and threw it over the body.

When a great pile of heather had been gathered, he threw petrol over it and struck a match. 'They should see that,' he said. 'Keep getting more heather.'

An hour passed while they desperately fed the fire, and all the time Hamish prayed for the life of his dog.

He could have cried with relief when he heard the whirr of a helicopter soaring over the mountains. Then came another.

They both set down in the heather. Police poured out, headed by Jimmy Anderson.

'It's Lugs,' cried Hamish. 'He's mortal bad. Got to get him to a vet.'

Jimmy's sidekick, MacNab, was there with him. 'Hamish, we've got to get a full statement. We've got to wait for the pathologist . . .'

'We've got two helicopters,' said Jimmy, 'and Macbeth here needs hospital treatment.'

'For what?' asked MacNab.

'I'll think o' something. Get along, Hamish.'

Hamish lifted Lugs tenderly into the helicopter. 'Hospital?' asked the pilot.

'No, the vet,' said Hamish.

All the way to the small airport at Strathbane, Hamish held Lugs. The pilot had radioed ahead and a police car was waiting for them. There was a vet in Strathbane. Hamish knew where he lived, so he directed the driver to the man's house. Once there, he hammered on the door until the vet, blinking sleepily, answered it.

'It's my dog, Fred,' gasped Hamish. 'He's dying. Someone hit him. I don't want him to die.'

'Take him round to the surgery next door. I'll need my coat.'

In the surgery Lugs was laid out on a table. 'Pretty bad,' murmured the vet. 'You'll need to leave the animal with me, Hamish. No, there's nothing you can do here. Go and get some sleep.'

Hamish reluctantly went back to the police car. 'They've just radioed,' said the driver. 'Mr

Daviot's out of his bed and heading for head-quarters. He wants a full statement from you.'

Hamish groaned.

Superintendent Daviot saw Hamish in an interview room, not in his office. Another detective was there, a new one Hamish did not recognize, and the tape was started as Daviot explained. 'I want you to give me a full report. I gather he was the only survivor from that boatload of Germans. The two hillwalkers say you pulled a shotgun out of the police Land Rover and shot him. They do say he was ready to kill all of you. But what we must know for the record is why you took a police vehicle with you when you were supposed to be on leave and why you had a loaded shotgun in an unlocked vehicle with a window open.'

I must make this good, thought Hamish. I can't afford to lose my job.

'A friend gave me a lift a good bit of the way when I started my leave,' said Hamish. There was a short silence. The tape whirred. I must get Angela to say she drove me, thought Hamish. He began again. 'I took my camping equipment in a rucksack. My dog and I were walking up in the hills above Stoyre when I thought I saw a man skulking about in the distance. I began to wonder if they had all drowned.'

'For the tape, Macbeth. You mean the Germans from the wrecked boat who had been diving for the gold?'

'Yes, that is so. I phoned my friend Angela Brodie and asked her to take me back to Lochdubh. I have been suffering from exhaustion and thought I was imagining things. But I thought I would go back up and see if I could find that man. I took my shotgun with me. I knew if he was one of them, he would be desperate. I went back there to search but found no one. I thought I heard a noise in the middle of the night and went out and opened up the Land Rover and loaded my shotgun. At that point, Lugs, my dog, rushed off barking into the night. I heard a crack. That must have been when Lugs got hit on the head. I ran in the direction of the noise and found Lugs lying in the heather and the German pointing a pistol at me. He ordered me back to the tent. I picked up my dog and carried him. Outside the tent, he ordered me to put the dog down and go into the tent and make him some food. Then when I was just beginning to cook eggs and bacon for him, we heard Linda and Peter, the hillwalkers, exclaiming over the dog. He ordered me outside. He told us he was going to shoot us all. I asked if I could turn my back. He agreed. I reached into the Land Rover, grabbed the shotgun, fell to the ground, and twisted round and shot him.'

'But if you thought there was a dangerous criminal loose in the heather, why did you not report it?'

'I am not myself, sir,' said Hamish weakly. 'I've been feeling weak and shaky.'

Daviot turned to the detective. 'Switch off the tape and wait outside.'

When the detective had left, Daviot looked at Hamish and sighed. 'What am I to do with you? We have already issued a statement to the press that you are on leave. We do not want them to know that you have been going around like a Wild West sheriff. We will issue a statement saying a stranger had been seen up on the hills and you had gone to investigate. Make it official. But tell me this. What on earth was the German doing to give you time to reach into the Land Rover, get out the shotgun, and turn round and shoot him?'

'I asked to say a prayer. I think that threw him. I am very fast with a shotgun, sir.'

'So I've heard, now come to think of it. You used to win all the prizes at the clay shoot down at Moy Hall. Why did you stop competing?'

'Give someone else a chance,' said Hamish with a simple Highland vanity. 'I'm too good for the others.'

'You look a wreck. We'll give you a lift back to Lochdubh. A policeman has been ordered to drive your vehicle back to your station.'

'Sir, if you don't mind. I have to stay here the rest of the night. My dog's at the vet.'

'Of course,' said Daviot quickly, and Hamish was grateful that his boss was sentimental about animals.

'I'll see if one of the cells is free.'

'Just this once, you may put up at a hotel. Charge the room on your credit card and then put the bill in with your expenses. You do have your credit cards with you?'

Hamish felt in his pocket. 'Yes, I still have my wallet.'

'Off you go.'

Hamish chose a small hotel near the vet's. He phoned Angela Brodie, who said, yes, she would swear blind she had driven him. It was six in the morning when he climbed into bed. He'd asked for an alarm call at nine.

After the call had come in, he washed and put on his clothes, ruefully feeling the red bristles on his chin. He tried to eat a quick breakfast in the small dining room but the food seemed to stick in his throat. He was just pushing his plate away when Angela walked in. Her thin face lit up when she saw him. 'I thought I'd better come and drive you around and make it official. Let's go and see Lugs.'

All the way to the vet, Hamish sat hunched up in the passenger seat. After his last dog, Towser, had died, he hadn't wanted another.

But fisherman Archie Maclean had found Lugs wandering up on the moors and had given him to Hamish as a Christmas present. Hamish had been captivated from the first by the dog with large ears and odd blue eyes.

'Do you think he'll be all right?' he asked Angela.

'Can't say until we hear what the vet's found out about his condition,' she answered.

'Here we are. Take it easy, Hamish. Don't try to get out of the car until I've parked it.'

Hamish walked into the waiting room. It was full of people, sitting with their animals. He headed for the surgery door. 'Take your turn!' shouted an angry woman. Hamish and Angela walked straight in.

'Don't you ever knock?' asked Fred crossly as he stood over a cat, about to give it an injection. 'Oh, sit over in the waiting room and I'll call you.'

'My dog?'

'Your dog's fine.'

'Let the vet attend to my cat,' said a thin woman, hovering beside the table.

They retreated to the waiting room. Angela held Hamish's hand in a reassuring clasp. By evening, it was all over Lochdubh that Hamish had been holding hands with the doctor's wife.

The thin woman finally emerged with her cat. She glared at Hamish. 'You could have harmed Tiddles with your interruption.'

She was followed by the vet.

'Come along, queue jumpers that you are,' said Fred. 'He's through here. That dog of yours must have a skull like iron. I X-rayed him. He took a sore dunt but no bones broken in his skull. Just a bad concussion.'

There were various large pens holding sick animals. 'Here we are,' said the vet. Lugs had a white plaster on the crown of his head. He was lying on his side with his eyes closed.

'Lugs,' said Hamish softly.

The dog opened one blue eye and feebly wagged his tail.

'Can I take him home?'

'No, you'll leave him here until I phone you. Now run along. I have other animals to see to.'

Back in Angela's car, Hamish said, 'I could sleep for a month but I'd better get back to Lochdubh and write up my full report.'

'I tell you what, I'll type for you. You dictate. You're so tired your fingers will fall between the keys.'

'Elspeth all right?'

'I think she was coming round,' said Angela. 'But she'll be mad again when she hears the news. More drama and you didn't even let her know.'

'I hadnae time to let her know!'

'Let's hope she sees it that way. They phoned up to check I had driven you and I confirmed that, and then, you'll be glad to know, my excellent husband got on to Daviot and told him you definitely needed peace and quiet and rest. So you're still off work. Once we get the report off, you can sleep for days if you like.'

The Land Rover was standing outside the police station. Hamish collected his things from it and he and Angela went inside. He dictated his report, which she neatly typed up on the computer and sent to Strathbane. All the time, the phone rang with requests from newspapers for an interview. 'It won't be Blair who leaked it this time,' said Hamish. 'He'll think I've had enough publicity. Have you heard how things are in Stoyre?'

'There was a really moving piece about the villagers on Strathbane telly. Cheques are starting to pour in from well-wishers. They'll need to set up a trust. Oh, and some lassie called Elsie Queen who sang a Gaelic song has been signed up by a London agent. Stoyre will never be the same again.'

'Yes, it will,' said Hamish. 'The world will move on and Stoyre will be forgotten. Isn't it sad that we only get upset about nasty things happening to people and places if television decides we should?'

'Did you have anything to do with that business in Stoyre? I'm sure they would never have thought to stage anything like that themselves. It was like a sort of *Brigadoon* setting. Whiff of Hollywood about it all.'

'Oh, really? Sorry I missed that.'

'So you didn't have anything to do with it?'

'Gosh, I'm tired. If you don't mind, Angela, I'm off to bed.'

But when Hamish finally stretched out on his bed, he found his mind was racing with worries about Lugs (would the dog really be all right?), Priscilla (was she really going through with getting married?), and Elspeth (would she ever speak to him again?).

He picked up an American detective story and began to read from where he had left off. The American detective had been beaten up with an iron bar, had gone two nights without sleep, and was still soldiering on. Makes me feel like a wimp, thought Hamish. The book slid from his hand on to the floor, his eyes closed, and he was asleep at last.

Hamish slept right through until the next morning and found to his irritation that the press were outside the police station again.

He phoned Strathbane and asked for permission to speak to them because he knew they would not go away until he did so, and he was anxious to get on with his normally quiet life.

The word came back from Daviot that as he was supposed to be ill, Detective Chief Inspector Blair would be over to have a word with them.

Blair eventually arrived. He looked in high good humour. Hamish opened the kitchen door a crack and listened.

'You lads want a statement,' said Blair, 'so I suggest we all go to the pub and I'll give you one.'

'What about Macbeth?' shouted one.

'You won't get him. He's off on vacation. Come along.'

Hamish waited until they had gone, then phoned Archie Maclean. 'Blair's taken the press along to the pub to make a statement. Could you do me a favour and get along there and see what he's saying?'

'I'll do that,' said Archie. 'But you owe me a dram.'

Hamish waited patiently that morning until he heard a knock at the kitchen door. He opened it and Archie slid in.

'I haff neffer heard such a load o' twaddle,' said Archie. 'I doubt if thae press'll be bothering you for a long time.'

'What did Blair say?' asked Hamish, lifting down the whisky bottle and setting a glass in front of Archie. 'Help yourself.'

'The big man started off by telling them you still had the exhaustion but would be back at work in a couple of weeks. Then he began to tell them what a great detective he was, getting drunker and louder by the minute. One by one they left and by the time they had all gone he was bragging away to an empty space. Then he got in his car and drove off.'

'*He* drove?'

'Aye, but he won't get very far.'

'Why?'

'I phoned Strathbane and said there was a fat man drunk as a skunk that had just left the pub and taken the Strathbane road, driving a W-reg Volvo. You look fine tae me. Are you suffering from the exhaustion?'

'Not really. Just want a holiday.'

'Are you going away?'

'I might. My dog got injured.'

'Lugs! What's been happening? There wass a bit in the papers, they say, but I havenae seen them yet.'

Hamish told Archie about his adventures. 'So,' he finished, 'I'd better enjoy my bit of rest because I'll be spending a lot of time in court giving evidence.'

'Do you know it's all around Lochdubh that you and Angela Brodie were seen holding hands?'

'Oh, for heaven's sake,' said Hamish crossly.

'The Currie sisters tackled her with it and she telt them herself had been in love wi' you for years.'

'I'd better see Angela and put a stop to it. She never did realize what a lot of damage a misplaced sense of humour can do in a village.'

* * *

Angela, confronted by him half an hour later, looked guilty. 'You know how it is, Hamish. They are so gossipy and righteous, I couldn't resist it.'

'The trouble is, Angela, if I go around denying it, folks will really begin to think there's something in it.'

'Maybe you should be seen around with Elspeth.'

'I tried to phone her but she hung up on me.'

'Have a word with her. She's a pretty, clever girl. You couldn't do better than that.'

'I've had enough of women.'

'Then stop chasing after the unavailable ones.'

'I'll have a chat with her anyway.'

'Coffee?'

Hamish eyed the cats strolling across Angela's kitchen table. 'I'll maybe drop by and have some later.'

He walked along to the newspaper offices. The air was clear and sharp. The loch lay glassy and still as if not even a breath of wind had ever disturbed it. The sound of chain saws echoed across the loch where the forestry workers were clearing the debris of fallen trees. Peat smoke rose from cottage chimneys, straight up into the air. A pale blue sky stretched overhead and the sun was a hazy yellow, as if it were losing its strength before the Highland winter had even arrived.

He was told Elspeth was out reporting but expected back soon. He turned up the lane past the Currie sisters' cottage and round to where the Bains lived.

Mr Bain answered the door. He looked shamefaced when he saw Hamish and said, 'You must think me a right fool. Come in.'

Hamish followed him into the living room. 'Is that why you left Stoyre?' he asked.

'Aye. Sit down and take the weight off your feet. I was right scared. I didn't want to have a part of it. They all believed, you see, that they would get the Holy Grail, drink from it, and live forever.'

'Didn't you believe it yourself?'

'I thought it was meddling in things best left alone but I was taken in by it all. I thought it best to clear out of Stoyre to where life was normal. But it had frightened me enough to be terrified to speak of it. I'm glad you found out it was a trick or there would be some children like my wee girl having nightmares for the rest of their lives. Can I get you something? Coffee, tea, drink?'

'No, I'm fine. I'll be on my way.'

Harry Bain looked at him awkwardly. 'I hope it works out for you.'

'Oh, the case is finished and I'm on holiday. All over now.'

'I didn't mean that.'

'What did you mean?'

'It's just it must be hard on you being in love with a married woman.'

'I AM NOT IN LOVE WITH ANGELA!' howled Hamish.

'Oh, the poor woman. She's in love with you and you don't want to know.'

'Use your wits, man. She was teasing the Currie sisters. Angela was with me at the vet's. I was sore upset because I thought Lugs wasn't going to make it, and being the warm-hearted person she is, she held my hand.'

'Is that a fact? You'll disappoint a lot of people,' said Harry.

'Why?'

'My wife was just saying how they were all enjoying a good gossip.'

Hamish groaned. 'Visions o' God, Holy Grail, shipwreck, murder and mayhem, and all you lot can find to talk about is a mythical affair.'

'I suppose. You know how it is. Anyway, turns out I missed out by leaving Stoyre. The money's pouring into the village after that television programme. Still, it's better in Lochdubh. There's more life here.'

Hamish left him and then walked to Mr Jefferson's cottage. He knocked on the door and Mr Jefferson answered it. 'Oh, it's you,' he said. 'I read all about you in the papers. You might have let me in on the action.'

'If you mean the latest fright, how was I to guess some murderous German would still be roaming around? How are you doing? Still going south? Back to the city?'

'I keep putting it off. There's more things happen in this village than I could have guessed. Archie Maclean took me out fishing one night. Dr Brodie took me over to Strathbane for a round of golf, and various ladies of the village have been inviting me for meals. I'm beginning to enjoy myself. Sometimes I think of Annie and feel guilty.'

'Annie Docherty is the one person who would have loved the idea of you enjoying yourself in Lochdubh,' said Hamish.

'True. There's a lot goes on in the village. What's this about you having an affair with the doctor's wife?'

After he had put Mr Jefferson straight on the matter of Angela, Hamish headed back to the newspaper office This time Elspeth was sitting at her computer, a pencil stuck in her hair.

'Oh, it's you,' she said curtly. 'Any more stories you want to keep from me?'

'Elspeth, I'm right sorry. But look at it this way. I'd been up all night in the hurricane and then they all arrived from Strathbane. There wasn't time. Did you get my flowers?'

'Yes, and your soppy message.'

Hamish's hazel eyes sharpened. 'What message? I simply apologized.'

'And sent me all your love.

'That was Jimmy Anderson. He must have decided to spice up the message.'

'So you couldn't even send them yourself.'

'Elspeth, this is ridiculous. What on earth are we quarrelling about?'

She stared down at her computer for a long moment. Then she raised her eyes. 'Okay, buy me dinner.'

'When?'

'Eight o'clock tonight.'

'I'll be there. The Italian's?'

'That'll do.'

That evening, Hamish phoned the vet and was told that he could pick up his dog on the following day. 'The thing I don't under-stand, Fred,' said Hamish, 'is why Lugs did not bark. That German said he lured him with a piece of cheese. But Lugs has a sixth sense for danger.'

'I think I can answer that. I was busy today and had only time to grab a bite to eat in the surgery. I took out some crackers and a piece of Stilton I had in the surgery fridge and the most terrible howling and barking came from the pens next door. I went through with the cracker and Stilton in my hand and there's Lugs, going frantic. I opened the pen and offered him the cracker and Stilton and he fair gulped it down and nearly took my fingers with it. Did you ever find out where Lugs came from?'

'No, just that he was lost up on the moors.'

'Maybe his previous owner had rich tastes. Your dog'll be looking for the port to go with it next.'

Hamish laughed and promised to be over the next morning.

He took out his one good suit and brushed it carefully, his one good shirt, and one good silk tie. He hadn't a decent pair of shoes so he wore his regulation boots. His feet would be under the table anyway.

Elspeth in a cherry-red wool dress and black mohair stole made her way along the waterfront to the restaurant. She was looking forward to the evening. She was glad their quarrel was over.

She was so absorbed in happy thoughts that she did not notice the approach of the Currie sisters until they bobbed up in front of her, the lights on the waterfront shining on their thick glasses.

'And where are we off to tonight?' asked Nessie.

'I'm joining Hamish for dinner.'

'A young lassie like you could do better for herself than hang around with that adulterer, adulterer,' said Jessie.

'I don't know what you're talking about,' said Elspeth, trying to walk round them, but Nessie clutched her arm.

'Did no one tell you? It's all over the village.'

'No, folks wouldn't tell *you*,' said Nessie. 'You'd be the last to know.'

'Last to know,' prompted Jessie.

'Know what? Look, it's getting late . . .'

'Hamish Macbeth is having an affair with Angela Brodie.'

'And who told you that?' demanded Elspeth scornfully.

'Why, Angela herself. Did she not tell us, bold as brass, that she had been in love with him for ages?'

'I've got to go,' said Elspeth, tugging her arm free. She walked towards the restaurant and then stopped. Hamish seemed to confide in Angela a lot. She remembered days when she would see them standing together on the waterfront, talking, their heads together.

All her resentment at Hamish came flooding back.

She turned on her heel and went home.

'Are ye no' going to order?' asked Willie Lamont.

'Not yet,' said Hamish. 'I'm waiting for Elspeth. She's late. I'll give her a ring.'

He waited until Willie had retreated, then he

took out his mobile phone and dialled her home number.

'Yes?' came Elspeth's voice on the phone.

'Where are you?' asked Hamish. 'I mean aren't you coming?'

'No, and I don't suppose you'll be lonely for long. Why don't you ask Angela Brodie, or have you finally had some decent consideration for her husband?'

Hamish did not often lose his temper but he lost it now. 'For God's sake, you silly cow . . .'

'*What* did you call me?'

'I'm sorry, Elspeth. It's just that –'

She slammed down the phone. He tried ringing several times again but got the engaged signal.

He waved Willie over. 'She's not coming. I'll just have a bowl of spaghetti and a glass of your house wine.'

'Right, Hamish. You know, Hamish, I'm always here for you.'

Hamish looked at him in surprise. 'Thanks, Willie.'

'I mean, a man in trouble could always do with someone to speak to.'

Hamish's eyes narrowed.

'Out with it, Willie.'

'I know the kirk says that adulteration is a bad thing, but . . .'

'The word is adultery!' shouted Hamish.

There was a silence in the restaurant as the other diners stared at him.

'Forget my order,' said Hamish Macbeth, and slammed out of the restaurant door.

The following day, he collected Lugs and drove back towards Lochdubh with the dog beside him on the passenger seat.

'Now, what'll we do with our vacation, old friend?' said Hamish. 'I feel like going down to Inverness and picking up some pretty girl.'

Lugs let out a low growl.

'Oh, you got that one all right,' said Hamish. 'But you couldn't even sniff out a murder, you were that keen on Stilton.'

I'm really going barmy, he thought sadly. I'm talking about holidays with a dog.

If you enjoyed *Death of a Village*, read on for the first chapter of the next book in the *Hamish Macbeth* series . . .

DEATH of a
POISON PEN

Chapter One

I'm not a jealous woman, but I can't *see
what he sees in her, I can't see* what *he sees
in her, I can't see what he* sees *in her!*
— Sir Alan Patrick Herbert

Jenny Ogilvie was curled up on a sofa in
her friend Priscilla Halburton-Smythe's London
flat. They had been talking for most of the
evening. Jenny was secretly jealous of Priscilla's
cool blonde looks. Although an attractive girl
herself with her mop of black curls and rosy
cheeks, she longed to look as stylish and composed as her friend.

A desire to rattle her friend's calm prompted
her to say, 'You've talked an awful lot about
this village policeman, Hamish Macbeth. I
mean, you've barely mentioned your fiancé.
Come on. What gives? I think you're still in
love with this copper.'

A faint tide of pink rose up Priscilla's face. 'I
was engaged to him once and we shared a
lot of adventures. But that's all. What about

your love life? You've been letting me do all the talking.'

'Oh, you know me. I like to shop around,' said Jenny. 'I'm not prepared to settle down yet.'

'What happened to Giles? You did seem frightfully keen on him.'

'He bored me after a bit,' lied Jenny, who had no intention of letting Priscilla know that Giles had broken off with her the minute she had hinted at marriage.

'You'll find someone. Don't worry,' said Priscilla with all the calm assurance of someone about to be married.

Jenny returned to her own flat, feeling jealous and cross. It was a pity, she thought, that Priscilla's policeman should live in some remote Highland village or she would be tempted to have a go at him herself. He must be one hell of a man to occupy so much of Priscilla's thoughts. She went to her bookshelves and pulled down an atlas of the British Isles. Now, where had Priscilla said that village was? Lochdoo or something. She scanned the index. There was a Lochdubh. That must be it. Maybe like 'skeandhu', the dagger Highlanders wore with full dress. She looked it up in the dictionary. That was pronounced *skeandoo*. Also spelt 'skeandubh'. So it followed that Lochdubh must be the place. She knew

Priscilla's parents owned the Tommel Castle Hotel there. Just to be sure, she phoned directory inquiries and got the number of the Tommel Castle Hotel and asked for the exact location of Lochdubh. Got it! She replaced the receiver.

She put down the atlas and sat cross-legged on the floor. She had holiday owing. What if – just what if – she went to this village and romanced the copper? How would Priscilla like that?

Not a bit, she thought with a grin. She would ask for leave in the morning.

The subject of Jenny's plotting took a stroll along Lochdubh's waterfront the next morning with his dog, Lugs. PC Hamish Macbeth was preoccupied with a nasty case. The nearby town of Braikie had been subjected to a rash of poison-pen letters. At first people had ignored them because the accusations in some of them were so weird and wild and inaccurate that they hadn't been taken seriously. But as the letters continued to arrive, tempers were rising.

Mrs Dunne, who owned a bed and breakfast on the waterfront called Sea View, hailed him. She was a fussy little woman who looked perpetually anxious and tired.

'Morning,' said Mrs Dunne. 'Terrible business about those nasty letters.'

'You havenae had one, have you?' asked Hamish.

'No, but I just heard that herself, Mrs Wellington, got one this morning.'

'I'd better go and see her. Business good?'

'Not a bad summer, but nobody really books in now it's autumn. I've got a couple of the forestry workers as regulars. Though mind you, a lassie from London is coming for a couple of weeks, a Miss Ogilvie. She phoned this morning.'

Hamish touched his cap and walked off in the direction of the manse, for Mrs Wellington, large, tweedy and respectable, was the minister's wife.

Mrs Wellington was pulling up weeds in her garden. She straightened up when she saw Hamish.

'I've just heard you've had one o' thae letters.' Hamish fixed her with a gimlet stare to distract her from the sight of his dog urinating against the roots of one of her prize roses. 'Why didn't you phone the police station?'

She looked flustered. 'It was nothing but a spiteful piece of nonsense. I threw it on the fire.'

'I can do with all the evidence I can get,' said Hamish severely. 'Now, you've got to tell me what was in that letter. Furthermore, I've never known you to light a fire before the end of October.'

Mrs Wellington capitulated. 'Oh, very well.

I'll get it. Wait there. And keep that dog of yours away from my flowers.'

Hamish waited, wondering what could possibly be so bad as to make the upright minister's wife initially lie to him.

Mrs Wellington came back and handed him a letter. On the envelope was her name and address in handwriting now familiar to Hamish from the other letters he had in a file back at the police station. He opened it and took out a piece of cheap stationery and began to read. Then he roared with laughter. For the poison-pen letter writer had accused Mrs Wellington of having an adulterous affair with the Lochdubh policeman – Hamish Macbeth.

When he had recovered, he wiped his eyes and said, 'This is so daft. Why didnae you want to show it to me?'

'I know your reputation as a womanizer, Hamish Macbeth, and I thought this letter might give you ideas.'

Hamish's good humour left and his hazel eyes held a malicious gleam. 'I am in my thirties and you are – what – in your fifties? Don't you think you are suffering from a wee bit o' vanity?'

Her face flamed. 'There are winter–summer relationships, you know. I read about them in *Cosmopolitan* – at the dentist's. And when I was in the cinema with my husband the other week, a young man on the other side of me put a hand on my knee!'

'Michty me,' said Hamish. 'What happened when the lights went up?'

'He had left by that time,' said Mrs Wellington stiffly, not wanting to tell this jeering policeman that during a bright scene on the screen, the young man had leant forward and looked at her and fled.

'And I am not a womanizer,' pursued Hamish.

'Ho, no? You broke off your engagement to poor Priscilla, and since then you've been playing fast and loose.'

'I'll take this letter with me,' said Hamish, suddenly weary. 'But rest assured, I have not the designs on you, not now, not ever!'

Back at the police station, he added the letter to the others in the file. There was a knock at the kitchen door. He went to answer it and found Elspeth Grant, the local reporter and astrologer for the *Highland Times*, standing there. She was dressed in her usual mixture of charity shop clothes: old baggy sweater, long Indian cotton skirt and clumpy boots.

'What brings you?' asked Hamish. 'I havenae seen you for a while.'

'I've been showing the new reporter the ropes.'

'Pat Mallone,' said Hamish. 'The attractive Irishman.'

'Yes, him. And he is attractive. Are you going to ask me in?'

'Sure.' He stood aside. Elspeth sat down at the kitchen table. The day was misty and drops of moisture hung like little pearls in her frizzy hair. Her large grey eyes, gypsy eyes, surveyed him curiously. He felt a little pang of loss. At one time, Elspeth had shown him that she was attracted to him but he had rejected her and by the time he had changed his mind about her, she was no longer interested.

'So,' began Elspeth, 'I hear Mrs Wellington got one of those letters.'

'How did you learn that?'

'She told Nessie Currie, who told everyone in Patel's grocery. What on earth was in it?'

'Mind your own business.'

'All right, copper. What are you doing about these letters? They're weird and wild in their accusations, but one day one's going to hit the mark and there'll be a death. Haven't you asked for a handwriting expert?'

'Oh, I've asked headquarters, right enough, but it is always the same thing. Handwriting experts cost money. The budget is tight. It's chust a village storm in a teacup and will soon blow over, that's what they say.' Hamish's Highland accent always became more sibilant when he was excited or upset. 'So I sit on my bum collecting nasty letters.'

'There is something you could do and I'll tell you if you make me a cup of tea.'

293

Hamish put the kettle on top of the stove and lifted down two mugs from the kitchen cabinet. 'So what's your idea?'

'It's like this. Someone always knows something. You could call an emergency meeting at the community centre in Braikie and appeal to the people of Braikie to help you. I could run off flyers at the newspaper and we could post them up in shops and on lamp posts. Someone knows something, I'm sure of that. Go on, Hamish. I feel in my bones that death is going to come and come quickly.'

Hamish looked at her uneasily. He had experienced Elspeth's psychic powers and had learned that, at times, they were uncanny.

'All right,' he said. 'I'll do it. Let's see. This is Monday. We'll make it for next Saturday evening.'

'No, make it around lunchtime, say one o'clock. There's a big bingo game on Saturday evening.'

'Okay. I'll leave it to you.'

Hamish made tea. 'What sort of person would you say was behind these letters?'

'Someone living alone, no family. Maybe someone retired who once had some power over people. Probably a woman.'

'There are an awful lot of widows and spinsters in Braikie.'

'Never mind. Let's hope this meeting flushes something out.'

* * *

After Elspeth had left, he noticed she had left him a copy of the *Highland Times*. Curiously, he turned to her astrology column and looked under 'Libra'. He read: 'Romance is heading your way but it is a romance you will not want. You will suffer from headaches on Wednesday morning. You are not working hard enough. You are congenitally lazy, but remember always that mistakes caused by laziness can cause death.'

Hamish scratched his fiery hair. What on earth was the lassie on about?

On Saturday morning, Jenny Ogilvie looked out of the window of the bus that was bearing her northwards and felt she was leaving civilization behind. She had flown to Inverness and caught the Lochinver bus. She had been told, however, that the bus to take her on to Lochdubh from Lochinver would have left by the time she arrived, but a local taxi could take her the rest of the way. Moorland and mountain stretched on either side. Foaming waterfalls plunged down craggy slopes. Red deer stood as if posing for Landseer on the top of hills as the bus wound its way round twisting roads, breaking sharply to avoid the occasional suicidal sheep.

She had decided to book into a bed and breakfast in Lochdubh rather than stay at the Tommel Castle Hotel, in case Priscilla might learn from her parents of her arrival. The bus finally ground its way down into Lochinver and stopped on the waterfront. It was a fine day and sunlight was sparkling on the water.

Jenny climbed stiffly down from the bus and retrieved her luggage. She took out her mobile phone and dialled the number of a taxi service in Lochdubh she had tracked down by dint of phoning the Sutherland tourist board. Better to have someone from Lochdubh to collect her than get a cab from Lochinver.

A pleasant Highland voice on the other end of the line informed her that he would be with her in three-quarters of an hour and if she sat in the café on the waterfront, he would find her.

Jenny went into the café and ordered a coffee, forcing her eyes away from a tempting display of home-baked cakes. It was all right for Priscilla, she thought bitterly. Priscilla could eat anything and never even put on an ounce, whereas she, Jenny, could feel her waistband tightening by just looking at the things.

She was the only customer in the café. She noticed there was a large glass ashtray on the table in front of her. Jenny was trying to cut down on smoking, but she hadn't been able to have one all day. She lit one up and felt dizzy, but after two more, felt better. The sun was already disappearing and the water outside darkening to black when a man popped his head round the door. 'Miss Ogilvie?'

Jenny rose and indicated her luggage. 'The cab is outside,' he said. 'I would help you with your luggage, but my back's bad.'

Hoisting her two large suitcases outside, Jenny stared in dismay at the 'cab'. It was a minibus painted bright red on the front, but because the owner, Iain Chisholm, had run out of paint, the rest was painted a sulphurous yellow. Inside, the seats were covered in brightly coloured chintz with flounces at the bottom of each seat.

Jenny heaved her luggage in the side door and then decided to sit up in the front with Iain and see if she could pump him for some information.

The engine coughed and spluttered to life and the bus started its journey out of Loch-inver and headed up the Sutherland coast to Lochdubh. 'I'm up from London,' said Jenny.

'Is that a fact?' said Iain, negotiating a hair-pin bend. Jenny glanced nervously down a cliff edge to where the Atlantic boiled against jagged rocks.

'What's Lochdubh like?' asked Jenny.

'Oh, it's the grand place. Nice and quiet.'

'No crime?'

'Nothing much. Bit of a scare now, mind you. Some damp poison-pen letter writer's on the loose.'

'How scary. Do you have a policeman?'

'Yes. Hamish Macbeth.'

'What's he like?'

'A fine man. Solved a lot of crimes.'

'What's such a clever copper doing being stuck up here?'

'He likes it and so do I,' said Iain crossly.

Jenny was dying to ask what Hamish looked like, but she didn't dare show any more curiosity. Surely, someone who could attract such as Priscilla must be really handsome. He was probably tall and dark with a craggy Highland face and piercing green eyes. When not in uniform, he probably wore a kilt and played the bagpipes. Jenny clutched the side of the old minibus as it hurtled onwards towards Lochdubh, wrapped in rosy dreams.

Earlier that day, Hamish addressed the inhabitants of Braikie in the community hall. 'Some of you must know something – have an idea who is sending out these poisonous letters,' he said. He noticed uneasily that people were beginning to glare around the hall. 'Now, don't go leaping to conclusions because you just don't like someone,' he said quickly. 'Maybe if you all go home and think hard, you might remember –' he held up an envelope – 'someone posting one of these in a pillar box. Just on the chance that our letter writer is here in this hall, I would caution you that when you are caught – and you will be caught, mark my words – then you will be facing a prison sentence. I am going to engage the services of a handwriting expert –'

'What took ye so long?' demanded an angry voice from the front. 'You should ha' done it afore this.'

'I was told that because of cutbacks in the police budget, they were not prepared to let me hire one,' said Hamish. 'On your way out, you will see a petition on the table at the door requesting the services of a handwriting expert from police headquarters. I want you all to sign it.'

Hamish was mildly annoyed to see Elspeth in the front row accompanied by Pat Mallone, the new reporter. It only took one reporter to cover this. Did she have to go everywhere with him? He was whispering in her ear and she was giggling like a schoolgirl.

'This is a serious matter,' he went on, raising his voice. 'And should be taken seriously by our local press as well.' Elspeth looked up and composed her features and made several squiggles in her notebook. 'The accusations in these letters so far are silly and untrue, but if by any chance this poison-pen letter writer should hit on the truth about someone, maybe by accident, then at the least it could cause misery and at the worst, death. Now sign that petition. It is your civic duty.'

The audience rose to their feet. Aware of Hamish, still standing on the stage watching them, one by one they all signed the petition as they filed out.

When the hall was empty, Hamish leapt down from the stage and collected the petition. He would take it down to Strathbane in the morning and see if it prompted them to give him a handwriting expert.

Jenny Ogilvie was dropped outside Sea View. She hefted her suitcases up to the door, rang the bell, and waited. The village was very quiet and great stars blazed in the sky above. A chill wind was blowing off the loch. She shivered and rang the bell again. At last she heard footsteps approaching the door from the other side. 'Who is it?' called a voice.

'It's me. Jenny Ogilvie from London.'

The grumbles coming from the other side of the door reminded Jenny of the cartoon dog Muttley. Then the door opened. 'What time of night d'ye call this?' demanded Mrs Dunne.

'I have come all the way from London,' said Jenny coldly. 'And if this is the sort of welcome you give visitors, perhaps I would be better off at the hotel.'

In the light streaming out from the door, Jenny had seemed to Mrs Dunne like a small girl. But the cold authority in Jenny's voice made her say hurriedly, 'Come in, lassie. You must forgive me. We aye keep early hours. I'll show you to your room. I only serve the bed and breakfast, mind, but if you're hungry, I've got some food I can give you.'

'Just a sandwich and some coffee would be fine,' said Jenny.

'Right. Pick up your suitcases and follow me.'

This was obviously a world where no one carried anyone's luggage, thought Jenny as she struggled up the wooden staircase after Mrs Dunne.

Mrs Dunne opened the door. 'This is your room. I've given you the best one, it being quiet this time of year.'

Jenny looked dismally round, wondering, if this was the best room, what on earth the others were like. A forty watt bulb burned in a pink and white glass shade. There was a narrow bed under a slippery quilt against one wall. A closet covered by a curtain, which Mrs Dunne pulled back with a magician's proud flourish, was where she would hang her clothes. A wash-hand basin of Victorian vintage with a pink glass mirror above it was over in one far corner, and in the other stood a desk and a hard upright chair. In front of the fireplace, filled with orange crêpe paper in the shape of a fan, stood a one-bar electric heater. The floor was covered in shiny green linoleum, on which were two islands of round rugs.

'You put fifty pence in the meter to start the fire,' said Mrs Dunne. 'Breakfast is from seven o'clock until nine o'clock, no later. I'll expect you to be out of your room by ten because I have to clean it and I don't want guests under-foot. You can sit in the lounge downstairs if it's a wet day. We have the telly – colour, it is. Now I'll show you the bathroom.'

Jenny followed her along the corridor out-side to a room at the end of it. The bathroom held an enormous Victorian bath. Above it was a cylindrical gas heater. 'When you want a bath, put fifty pence in the meter above the door, turn this lever to the right, and light the geyser.'

'Do you mean I don't have my own bath-room?' asked Jenny.

'No, but there's only the two forestry workers and they're out early and don't use the bath much.'

Jenny repressed a shudder. 'What about laundry?'

'What about it? Can't you be doing your smalls in the hand basin?'

'No, I would prefer to do them in a washing machine with a tumble dryer.'

Mrs Dunne sighed. 'Well, you can use the one in the kitchen downstairs, but only if I don't need it. There's no tumble dryer but you'll find a clothes line in the back garden. Go and unpack and come downstairs and have something to eat.'

Jenny returned to her room. She felt thor-oughly tired and depressed. She hoped this policeman would prove to be worth all this suffering. She opened one suitcase and unpacked a diaphanous nightgown and a silk dressing gown and laid them on the bed. Then she began to hang away some clothes and put underwear in the drawers.

When she heard Mrs Dunne calling her, she went reluctantly downstairs. 'I've put your food on a tray in the lounge,' said Mrs Dunne. 'When you're finished, put the tray in the kitchen – it's at the back of the hall – and don't forget to switch out all the lights. Good night.'

'Good night,' echoed Jenny. She went into the lounge. It was an uncomfortable-looking room with an acid three-piece suite which seemed to swear at the orange and sulphurous-yellow carpet. Above the cold fireplace some amateur had tried to copy the *Stag at Bay* and failed miserably. The television was operated by a coin box. A tray on the coffee table held a plate of ham sandwiches, two fairy cakes and a pot of tea. The ham sandwiches turned out to be delicious and the tea was hot and fragrant. Slightly cheered, Jenny finished her supper and carried the tray through to the kitchen. Then, carefully switching out all the lights behind her, she made her way up to her room.

It was very cold. London had been enjoying an Indian summer. She had not expected it to be so cold. She scrabbled in her purse looking for a fifty-pence piece but could not find one. She washed her face and hands, deciding to put off a bath until the following day. Shivering in her flimsy nightgown, she crawled into bed. There were two hot-water bottles in the bed and the sheets smelled faintly of pine soap. The bed was amazingly soft and comfortable. Jenny, normally a restless sleeper, plunged down into a deep and dreamless sleep.

Hamish drove towards Strathbane the following morning with Lugs beside him on the passenger seat of the police Land Rover and with the petition in a briefcase in the back. It was a beautiful clear day. Not even a single cloud wreathed the soaring mountain tops. A heron flew across the road in front of him, slow and graceful. The air was heavy with the smells of pine, wood smoke and wild thyme.

But his heart sank as the Land Rover crested a rise on the road and he saw Strathbane lying below him – the City of Dreadful Night. It had originally been a thriving fishing port, but European Union regulations and a decline in fishing stocks had put the fishermen out of business. Stalinist tower blocks reared up to the sky, monuments to failure and bad architecture.

He was lucky it was a Sunday. The bane of his life, Detective Chief Inspector Blair, hardly ever worked on Sunday. Hamish knew Blair would block any proposal of his out of sheer spite. He was even luckier to meet Chief Superintendent Peter Daviot in the reception area.

'What brings you, Hamish?' asked Daviot.

It was a good sign that he had used Hamish's first name. Hamish held out the petition and explained his need for the services of a handwriting expert.

'We have an overstretched budget,' said Daviot. 'Don't you think it'll just blow over?'

'No, I don't,' said Hamish.

'Don't what?'

'I mean, I don't think it'll blow over, *sir*. It's been going on for some time. My concern is this: If we don't track down this poison-pen letter writer soon, he or she, instead of wild accusations, might hit on a truth that someone doesn't want known. Braikie's a very churchy place. Everyone prides themselves on their respectability. It could be that one of these letters could drive a man or woman to suicide.'

Daviot looked at the tall policeman with the flaming-red hair. He knw that when it came to cases, Hamish Macbeth often showed remarkable powers of intuition.

'Type up a report and give it with the petition to Helen.'

'Thank you, sir.'

Hamish made his way up to the detectives' room where Detective Jimmy Anderson sat with his feet up on his desk.

'I was just thinking of going out for a dram,' he said when he saw Hamish.

'Give me a minute, Jimmy,' said Hamish. 'I've got to type something out for Daviot.'

'So what's so important the big cheese has to see it himself?'

Hamish told him as he switched on a computer.

'Hardly earth-shaking stuff, laddie. Tell you what. I'll be along at the Wee Man's. Join me when you're finished.'

No one could remember why the nearest pub, the Fraser Arms, had been nicknamed the Wee Man's.

Jimmy left. Hamish rapidly typed up his report and nipped up the stairs to where Helen, Daviot's secretary, gave him a sour look.

'Working on the Sabbath, Helen?' asked Hamish.

'If you have something for Mr Daviot, leave it with me and do not waste my valuable time.'

Hamish gazed on her fondly. 'You know something, Helen? You're right ugly when you're angry.' And then he scampered off before she could think of a reply.

Despite Jimmy's urging, Hamish would only drink mineral water at the pub. He often wondered why Jimmy had never been done for drunk driving. He set off again, stopping outside the town to give Lugs a walk on the heather. As usual, when he approached Lochdubh, his spirits lifted even though the day was darkening. Mist was rolling down the flanks of the mountainsides, and thin black fingers of rain clouds were streaming in from the west on a rising wind. The crisp feel of the day had gone and he could feel a damp warmth in the air blowing in from the Gulf Stream.

He parked outside the police station and went into the kitchen – and glared at the figure of Elspeth Grant, sitting at his kitchen table.

'How did you get in?' he demanded.

'You left the door open,' said Elspeth. 'An open invitation.'

'Well, next time, wait until I'm at home.' I'll need to keep remembering to lock the door, thought Hamish. He was so used to leaving it open while he went to feed his hens and check on his sheep that he often forgot to lock it when he was out at work.

'How did you get on with the petition?'

'I gave it to Daviot. He says he'll see what he can do.'

'It'll be too late,' said Elspeth, looking at him with her silver eyes.

'I think he'll get moving on it.'

'Oh, Hamish, you know what the red tape is like. They'll pass memos back and forth and it'll take weeks.'

'Well, let's see how it goes.'

There was a knock at the door. Hamish opened it and found an attractive face staring up at him. Jenny Ogilvie held out one small hand. 'I would like to speak to Hamish Macbeth.'

'I am Hamish Macbeth.'

He was surprised to see disappointment flash across her large brown eyes. The pair surveyed each other.

Jenny *was* disappointed. Gone was the craggy Highlander of her dreams. She saw a tall, gangling, red-haired man with hazel eyes and a gentle face. Hamish, for his part, saw an attractive girl with black curly hair, large eyes and a curvaceous figure. She was dressed in a smart skirt and jacket and flimsy high heels.

'What can I do for you?' he asked.

'I'm a tourist here,' said Jenny, 'and I arrived yesterday. I don't know this neck of the woods and I wondered if you could tell me good places to visit.'

'Come in,' said Hamish.

He introduced Jenny to Elspeth. 'Sit down,' said Hamish. Both regarded each other with the wary suspicion of cats. 'Drink?'

'Yes, thank you.'

'Jenny here is a tourist and wants to know where she should visit,' said Hamish, lifting down a bottle of whisky and glasses. 'Elspeth here is our local reporter. She'll help you out.' Elspeth glared at Hamish's back.

Lugs, roused from slumber by the sound of voices, came up to the table, put a large paw on Jenny's leg, and drew it downwards, leaving white ladders on her ten-denier tights.

Jenny squeaked with alarm and drew her legs under the table. 'Come here, Lugs,' ordered Elspeth. 'Good dog. Settle down.' She turned her clear gaze on Jenny. 'If you really want to sightsee, you'll need a car. Do you have one?'

'No, I did the last of the journey by taxi, a chap called Iain Chisholm.'

'I think you'll find he has a spare car to rent, and his prices are low.'

'Thank you. I'll try him in the morning.'

'Mostly, people who come up here are walkers, hill climbers or fishermen. They have some sort of hobby. But if you drive around, there's some wonderful scenery. Where are you staying?'

'Sea View.'

'You're right next to the *Highland Times* offices. Drop in tomorrow morning and I'll give you some maps and tourist brochures.'

Hamish joined them at the table and poured whisky into three glasses. 'Do you drink it neat?' asked Jenny.

'Aye, but I can put water in it if you like.'

'It's all right,' said Jenny quickly, not to be outdone by Elspeth. Was Elspeth his girl-friend? If she was, then her plot was doomed from the start.

'So what made you decide to come this far north?' asked Hamish. His Highland voice was soft and lilting. Jenny began to understand a little of why her friend Priscilla appeared to be so fascinated with this man.

'I came up from London. Just felt like getting as far away as possible.'

'Broken heart?' asked Elspeth.

'No,' said Jenny crossly.

Elspeth finished her whisky and stood up. 'I'd best be getting along.' She walked to the door and then turned and said to Jenny, 'Good hunting, but you'll find the prey is difficult to catch.'

Jenny's face flamed. 'What do you mean?'

'Just a Highland expression,' said Elspeth, and she went out and closed the kitchen door behind her.

'I'm sorry I butted in on you and your girlfriend,' said Jenny.

'Just a friend. So what do you do in London?'

'I work for a computer company.'

'And what's the name of it?'

Jenny looked at him, startled. She worked for the same company as Priscilla. 'I work for Johnson and Betterson in the City,' she said, inventing a name.

'Ah. If you've finished your drink, I'll walk you back. Lugs needs some exercise.'

Lugs needs to be put down, thought Jenny, standing up and ruefully looking down at the wreck of her tights.

Hamish opened the door. The rain still hadn't arrived, but he could sense it coming.

They walked together along the quiet waterfront. 'I hope you won't be too bored here,' said Hamish as they approached Sea View.

Jenny stopped suddenly and stared.

'What's the matter?' asked Hamish.

He looked and saw Jessie and Nessie Currie, the local twin spinsters, the minister's wife, and Mrs Dunne, standing together at the gate of the boarding house. Mrs Dunne was holding up a piece of Jenny's underwear, a black silk thong. 'Now, what in the name o' the wee man would you say that was?' she was asking.

Hamish reached out a long arm and snatched it from Mrs Dunne. 'That is the makings of a catapult for Miss Ogilvie's nephew. You should not be going through her things.'

'I didn't,' protested Mrs Dunne. She turned to Jenny, who was standing there wishing an earthquake would strike Lochdubh and bury them all. 'It was lying in the corner of your room. I found it when I was cleaning. I didn't know what it was and I thought it might have been left by the previous tenant.'

Hamish handed the thong to Jenny. She stuffed it in her handbag, marched past them, and went up to her room. She sank down on the edge of her bed and buried her head in her hands. This holiday had all been a terrible mistake.

Hamish went back to the police station, mildly amused. From the washing lines of Lochdubh, he knew that the usual female underwear consisted of large cotton knickers with elastic at the knee.

When he walked into the police station, the phone in the office was ringing. He rushed to answer it.

It was Elspeth. 'You'd best get over to Braikie,' she said. 'Miss Beattie, who worked in the post office, has been found hanged. And there's one of those poison-pen letters lying on the floor under her body.'

To order your copies of other books in the Hamish Macbeth series simply contact The Book Service (TBS) by phone, email or by post. Alternatively visit our website at www.constablerobinson.com.

No. of copies	Title	RRP	Total
	Death of a Gossip	£6.99	
	Death of a Cad	£6.99	
	Death of an Outsider	£6.99	
	Death of a Perfect Wife	£6.99	
	Death of a Hussy	£6.99	
	Death of a Snob	£6.99	
	Death of a Prankster	£6.99	
	Death of a Glutton	£6.99	
	Death of a Travelling Man	£6.99	
	Death of a Charming Man	£6.99	
	Death of a Nag	£6.99	
	Death of a Macho Man	£6.99	
	Death of a Dentist	£6.99	
	Death of a Scriptwriter	£6.99	
	Death of an Addict	£6.99	
	A Highland Christmas	£5.99	
	Death of a Dustman	£6.99	
	Death of a Celebrity	£6.99	
	Death of a Village	£6.99	
	Death of a Poison Pen	£6.99	
	Death of a Bore	£6.99	
	Death of a Dreamer	£6.99	
	Death of a Maid	£6.99	
	Death of a Gentle Lady	£6.99	
	Death of a Witch	£6.99	
	Death of a Valentine	£6.99	
	Death of a Sweep (hardback)	£18.99	
	Grand total		£

FREEPOST RLUL-SJGC-SGKJ, Cash Sales Direct Mail Dept., The Book Service, Colchester Road, Frating, Colchester, CO7 7DW. Tel: +44 (0) 1206 255 800.
Fax: +44 (0) 1206 255 930. Email: sales@tbs-ltd.co.uk

UK customers: please allow £1.00 p&p for the first book, plus 50p for the second, and an additional 30p for each book thereafter, up to a maximum charge of £3.00. Overseas customers (incl. Ireland): please allow £2.00 p&p for the first book, plus £1.00 for the second, plus 50p for each additional book.

NAME (block letters): _____

ADDRESS: _____

_____

_____ POSTCODE: _____

I enclose a cheque/PO (payable to 'TBS Direct') for the amount

of £_____

I wish to pay by Switch/Credit Card

Card number: _____

Expiry date: _____ Switch issue number: _____